The Translator's Tale

Her name was Nionc Tigo. Maybe you've heard of her, maybe you haven't.

Tigo was the most accomplished writer of her generation. Only problem is, her generation grew up in Slothin, a country so small it is tucked away between two other countries and most people don't know it even exists.

Nevertheless, Tigo was a prolific chronicler of her place and time. She wrote reams of material: novels, plays, essays, poetry, reviews, presidential speeches, recipes, and advertising copy. A true woman of letters.

Most of her work went unpublished. The parts that were published convinced the literary world that she was a talent of enormous significance.

When she died, there were calls for publishing her writings. All of it. Many lusted after her collected works, which were, unfortunately, stashed away in her nephew's attic. He was her sole heir.

The nephew, for his part, had no interest in his aunt's literary endeavors, but reasoned that since there was so much interest on the part of others, he would keep the papers to himself for a few decades to drive up the price and cash in when he retired.

Years passed. The papers, filling a dozen good-sized boxes, moldered in the nephew's attic. Scholars from around the world offered to buy them. The nephew did not budge from his original position, and, seeing all the interest, reasoned that his reasoning was sound.

However, he was a reckless young man, given to extreme sports. One bright October morning he got it into his head that he would free dive from the tallest building in Slothin. This was a critical error.

Slothin has few tall buildings of any kind, and the one the nephew chose was a mere seven stories tall. Not enough height, really, to allow time for his parachute to deploy properly, but plenty of altitude to kill him, which, when he reached the ground, it did.

The nephew left no will. His possessions passed to the state of Slothin. Tigo's literary estate went into legal limbo. A government official determined that some of Nionc Tigo's writings were detrimental to the well-being of the state of Slothin.

She decreed that the papers be locked away for some time. Perhaps a couple of centuries or so.

When that time had elapsed, the then government of Slothin might decide to publish them, or might decide to lock them up for another couple of hundred years.

Things remained like this for decades. The few works of Nionc Tigo's that had been published were reissued in numerous editions with plenty of supporting material in the form of introductions, afterwards, forwards, footnotes, analysis and so on.

You could read between the lines of all this ephemera to see how much the literary community lusted after getting their hands on Tigo's unpublished works.

It was about this time that I first heard of Tigo. I acquired one of her books in the original Sloth, the language of Slothin, and used it to learn the language. I decided it would be in my interest to translate the balance of Nionc Tigo's works.

I also decided I would do what needed to be done to get the ones locked away in Slothin.

My husband doesn't understand me. I think about that sometimes when I see him in the late afternoon light, sitting on the couch after a day of labor, the cool air coming off the ocean and filling the house with a kind of frigid presence, like some creature has emerged from the waves and filled the house.

At these times he is oblivious to me, my husband is, but that doesn't bother me. Much. Other times he is attentive enough to make up for it. Husband's not understanding their wives is nothing new, after all. Does any husband possess that ability to any meaningful degree? I doubt it.

I'm a translator. He says my profession caters to lazy people. He says this in a challenging way, but I usually don't rise to the challenge. It's one of those husband-wife things that only the participating couple get. People observing the so-called battle of wits when we get into the subject would be baffled by it.

In any case, I have to mention that his job caters to lazy people as well. He's a heavy equipment operator. Moves earth around for a living because if he doesn't do it, then someone else would have to, and, let's face it, most people don't want to put in the work necessary to move earth around all by themselves. Lazy. Really, don't all jobs cater to lazy people, if one is inclined to think of it in that way? I think so.

We josh each other about this all the time, but we don't go too far. After all, I haven't killed anyone by practicing my profession. My husband has.

Oh, it was a long time ago, but it's still raw for him. He was working a road project a couple of counties over. It was winter, the ground was wet. His excavator hadn't been anchored properly and it slid on the slick mud and a fellow worker got trapped under it and was crushed to death. A very grisly demise.

My husband, so witnesses said, was completely distraught. He cried to the heavens and pulled at his hair and dragged his fingernails over his face, scraping the skin and drawing blood. I saw the scars, so I knew something happened.

The investigation absolved my husband of any guilt. At least legally. The official report said the dead man was at fault. He should have known better than to be standing where he was, given the conditions extant at the time. Blame the dead victim. Always the easiest way to go. Clean and decisive.

My husband, though, fell into a long depression. It lasted years and when it finally lifted, he was functional and reasonably intact, but could never shake the guilt. I still see it eating at him. It is only relieved when he talks to the walls. I'll get to that later.

In the meantime, just know he's a fragile person. Sometimes, in an effort to prove that he *isn't* fragile, he likes to kid me about stuff. Usually about my livelihood, as I've indicated. I see right through it, but I don't feel the need to tell him I see right through it. It's difficult to be constantly vigilant about another person's feelings, even someone you love. It would be pure joy and freedom to be able to tell him to get over it. But I know that would do him no good.

The only reason there's a call for your skill, he says, referring to my translation abilities, is that people don't want to put in the work to learn new languages. He has a point, of course, but no one can know every language. That's why there are people like me, to help everyone understand each other.

And even I need some help sometimes. I'm a language expert and there are still languages I don't understand. Here's a perfect example: I don't understand my husband's language.

You would think after thirty years of marriage that we would know each other quite well. We would have the capacity to learn about and understand everything there is to know about the other person. Not so.

My husband talks to ghosts. I don't know what he says or what they say to him. Even with my translation skills, his conversations are a total mystery to me.

He laughs when I ask him to teach me the ghost language. He says it isn't something you can learn. It's something you have to be born with. This only makes me grit my teeth.

All I do is learn. I'm always learning. There is so much knowledge in the world that if you're not learning all the time, you're just existing.

It's innate, he says, serenely, happy that he learned that word. My husband has not had much formal eduction. Nothing wrong with that. I'm just letting you know that he believes all he needs to know he's been born with. Except for heavy equipment operation.

He took a three week course to learn that. Beyond high school, that's all he's ever learned. I don't like hearing about innate abilities. If the world was all about innate talent, then learning would be useless. Education would be a waste of time.

I've tried to learn ghost. I've sat with my husband as he talks to the walls and the walls (presumably) talk to him. I haven't heard them, so I can only take his word for it. What I hear is nonsense syllables coming out of his mouth, then a long pause as he turns his ear to the wall, then more nonsense syllables from him. He goes into a kind of trance. After, I ask him what he was talking about. He says he asks the ghosts about the future. I ask him how they can know anything about the future. He says they're ghosts, of course they know.

And I say why? Why should ghosts know anything more about the future than we do? They're dead. They may know about the past, since they lived in the past. But the future? Even ghosts live in the now. The future is as much a mystery to them as it is to us.

I say this in all seriousness. It seems the most obvious of facts. It almost an axiom, in my mind. A perfectly obvious truth.

He looks at me then like I'm some kind of crazy person. They're *ghosts* he says again, as though emphasizing the word will make it clearer to me. When he does that, it can either make me mad or make me laugh. Usually I laugh, but not always.

So then I ask him what they're saying about the future and he shrugs. Oh, he says, it's general stuff. Everything is going to be okay.

That's something he needs to hear. Something he *craves* because then his killing of his fellow worker will be okay too, in the sense that he can let himself realize it was an *accident*. I would love for him to see that. But now. Not in some rosy future. *Now.*

I could tell you the same thing, I say. I could tell you the future is going to be okay.

Go ahead.

The future is going to be okay, I say. There.

Well fine, he says. You said it. But they *know*.

It goes around and around like that. I tell him to ask them for the winning lottery numbers and he shakes his head in this tut-tut fashion, like I'm some kind of rube. It doesn't work that way, he says.

Okay, but how does it work?

It's complicated, he says.

First thing: I'm not a rube. I've been making a living at doing translations of sophisticated documents in German, French, Farsi, Portuguese, Chinook, Italian, Serbo-Croatian, Russian, Hawaiian, Japanese, Spanish, and a few others for some years. I work quickly, too. I take a document in the original language and translate it on the fly, reading it aloud in English, no matter what language it was composed in, and recording my words.

I usually get about 98 percent accuracy on my first try. I give the result to any of a dozen or so assistants for final checking. They fix the few mistakes that are there and I look at it one more time for final tweaking, and I'm done.

As I say, I rarely make a mistake. I can master a language's grammar very quickly and acquire a good chunk of vocabulary in not much longer than that. Lots of lazy people pay dearly for my skills. I've done classic novels for publishers, training documents for multi-national companies, legal documents for law firms, so many things it's too much to enumerate here.

But the ghost talk, it eludes me.

I told my husband I was going to Slothin.

Slothin, he said. What's that?

It's a country.

Never heard of it.

Hardly anyone has. I hear they have lots of ghosts. Walls, too. Stone walls that criss-cross the country. The people who lived there thousands of years ago are mad for stone walls and they built lots of them. The country is practically a patchwork quilt of them.

And why are you telling me this?

I want you to go with me. I figure if you can find new ghosts to talk to, you'll want to.

He thought about this for a moment. I wouldn't mind talking to spirits in stone walls, but why do *you* want to go?

I told him about Nionc Tigo and her unpublished works.

But if the papers are hidden away—

Once we're there, I know I can find them. It's a small country.

And?

And—I don't know. I want to go there and see if I can get them.

He looked at me. My husband studied me like I was a piece of land he was charged with transforming. I didn't like the feeling it gave me. Made me see him in a new light, and not a flattering one. Also, his look made me think that maybe I was embarking on something that wasn't right.

You aren't proposing to go to Slothin and steal the woman's papers, are you?

They've already been stolen! I said. By the Slothin government.

I don't think they would see it that way. In any case, how would you get them out of the country?

I admit I don't have that all worked out, I sad. Not yet. But I will.

I'll only go if you promise you won't do anything illegal.

Now why would I do something illegal?

I don't know, but this is strange. You usually don't act this way.

You haven't read her poems.

True, he said. Are they good?

One of them is amazing. It's about this crow that flies into her skull.

He held up his hand. No more, please. It sounds awful.

It's not, I said. It's a marvelous poem. It's all about how the thoughts you have are really things other than thoughts. It should interest you, since you're all about voices and ghosts and such.

I see your point, and I'm convinced. Under one condition.

The illegal thing, right?

Right.

Okay, I said. I promise. I knew that would convince him. And it did.

The first time my husband had a conversation with walls was on our honeymoon. He sat up in bed early in the morning and looked directly at the picture hanging on the wall next to the television set.

What is it? I asked.

They're here, he whispered. This hotel is haunted.

I laughed. Should we cleanse the area? I asked.

I'm serious, he said. There's spirits in the walls.

He did indeed seem completely serious. I sat with him for a while, but he was already gone in that way I would become accustomed to over the next decades. He was *there*, but *not* there.

His mental faculties had left his body and they were somewhere else. At first I was confused. I had never witnessed that phenomenon quite so strongly. It was like daydreaming on steroids.

I stayed next to him for a few moments, but it was too difficult. I felt like I was a complete intruder. A stranger.

I got out of bed and went to the balcony. Our room overlooked the Pacific ocean. It spread out from the Washington coast as far as I could see. And then even farther. Seeing the expanse of water opened out before me like that, I felt as alone as I have ever felt. Even more alone, considering that my new husband apparently had a predilection for speaking with disembodied spirits.

This particular issue had not come up at any time during our courtship, engagement, or wedding. That probably had something to do with the fact that those three events spanned approximately two weeks. I was beginning to think that deciding to marry so quickly might not have been the best thing to do.

The sun was up, but on the other side of the hotel building. The air was still cool enough to make me wrap my arms around my shoulders and wish

I wasn't there. I stood shivering for a few seconds until I felt the pressure of his hands covering mine.

I turned around and faced him. He hugged me tightly. More tightly than he ever had before.

Bad news? I asked.

No, he said. I'm just thinking maybe I should have told you about this before.

You think? I said.

I've done this all my life.

So to you it's so normal that you think it would be abnormal to tell me about it?

No. Not exactly. Do you want out? We don't have to stay married. I should have told you earlier. I won't argue with you if you see it as a deal breaker.

I tried to look at him, but couldn't. I looked off to the side and considered the past two weeks.

We had an instant and intense attraction. We both, within a few days, knew we wanted to get married. It was as though something bigger than us was at work. After all, he was a heavy equipment operator and I was an intellectual, a language expert. He made his living with his body, I with my mind. What could we possibly have in common? How could we possibly make a union work?

And yet. The attraction seemed almost supernatural. It seemed petty and somehow aberrant to defy it when it first appeared, and still thought so on that honeymoon morning.

I looked at him again. I don't want out, I said.

He seemed relieved.

But maybe we should get some more information about each other?

Yeah, he said. Makes sense. We've only known each other for less than a month. There hasn't been time to tell everything. Do you like asparagus?

I take your point, I said, but spirit talking is a pretty big thing to leave out. I love asparagus.

It's been part of my life ever since I was a kid. I learned to hide it, you know, because people think you're weird if you practice it. How about children? You want any?

I had an imaginary world when I was a kid, I said. Filled with dinosaurs. I can do without children.

Dinosaurs? Weird. Most little girls are into horses. How about pets? Dog or cat?

Oh, I liked horses too. But I liked dinosaurs more. I always imagined them like bears. Fiercely protective of their children. And themselves. Cat. Definitely cat.

Me too, he said. Here's the thing about the spirits. I don't hear them *all* the time, but I do a *lot* of the time. And it's always in walls. They seem to love walls for some reason. Or maybe that's just where I find them. Maybe that's where my particular ability sees them. I don't know. But walls are everywhere, so I guess you should know that a lot of them are going to be talking to me and I'm going to be talking back.

We stood on the balcony for a long time. I wanted to believe I had made the right choice and he tried to convince me I was right to try.

I couldn't stop thinking about the walls, though. So many walls everywhere. I realized that night, I think, that part of him was always going to be separate from me because of all the walls.

Promise me one thing, I said.

Of course, he said. Whatever you want.

Promise me that I come before the spirits.

He said yes. Right away. He didn't hesitate. But I could tell he wanted to.

We arrived in Slothin by train. The country does not have an airport. I found this charming. My husband thought it too backward to even comment on. I could feel him seething in the seat next to me as we crossed the border into Slothin. Waves of discomfort rolled off him like clouds of steam.

I patted his hand. Relax, I said. It's not so bad, the train.

People were not meant to travel like this. If God had wanted us to travel on rails, he would have given us metal wheels.

Very funny, I said.

How many people live in this country? If it's even a country.

Slothin has a fluctuating population, I said, remembering what I read about it in some stuff I found online. It goes up and down with the sheep flocks.

Sheep flocks?

Sheep shearers come in the fall, I said.

There are enough sheep shearers that it significantly affects the population count?

I nodded. The Slothinites number between fifty and fifty five thousand.

And five thousand of those are sheep shearers?

Honestly, you could feel the contempt drip off his words.

Something like that, I said. Though some of that number are support people for the shearers.

Of course, he said.

I turned from him and looked out the window. Green hills passed by in a stately procession. I saw flocks of sheep, of course. One of Tigo's published works was an extended essay on the philosophical aspects of keeping sheep. She discussed the moral implications of raising animals only to take their wool for your own benefit. Didn't I tell you she was the voice of her generation? Maybe all Slothin generations.

I also saw some of the walls. They hugged the hills like inverted furrows. I imagined all the spirits of all the Slothinites over the centuries living in those walls. How many could there be? A million? Perhaps. Maybe less. My mind couldn't do the calculations of the estimates. I settled on a million. A million voices for my husband to ask about the future.

He tried to look past me through the window. I leaned back to give him room. The seat-back supported me in a way that felt very comforting. The landscape held his attention for a few minutes. I closed my eyes. The motion of the train soothed me. It felt like I was being rocked to sleep.

This Tigo person, he said.

I opened my eyes. Yes?

She's a big deal?

She is in Slothin. And she's considered quite the writer by literary experts.

Why do you want to translate her?

She's got a unique perspective. She's a cosmopolitan soul that came from a hidden, maybe even backward, country. Plus, if I became her translator, it would be very good for me. It would make my reputation in literary circles. I'd have more work than I could use. I would have to turn away translation jobs. I could set my own price.

This he seemed to understand.

She might be living in one of those walls, he said. Those stone walls. He gestured towards the landscape beyond the window.

It's quite possible, I said.

Once, picking up on the theme of where spirits like to reside, I asked my husband why the walls were such a popular location for the spirits. Did they ever live in other places?

Sometimes in the hulls of boats, he said. Although that's really just a kind of wall anyway. Also, you'll sometimes find them in fences. Sometimes. Very very rarely, though. Fences are too flimsy for them. They slip out of them because there's nothing to hold them. It's like trying to catch mist with a net.

I see, I said. These spirits, they don't get tired of hanging around?

Oh sure, he said. They come and they go. Some will stay for years and years. Others will be there for a short time, then I'll never hear from them again.

We bought a house in Seagull Cove soon after we were married. Near the ocean, just like on our honeymoon. We both found that the ocean fed us. Its rhythms and strengths built our souls. Not to mention the house, bathed in fog most mornings, taking salt spray during the day. It didn't take long for my husband to find the spirits.

The house was saturated with them. Every brick was haunted. My husband could hardly keep up. He was inundated with conversation. I told him that would never do. I could not have him talking to spirits every minute of every day. I would go mad.

So we sold that house and moved to another in town. It was only slightly less haunted. We moved again. And again.

I was looking for a place that had only very few spirits, or maybe none at all. Finally, after two years of searching, and after going through a good half dozen houses, we found one, on Starfish Drive, up on the bluff overlooking downtown Seagull Cove.

In this house, the spirits tended to hang back a great deal. They did not contact my husband all that much. Maybe a couple of times a week. I could live with that. I asked him if the frequency of contact was okay with him.

Oh, sure, he said. It's not like I *need* to talk to them. It's just kind of nice when they do. And I can't say no.

So my husband had a hobby that didn't take up a lot of his time. That was okay with me. Everyone needs a hobby, and most of the time he was available to me. I felt like the kind of woman who needed her man a little too much. It bothered me, at first, but I let it go.

Meanwhile, my translation business took off. I had discovered my talent for languages in college. After I graduated, and before I met my husband, I had gotten work translating owners manuals for cell phones. It was boring work, but very fast and lucrative. Once I did a few, a whole world opened up to me. Soon I was deep into translating all kinds of documents. It became my world.

I can't explain what it did to me, but it transformed my view of the universe. Suddenly, the babble of voices all around me were tamed. I could navigate the ins and outs of meaning with little problem. Nothing was difficult for me anymore. People and their ways of speaking were an open book to me. It was as though the incomprehensible babble of the world flowed from the chaos of the air and coalesced in my brain.

I took on more work. I spit out more words. It got to the point where I was translating every phrase I saw on a road sign or a billboard. I could not pick up a utility bill without seeing the words in a dozen other languages.

I saw that I was going to harm myself if I continued. I sought to tame my predilection for translation, but it didn't work. Not really. Something had turned my brain over, or slipped it into another dimension. Something. My mind became a translating machine.

And that's when I met the love of my life.

The train pulled into the station of the capital city of Slothin, also named Slothin. Maybe such a small county has room for only a small imagination? Not that I was being critical. It just gave the impression of being even more provincial than I had expected.

We got off the train and a young man with a bicycle pulling a two-seat trailer approached us and asked, in broken English if he could take us to our hotel.

I answered in perfect Slothin that we would be happy to take him up on his offer.

His face brightened considerably and began talking in rapid Slothin, asking me who my relatives were. He assumed I must be a native. I assured him that I was merely a visitor to his fine city and country.

But you know our language. he said.

I do.

He smiled. *Please get in,* he said. *I will take you to your lodgings.*

My husband and I climbed into the trailer and the man exerted himself considerably to get the pedals moving. I saw the sinews on his arms raise themselves like snakes writhing. We went perhaps three blocks. Slothin is not a large city. We stopped in front of a seven story building.

Is this the building where Nionc Tingo's nephew died? I asked.

The man nodded. *Yes, yes,* he said. *Very sad situation. Do you know him?*

I know about his aunt.

His aunt, said the man, *was a great woman. She makes Slothinites very proud. She makes the sheep magical.*

Yes she does, I said.

What's all the chatter about? asked my husband. He was cranky and tired.

Shush, I said to him. I'm getting a feel for the country.

Your bags will arrive in a few minutes, said the man. *They will be delivered to your room.*

I thanked him and handed him a few dollars. He put up his hand. *No need,* he said. *I am paid by the government of Slothin.*

I put my dollars in my pocket. *Perhaps,* I said, *you can tell me where Tigo's papers are kept.*

He nodded vigorously. *Yes, of course,* he said. *They are in a safe location outside of town, near the cemetery. Kept in the mausoleum.*

Truly? I asked.

Yes indeed, he said. *Very truly indeed.*

I thanked him and me and my husband checked in and took the the stairs to our sixth-floor room. Slothin, it appeared, did not abide elevators.

We should have gotten a lower room, said my husband.

I agreed with him. I wanted the view, I said. I didn't know about the elevator situation.

He wanted to tell me I *should* have thought of it, but he refrained. He could be polite that way, when he wanted to be.

Our room was pleasantly spacious. A big window opened up onto the city below and the countryside beyond. Really, it was more appropriate to call Slothin a town, not a city.

The stone walls looked even more breathtaking than I imagined they would. They spread out beyond the town limits like an art piece. Both my husband and I stood at the window looking at them for a long time. Sheep dotted the spaces between the walls.

We also saw a few people walking with the sheep, and some dogs. But it was the walls, more than anything, that stood out.

I looked over at my husband. He licked his lips and got this blank look in his eyes.

You think there's spirits there? I asked, knowing the answer.

Without a doubt, he said.

Before we knew each other, we were walking the shores of a beach in Washington state at the same time. Of such coincidences are lifelong partnerships generated and sustained.

Both of us were on vacation. Both of us were passing the time aimlessly, walking on the beach. We had both been attracted by a particular rock in the sand. It rose up to a dozen feet or so and was encrusted with moss, seaweed, and barnacles. We stood beside each other, admiring the rock.

I wonder what it would take to move it, he said.

I wonder what it's trying to say to us, I said.

We looked at each other, forgot about the rock, and began walking along the waterline together. We fell into an easy pace, immediately comfortable with each other.

He spoke in English. I heard him in at least seven other languages. This was becoming a problem for me, but with him, it wasn't. With him, I felt completely at home. He sensed *something* in me. He couldn't put it into words, but he knew I was something special.

Nothing more appealing than a man who thinks you are exceptional. Without that, well, where can a relationship go? Without that, it can only devolve into bickering and resentment.

I think. At least, that's what I've seen in others.

As for me, I'm not sure I saw anything exceptional in him. I did see that he was solid. He wasn't going to go off and behave in some strange manner, or do something that would harm him or me. I could see that immediately.

So we spent the rest of the day together. Then the next day, and that led to a few nights together. Before long our lives were divided into two: the time before we met and the time after. That's when we knew we were for each other.

The wedding was a simple affair. I had a friend with me and he had a friend with him. We didn't tell either of our families until it was all over.

Then we went on our honeymoon and I found out that he wasn't quite so rock-steady as I had thought.

But we got over that. I think.

Actually, I'm still not exactly sure of that because soon after, maybe a month into our marriage, his accident happened.

That night, after he had talked to police and the accident investigators, after he had apologized to the dead man's family, tearfully and with heaving convulsions, he returned to our house and spent the remainder of the day not in the comfort of my arms but with the spirits in the walls.

I'll leave you with that picture for the moment. Imagine him in the twilight of the evening hours, sitting alone in the dark.

I had offered him some food, but he wasn't hungry. I had offered him an embrace, which he accepted, briefly, but which did not comfort him as I had hoped it would. I even offered him a drink, but he refused that as well. Instead, he immersed himself in the voices coming from the walls.

Now flash forward three decades.

I think I want to go down to those rock walls, he said.

Of course, I said. Let's go.

We navigated the stairwell again. It was much easier going down. The kid who took us from the train station was there waiting for us. He offered to take us out of town to some of the rock walls.

Some are better than others, he said. *I can show you the really good ones.* He didn't exactly grin at us, but he did have this ebullient air about him. It was as if he really wanted to help us, even though I knew he was only doing this for the money. He couldn't really *like* helping visitors to Slothin. Could he?

Well, I won't try to fathom the minds of people working in the tourist industry. Instead, I asked him to steer us toward a good wall near the cemetery. He grinned and nodded. *No problem,* he said.

My husband would just as soon have gone out to the countryside on his own, but he reluctantly agreed to accept the young man's help and we got in the trailer of his bicycle again and off we went.

Slothin City had no outskirts. It wasn't big enough for that. The central core of the city was about four blocks wide and six blocks long. Once we were out of that grid, we were in the green hills.

We went past many stone walls. They rose to about six feet or so. Plenty big enough to hide a view of the countryside from our eyes.

We were forced to consider the land of Slothin in little chunks, surrounded by stone walls. Each enclosure was a few acres. The kid stopped at gates, got off the bicycle, opened the gate, got back on the bicycle, rolled through the entrance, got out, closed the gate, got back on, and continued pedaling.

It was a decidedly slow means of transport, but it had its charms nonetheless, chief among them a view of the walls. They soon seemed to tower above us. The rest of Slothin disappeared from my imagination just as much as from my view.

The country, so small to begin with, created an illusion of expanse by closing off the view. It made your mind think there was an immensity beyond the walls.

Hearing any voices yet? I asked my husband.

He had his senses tuned to the stones, piled up all around us in stately walls.

Nothing yet, he said.

Sorry, I said.

The kid kept up a chatter as we went slowly along the roads. *The walls are thousands of years old,* he said. *Sometimes rocks fall to the ground. People put them back. All of Slothin works to keep the walls in good repair. The rocks don't come from Slothin. They were brought here from other parts of the world. Early Slothinites spent their days collecting rocks. We don't know why. The sheep came next. We love to have sheep in Slothin. It is every Slothinite's dream to have a flock of sheep. Are you comfortable? There is a small inn up ahead. We can stop and have refreshments. You must be warm.*

I translated some of this chatter for my husband. He took it in but seemed distracted. Uncomfortable, actually.

Everything okay? I asked.

He waved his hand with some irritation, as if to say something like: Stop pestering me. I recognized the gesture, but didn't press it. He wanted to be left alone for a while, that was fine with me.

Tell me more of what you know about Nionc Tigo, I said to our tour guide.

She was a great writer, he said.

Have you read her books?

All Slothinites read her books. She wrote the poetry of the sheep. He reached into his back pocket and retrieved a slim volume of her poetry. I recognized it. It was, indeed, a collection of poems on sheep and sheep herding.

We came to another enclosure. The tiny nation of Slothin suddenly felt bigger than China. Could any place have so many fenced off bits of land?

Isn't it difficult to keep sheep in such an environment? I asked. *After all, if the country removed all these fences, the sheep would have room to roam.*

What you say is true, he said. *But Slothinites love their walls. They are beauty. They are like the sculpture of the nation. Our country is a kind of sculpture. A kind of art piece.*

I nodded.

We continued for another half an hour or so, then we entered a stone enclosure with a building. It was so startling that I thought I might be dreaming.

The building was round and domed. It was built of stone, but I could see immediately it was a sacred structure. It had an air of the protected about it.

Our guide stopped. We got out of the trailer and stood on the ground. Our guide indicated the building with a long arc of his hand. *The Mausoleum,* he said.

Can we go inside? I asked.

Of course. He walked up to the door and opened it. I stepped inside. My husband elected to remain outside.

I'll go see what the walls have to say, he said. Maybe if I get closer to them.

I nodded and followed the young man through the interior halls of the mausoleum. The lighting was dim. Marble faces with the names of dead Slothinites hid in the shadows. The walls also held dioramas of dead slothinites. Urns with ashes and some bits of that person's life. It was like looking inside aquariums and seeing not fish and water, but trinkets and kitsch. I saw someone's elementary school report card, another's tunic, another's baby shoes. Strange memorials to the dead.

Many slothinites are here, said my guide. *We don't bury our dead. The ground is for grazing sheep, you see.*

I do see, I said.

We took a few turns and soon my sense of direction was scrambled. I didn't know where we were and simply worked to keep up with the guide.

We came to a large vault. I saw Nionc Tigo's name in raised metal letters. My guide stopped and stood next to her name and grinned as widely as it was possible to grin. It looked like his face was about to be cut in two at the mouth.

I shook that disturbing image from my psyche and stepped forward to put my fingertips on the letters of Nionc's name. *Her papers,* I said. *They're in here?*

He nodded. *With her ashes.*

He let me study the marble face for a time. He probably thought I was having some reverential moment, but I was trying to ascertain the possibility of opening the vault on my own. I saw no mechanism for doing so. Surely it would be possible?

After a few moments, he said *we needed to get going.* Since I had seen all that I *could* see, I agreed, though reluctantly. We retraced our steps and emerged into the sunlight and fresh air.

We got back in the bicycle's trailer and the guide asked us if we wanted to go on. I said it was time to go back, so we started our return journey to Slothin City. I asked my husband if he had any more luck listening to the walls. He shook his head and didn't say anything. Fine. He was in a mood. I'd leave him for a while.

But as we journeyed back, my husband was growing more and more agitated. He could not keep still. His face was red and puffy. What is wrong with you? I asked him.

This land, he said. This land needs to be scraped away.

What are you talking about?

I need to find an excavator. There are rocks under here that need to be exposed.

I searched for something to say to him. I had never seen him so perturbed. We aren't going to find an excavator in this country, I said. Haven't you noticed it's almost completely rural?

They built those buildings in the city. They had to have moved some earth to do it.

I asked our guide to please hurry. He glanced back and saw my husband's face and complied immediately. He doubled his speed, which didn't mean he was going particularly fast, but it showed he understood we were in a hurry, which I appreciated.

Just get me on an excavator, he said. Find me one.

I asked our guide if he knew where I might find heavy equipment. He told me there was a place and gave me the address.

We got back to the hotel. The poor kid offered to *carry* my husband up the stairs. I paid him some money and told him that would be fine. We could manage from there. He refused my money again, but I persisted until he accepted. Then he disappeared.

I walked with my husband to a bench in the lobby of the hotel. There was no way I was going to have him navigate the stairwell. Not the way he was looking.

I sat beside him. Did the stone walls cause you some discomfort? I asked.

He shook his head. It's being here, he said. This country is—empty.

Empty?

He lowered his head and whispered to me. They have no spirits. It's completely material. Every bit of it.

But how can that be? I asked.

I don't know, but it is.

Are you okay to be alone for a few minutes? I asked.

He nodded. I think so.

I went to the desk. The woman behind the counter looked attentive, but vacant, like she was there because she had to be, but she didn't understand why all these people were always coming to her *asking* for things. People like me.

I showed her the address the other Slothinite had given me. *Where is this?* I asked.

She pulled out a piece of paper and drew a map for me. My destination was not too far away. How could it be? I went back to my husband and helped him to his feet. Come on, I said.

Where are we going?

Just follow me.

We went back out into the streets of Slothin City. There were a few people out and about. They all looked like they belonged in the fields. I didn't see a single suit anywhere. Mostly they wore ragged tunics and boots crusted with dirt. I only saw a few pairs of shoes.

Their demeanor followed no particular pattern. Some looked straight at us, even greeted us with waves of their hands or nods of their heads, but others would not look up from the ground as they passed. Indeed, it seemed they resolutely chose *not* to look up, as if they might break something with their eyes if they violated that principle.

A warm breeze, not unpleasant, brought the smell of the fields to our nostrils. It invigorated me. I could tell it was doing wonders for my husband as well. He was getting back some of his normal color and seemed not nearly as weak as he did before.

I looked down at my map. We rounded a corner and came to a short street that ended at a stone wall. Beyond the wall, the countryside of Slothin spread out far and wide. At the end of the street I saw our destination: a small shack of a building. We entered and found a dusty interior and an old man. He sat in at a small desk and popped to his feet when we entered.

I understand you have an excavator.

He glanced out a window in the back of the shack.

We're foreigners, I said, *but we know how to operate one. My husband would like to see it. He's a professional in his own country.*

The man looked doubtful, but escorted us to the back of the shack. He opened the door and we stepped into a stone-wall enclosure. Three excavators sat in the yard. They looked rusted and in disrepair. I asked my husband which one looked best.

None of them, he said.

Pick one, I said.

What's this about? he asked. Why are we here? I thought this was a vacation.

I don't know where you got that idea, I said. We're here for my work.

He sounded exasperated and lifted his hand and pointed to the one I would have picked as well. That one looks like it might not fall apart under me, he said.

Good, I said. Climb up into the cab.

He wanted to say no, I could tell, but he didn't. Instead he walked over to the excavator, and eased himself into the cab.

Despite himself, he grinned widely. I could tell he was happy to be there. His hands moved to the controls. His body language told me everything I needed to know.

I turned to the old man. *May we use it for the afternoon?* I asked.

He scratched his head. I produced some money and handed it to him. At first he didn't want to touch the cash, but, reluctantly, he eventually reached for it and put it in his pocket. *If you want to take it off the lot,* he said, *you'll have to give a reason to the authorities.*

Is there gas in it? I asked.

Most assuredly, he said. *Did you hear what I told you about the authorities?*

Of course, of course, I said. He seemed doubtful. *Most assuredly,* I said. At this, he smiled.

I left him and went to the side of the excavator and looked up at my husband. We were in a strange country. Culture shock had hit us both, but for him, things were looking up. He was in his element. How does it feel? I asked.

Like being home, he said.

I'm going to leave you here for a while, I said.

Where you going?

To check up on Nionc Tigo.

Who's she?

Why we came here, remember? The writer with the untranslated works.

Oh yeah, he said, but he was gone.

He was imagining working the ground with the excavator. He put his hands on the steering wheel and worked the levers a bit. Just a big overgrown kid, my husband. Like any boy, he wanted to work the big machines.

After we had been married a few years, and after my husband had the accident that killed his co-worker, we were in a strange place. My translation abilities were growing along with my commissions. I had so many that I couldn't keep up and had to turn some of them down. I developed a reputation sufficient to allow me to charge exorbitant rates for my services, with many people willing to pay those rates.

All this was good, because my husband took to the walls more and more. He missed weeks of work at a time. He got fired so many times for not showing up that I lost count. The spirits sustained him emotionally, but didn't do much for his bank account.

All of this put a strain on me. I wanted him to be healthy, but he didn't appear to have the same aspiration for himself. I knew men needed their work or they withered, but it was strange to see it happen so dramatically in my own man. I implored him to keep a job. He said he would try, but he didn't. Not for a long time.

I lost myself in languages. I knew living with a depressed man was not good for me or for him, but I didn't know what to do.

I sought advice from friends and they told me I had to lay down an ultimatum. Either he got his life together, or I would leave him. I resolved to do just that, but it never happened. I didn't have the heart. Or the will.

Mostly I fell into my translation. The catacombs of meaning in the labyrinth of other languages. Words floated through my world. They stamped everything with import. I left my husband to his walls, the ones that said everything was going to be okay, even if they weren't. Even if they couldn't *know*. None of that mattered.

We lived together but separately for some years. Maybe three. Maybe four. When he came out of his fog, finally, we were different people. It took us a while to come back together as a couple, but it happened. I learned that time can take care of just about anything.

I don't know what he learned. Patience, maybe. Or the power of the abiding love of his wife. Something. He never told me and after a while I stopped asking. I was just happy to have him back.

I assumed my husband would drive the excavator around the yard for a bit. Maybe lift the bucket. Maybe sit in the cab and soak in the surroundings. Something innocuous like that. I left him to his toy and returned to the hotel. I was dog tired for some reason I could not understand. I stretched out on the bed for a nap. My eyes closed almost immediately.

I was awakened by the sound of my door being pummeled by fists and the sound of a frantic voice shouting. *Wake up! Wake up! Foreigner, wake up!*

It took me a second to take in the words. They were not English. I forgot where I was, but got up out of bed and tripped over my feet as I made my way to the door and pulled it open.

The kid who had been helping us reached in and grabbed my hand and pulled me out of the room. Hey, I said in English, what's going on?

He didn't say anything. I didn't have any shoes on, but that didn't matter to him. He had surprising strength. It was like his arms were banded with steel. All that work pulling tourists around Slothin must build him up.

Stop, I said in Slothin.

No time, no time. Your husband is crazy man. Crazy.

What?

Follow me, just follow me. He hurried his pace and pulled me along with him. We pounded down the steps and got to the first floor.

I heard a sound, like things breaking. People were running in the street toward the shack where I had left my husband. Visions of him hurt and bleeding flitted through my brain but I suppressed them. Better to find out what happened before making myself frightened of what actually *did* happen. The guide dropped my hand, but kept running.

I worked hard to keep up with him. My bare feet were soon hurting from running on the sidewalk. I didn't care if they were torn up to hamburger. I ran faster than I had ever run before. We got to the shack and the old man who looked after it saw me and ran to me.

He tried to grab my shoulders. He was shouting something incoherent in Slothin but I didn't care what he had to say. I shook him off and ran through the shack. I called for my husband.

The excavator I left him in wasn't there. The stone wall on the other side of the yard was broken. A path had been pushed through it to the other side.

You didn't have to be Sherlock Holmes to piece together what had happened. My husband had run the excavator through the wall.

I ran to the gap and looked through it. Perhaps five acres of land separated me from the next wall, which had a similar hole in.

I sprinted across the grass toward the second break.

Sheep were everywhere. They came up to me as I ran. As though they wanted something. As though I could offer then anything. I made sheep noises at them, pretending I knew their language. After all, maybe I did.

I saw the puff of diesel emissions that poured out of the excavator. It stained the sky dark brown. I called to my husband again. I came to another break in the walls. The tracks of the excavator had left furrows in the ground. I saw where they had also crushed some of the rocks of the wall that had been loosened when my husband drove through the wall.

I leaned against the edge of the wall, breathing hard. Something about this felt awful. It wasn't just that my husband was behaving in a criminal manner, it was that the walls felt wounded, and the land felt wounded because of it. I felt the unravelling of Slothin.

The walls held the country together, and now they were being destroyed. The excavator puffed and chugged and grunted and roared, like a creature. Some marauding dragon, maybe. Did Slothin life admit of creatures such as dragons? Would dragons be troubled by stone walls? Probably not. They would push right through them.

I stepped over the rubble of crushed rock and kept running.

I caught up to the excavator after three more breaks in the walls. I ran next to the excavator and past it and then turned and stopped and waved at the cab. The excavator kept going. Not too fast, but fast enough to make my heart jump.

Was he going to stop? I made plans to jump out of the way at the last second, but before I had to implement those plans, the excavator belched and snorted and slowed to a halt, a mere three feet from me.

I climbed up onto the excavator and looked inside the cab. My husband was in there. Or something that looked like him. He was not behaving like my man, however. He was agitated and seemed to be breathing very hard. I pulled the door open and put my hand inside.

Turn it off, I said.

The excavator was still rumbling and shaking. I saw the keys hanging from the ignition. Off, I said again. Turn it off.

He looked at me. Something softened in him and in an instant he returned to the man I remembered.

The mausoleum, he said.

What?

The papers of that writer, I was going to push the mausoleum over and crush the vault and get the papers out.

I heard shouting behind me. Slothin citizens were on their way. An angry mob, I was sure. My husband and I were not going to be the most popular visitors to Slothin. I wondered what their jails were like.

As it turned out, Slothin did not have any jails. Not that there wasn't crime, and not that some people didn't need punishing, but they took care of matters in their own way.

When someone committed a crime, that person was billeted in someone's house where they could be watched over and nurtured back to some sort of civilized behavior. Often the host was the victim.

It was a strange form of justice to my sensibilities, but it seemed to work for them. The theory was that the perpetrator and the victim created a situation that needed resolving, and they needed to resolve it together. By living in the victim's house, the criminal learned that the victim was a person with rights and dignity. By hosting the criminal, the victim learned that the criminal was a person with rights and dignity.

Or something like that. I don't think I ever truly understood it. If the crime was particularly bad, or if the crime was against the state, the criminal was housed in a government official's house.

My husband and I ended up in the prime minister's residence since the destruction of the stone walls was considered quite a serious crime indeed.

The head of state of Slothin was a very nice old woman. She lived alone: Her husband had died some years before. She spent her days entertaining the requests of citizens who streamed through her door from early in the morning to late in the afternoon.

We arrived at her house the evening of my husband's rampage, escorted, as we were, by several Slothin citizens, including the old man at the excavator shack and the young man who had wheeled us around town. There was no force involved, merely a reassuring insistence that this was the best thing to happen.

We knocked on the prime minister's door. She opened it herself and welcomed us with hugs and kisses on our cheeks. Then she stepped back and surveyed us.

I tried to maintain a sense of decorum and dignity. My husband was not inclined to follow my example. He was rumpled and scowling.

Well, well, said the prime minister in perfect English, it seems our visitors have gone off the rails a little. She clucked her tongue. No matter. We'll fix you up. Are you hungry?

I am, I said. My husband said nothing. I elbowed him in the ribs and he grunted assent.

What is wrong with you? I whispered to him. He didn't answer, but the prime minister did.

Culture shock, I would guess, she said. It happens. Come in, come in.

She indicated the expanse of her house. It was not exactly a plush setting for the head of a state. The living room was small and looked smaller than it was by the deployment of a lot of brown in the decorating, and by the fact that all the windows were closed up and the heat was turned high.

Sit down, please, she said. I'll get a snack from the kitchen.

Can I help? I asked.

Oh, she said, as brightly as you please, I think you've helped more than enough for one day.

I couldn't argue with her. My husband and I sat on the couch, a wood-framed affair with a thin futon-like cushion on top of it. It felt like a prison cot. And yet, it also felt like home in a strange kind of way.

We heard a fridge door opening from around the corner. Jars on countertops, plates being slammed onto a table. It sounded like the prime minister was upset.

Where we going to sleep? asked my husband.

I don't know, I said.

This is crazy, he said. They can't make us live here.

They can and they have, I said. And I don't think you should be carrying on about craziness, not after the events of today.

He started to argue with me, then thought better of it and kept his mouth shut. I was irritated with him for putting us in such a position. My annoyance was compounded by the realization that I was now farther from my goal of acquiring Nionc Tigo's papers.

I was doing it for you, he said in a whisper.

For me?

I was going to knock down the mausoleum so we could get those poet's books.

I looked at him, incredulous, but he appeared completely serious. And you don't see how that is just a little bit nuts? I asked.

He shrugged. I didn't know what else to do. This place was making me antsy.

Antsy?

Yeah.

Maybe you should have taken a walk.

That would have been better, he conceded.

The prime minister returned to the living room carrying a tray laden with a plate of crackers, some dried meat I couldn't identify, and three glasses of cloudy water.

Lamb jerky, said the prime minister. A subject brought it yesterday. I tasted it. It's quite good. And the crackers are my own. All washed down with some limeade. She set the tray down on the small table in front of us. Go on, she said. What do they say in your country? Dig in?

Thank you, I said, and leaned over and took the glass in my hand. It was cool and wet. Everything in the room seemed unreal and every movement I made seemed to disturb some cosmic setting that the prime minister had set into place.

The house was inelegant, to be sure, but it felt like it had some semblance of perfection, as though it had been hewn by divine hands from an unruly rock.

I felt like we had already violated the land to such an extent that any other movement on my part would only add to the chaos. My husband must have felt the same sort of thing. He did not move from his position.

The prime minister noticed our hesitation. I don't mean to tell you what to do, she said, but you must be hungry. At least try some of the crackers if nothing else.

I dared disturb the tranquility of the setting by taking a cracker and biting off a small piece. It was dry and salty. I smiled at the prime minister.

You know, the first time I got caught doping mischief, back when I was a young girl, I was very hungry. My hosts offered me food and I didn't want it. I thought I would rather die. Perhaps you are feeling the same way now?

I nodded. I am filled with shame, I said.

The prime minister acknowledged my words with raised eyebrows. Indeed, she said. And what about you? She turned to my husband, who shrugged his shoulders.

He seems to have lapsed into a depression, I said.

Understandable, said the prime minister. I suspect our ways of punishment are foreign to you, am I correct?

I nodded.

Well, let me tell you a story. Then, after our story, I'll discuss Nionc Tigo with you. How would that be?

I'm not much for stories, I said.

She raised her eyebrows. Really?

I couldn't believe I had just said that. I was insulting the head of the country in which my husband had committed a pretty serious crime against property.

No offense, I said to the prime minister.

None taken. However, I'm going to insist on the story. In my capacity as prime minister and symbolic victim. When I was very young, I hated sheep. Why is not important. They are docile creatures, and kind of dumb. All they do is eat, poop, and grow wool. It seemed a wretched existence. Well, my attitude was not a good way to be in Slothin. We have based our entire economy on sheep. As you have seen, they are everywhere. I wanted nothing more than to leave the country and allÚ sheep. So, when I was only twelve years old, that is what I decided to do. I got up early one morning, before the sun, and before anyone else in the house, and I snuck out and walked the dew-soaked pastures of Slothin. I was not entirely rash. I waited until it was full moon so my way would be lit through the land. I went through gates, and climbed over walls. Sheep were all around me and I shooed them away. My mind, young as it was, convinced me that I had been traveling for some time. A very long time. But it wasn't so. The sun still had not come up and I was hungry. I climbed more walls. I was also cold. I shivered and looked back the way I had come, longing for the warmth of my bed and the comfort of a breakfast made by my father. I stood in the pre-dawn light and wondered if my adventure would have to be aborted. Slothin is a small country, as you know. It was not something I knew, then. I thought it was a vast wilderness of walls and sheep. I decided that I need sustenance for my journey and I found a darkened farmhouse, much like my own, though somewhat smaller. I approached it with trepidation, knowing I was doing wrong, and one level, caring deeply, but on another, not caring at all. I was on an adventure, after all. Didn't adventurers break rules? I certainly thought so. The front door was not locked, as was and is the custom in Slothin. I entered the house and crept through the front door and went into the darkened kitchen and looked through the shelves for something to eat. I found boiled eggs and smoked meat and stuffed them under my shirt. I found a loaf of bread and took that as well. I tiptoed out of the kitchen and opened the front door and was out of the house before a hand fell on my shoulder and grabbed my shirt with a force that felt like a noose around my neck. I screamed and dropped the food. The egg shells cracked, the meat fell into dust, and the bread, crusty and thick, broke into two pieces. I tried to run away but only succeeded in stepping on the bread and ruining it for anyone to eat. I was more frightened than I had ever been in my life. I had been caught. I was now a thief. And not even a grand or competent thief. I had stolen a few bits of food and was caught. The hand that held me yanked at my shirt and I turned around to face a very old man. At least, he seemed old to me.

You forgot to take strawberry preserves for the bread, he growled.

I didn't know if he was joking or serious. I didn't know if he was going to feed me or kill me. It was a most peculiar sensation, to exist on the knife edge of uncertainty like that. My whole being wanted to wrest itself from his grip and fly away. I tested the possibility by pulling away, but he was much too strong for me. I remember wondering how someone so feeble-looking could have such power in his arms. He pulled me inside the house and lifted me up on a chair. I started crying. I hated that I cried. I wanted to be stronger than that. I wanted to be in control and I wanted to be defiant. Yes, I was a thief, but that didn't mean I had to be weak.

What are you doing out on a night like this? he asked.

I hate sheep, I said, surprised by my words.

He nodded. That's a good thing. They smell and they don't know their own strength. Sheep are powerful creatures, but they are docile, as though they were weak creatures. Isn't that a sad thing?

I nodded, indicating that I thought it was, even though I had never given the matter much thought.

How about you? he asked. Are you strong or weak?

As he talked, he put wood into his stove and lit it and cut pieces of sheep meat from a slab that he had on the counter. When the pan on the stove got sufficiently hot, he put the slices in the pan and let them heat up. I watched him do all this with my mind in a dozen different places. I wanted to be back home, I wanted to be back on my adventure, and I wanted to eat this man's breakfast. I didn't know what I wanted.

No answer? he asked. Are you thinking about it? Are you a deep thinker, is that it? Should I wait for your wisdom?

He leaned on the counter of his kitchen and folded his arms over his chest and regarded me with the kindest eyes of anyone I had ever known.

I never meant to take your food, I said.

So, my house grabbed you from the fields and my cupboards forced food into your hands and under you jacket? *Bad* house!

I laughed. Not because I thought he was funny, but because I thought I should.

He waved his hand in the air, as though twirling a length of string. No matter, he said. What's done is done. You've committed a crime against me and now I must help set you back on a crime-free life. Not to mention, get you back to your parents. Do they know you're here?

I shook my head.

Are they wicked parents?

I shook my head again.

Is your home life awful? Do things happen there that would cause you harm or anguish?

I shook my head again.

Then there is no reason for you to leave your home. Do I have that right? At your age, you should not be on your own unless you have some means of support or are much better at stealing.

I thought maybe I should laugh again, but I did not. Instead I shrugged my shoulders. I was in a mess and didn't know what to do about it. I was at the mercy of this man, I suppose. But he was also well acquainted with our ways and and seemed to be behaving kindly toward me. He had the most soft eyes. They were filled with a kindness I did not know even existed in my short life up to then. He didn't say anything for a long time. He just held my gaze and I didn't have the power to look away, even though he was making me very uncomfortable with his kind eyes.

Finally, as much to end the silence as to confess my wrongdoings and shortcomings, I blurted out again that I hated sheep.

Ahhh, he said. A persistent issue, it seems. Why do you hate sheep?

They stink and they are cowardly.

I see. And this offends you?

I wasn't sure what he meant by that. They make me sick, I said. Is that the same as offend?

It'll do for now, he said.

It must be awful for you to live in Slothin, what with all the sheep around all the time, making you sick.

I nodded my head. I saw that I could have left, then. He was farther from the door than I was, by a good few strides. I was pretty sure I was a faster runner than he was, and I would have gotten a head-start if I chose to bolt from the house. I saw the way. I had nothing of his on my person any longer. All I had to do was run for all I was worth and I would be out of his house and out of his life for good. Then I could have continued my escape from Slothin.

But I didn't do that. He went to his coat rack and retrieved a hat and jacket of his own. He put them on and asked me if I would be so kind as to introduce him to my parents. He stood at the door, obviously expecting me to accompany him.

We walked through the fields together. The whole while he talked about Slothin. What a wonderful country it was. He mentioned the sky over Slothin, how it woke up the world every morning and filled all Sloth-inites with the love of life. He pushed out his chest and breathed in great gulps of air and told me the air over Slothin was the purest and freshest of any air anywhere. The rock that the ancient builders used to build the walls were the best hewn and most magnificent rocks anywhere. The very grass we walked on was the finest variety of grass ever known to anyone any-where. And so on. He did not stop talking about Slothin. He had me kick off my shoes and walk barefoot on the grass. Is that not the finest grass anywhere? he asked me. Why would you want to walk on any other grass?

I had no answer for him. By this time I was feeling as though I had stumbled into a mad man's clutches. A gentle mad man, but loopy nevertheless. How could anyone go on and on about Slothin, even if they truly did believe Slothin was a marvelous place?

He made a point of approaching sheep as we walked. The sheep seemed to cluster around him. Seemed to *want* to be near him. I didn't know what that was about. I had never known sheep to prefer one person over another. They even tried to group around me, but I had learned to keep them away. I gave them the stink eye and they retreated from me. I noticed the man noticing this and a look of amusement mixed with pity crossed his face. I saw immediately that the pity was aimed at me. And what was I to do with that? Why did he pity me? It seemed ridiculous.

We continued on. The sun was up. The grass was still wet with dew. Clouds blotched the sky and by the time we got back to my house, the world was bright and cheerful. My crime was not going to be hidden away, I could see that.

My parents ran to me when they saw me and the man approaching. They're going to hug me, I said to the man.

I expect so, he said.

Then they're going to punish me.

I expect so, he said.

I waited as they ran. I did not run toward them. I had no urge to do so. I believe I loved my parents as much as any child loved their parents, but I also believe I was ready to break from them. It's an inevitable part of life, of course, but also a sad part for both parties. The man patted me on the back, as if he understood. It felt like the first time someone had every understood me, although I know that was ridiculous. Know that *now*. Not then. At that time I wanted to replace my parents with the man.

My parents ran through herds of sheep. My mother was ahead of my father. He lumbered. He was not a good runner. My Mother, on the other hand, was animated by fear, I think. She was scared of what I might have turned into on my short sojourn. I was gone all of three hours, but to her, I think it must have seemed like three centuries.

We didn't so much embrace as collide. My mother slammed into me and she held me for a long time, crushing me against her. Above my head, I heard my father talking to the man who escorted me home. There was suspicion in his voice, but it faded as the man answered my father's questions and my father decided he was not a deviant or dangerous in any way.

When my mother finally pulled away from me, she brushed tears from her eyes and looked at my face.

Life brings us moments. They are separated by long stretches of noise, it seems. The moments are islands in the noise. They are what we live for, I think. When I looked at my mother then, it was one of those moments. I felt in my heart, perhaps for the first time, what it was to truly love another. How that love could easily cause grief.

The prime minister stopped talking. She stared away into space, as though chasing after a thought that had escaped her.

My husband and I looked at each other. My husband leaned close to me. She's listening for voices in the walls, he whispered.

She is not, I said. She's remembering her mother.

Same thing, said my husband.

The prime minister finally looked away from her distant object of attention. After that, she said, things were different. I never ran away from my house again. Of course, I eventually grew up and moved away, but I didn't *run* away. There's a difference.

Of course, I said.

The man that caught me stealing from him was obliged to cook me meals and offer me shelter. He did so quite willingly. I stayed at his house for a few nights and it turned out he was a pretty good cook. It was a humbling experience for us both. It brought us to a better understanding of each other and of humanity in general. At first it seems ludicrous to have the victim of a crime be obliged to help the perpetrator, but, you know, it has served Slothin well. Your crime has obliged me to help you. Do you understand?

I don't, I said. Not exactly.

The prime minister smiled. Well, maybe you don't have to.

I'm wondering what happened to the man, said my husband.

He lived a long life, and a good one, I think. After I became grown up, I lost touch with him for a while. I remember him fondly and when I heard that he was dying I went to visit him. He didn't remember me. His mind was foggy by then, drifting in and out of the twilight between worlds. I wished him the best on his journey. I want to think that he remembered me fondly as well, but I have no way of knowing, not really.

I think, said my husband, that his spirit must be in the land.

The prime minister looked puzzled. I suppose so, she said.

I also think, said my husband, that I may have hurt him on my rampage.

I squeezed my husband's hand.

Yes, said the prime minister, about that. Can you explain what happened?

Not really, said my husband. He seemed more animated and aware than he had been even a few minutes previously. It was as though the prime minister's story had awakened some spark in him. I was glad to see it, but also somewhat puzzled by it. Did my husband like the story because of the man or the young prime minister or the parents?

The prime minister wanted more from him. You were on the excavator, she said. And then . . .

I was on the excavator, said my husband, unconsciously imitating her voice. It felt comfortable. I operate excavators for a living in my own country.

The prime minster nodded. I thought as much.

The walls were wrapped around me in a kind of suffocating embrace.

I see, said the prime minister.

I thought that I should get off the excavator, but I couldn't. The walls seemed too menacing. They felt like the wanted to crush me.

I wasn't nodding. I felt the tension in the room. My tension. I was not at all sure that my husband could hold it together long enough to tell the prime minister anything of value.

The noise of the excavator, continued my husband, it felt right. It felt like something familiar and I revved up the rpms to make the noise bigger and then, well, I'm not sure I can explain it fully, but I suddenly realized I had an instrument to fight the walls with. Almost without thinking I turned the excavator on the nearest wall and knocked it down and kept going. I was heading for the mausoleum.

The mausoleum? said the prime minister. You were intending to demolish the mausoleum?

My husband was red-faced and blustery, as though he was facing a cold and wet wind and needed to guide his craft through the storm. A ridiculous image, but there it was in my head.

Not at first, said my husband. I had no wish to demolish *anything*, but once I got going, I remembered that poet's papers and, well, I figured I had the tool to extract it. So I kept going.

The prime minister had a look of amusement on her face. Do you really think the excavator could have crashed through the walls of the mausoleum?

My husband blinked. Well, yes, he said.

The prime minister shook her head. Emphatically. It is constructed of the finest concrete reinforced with steel. It has been built to withstand earthquakes of 9.5 on the richter scale.

Has there ever been a 9.5 earthquake? I asked.

Not that I know of, but if one ever strikes here, the mausoleum would be safe. It would take much more to destroy it than a single excavator.

My husband nodded. I see, he said.

If you wanted the papers of Nionc Tigo, you merely have to ask for them.

I wondered if she was kidding. I hadn't seen any instances of Slothin humor up to now, but it wasn't impossible.

Ask for them? I said.

Now that your husband has put me in the position of being caretaker of you, on account of our—how can I put this?—*peculiar* tradition of victims helping perpetrators, I feel I can help you *both*.

That's very generous, I said.

She shrugged. I know it is.

I didn't want to appear pushy or ungrateful. I was not sure how to proceed, but decided it was best simply to plunge in. When can we get them? I asked.

She looked through her window. There's still a few hours of daylight left. How about now?

I tried to keep my cool, but I failed miserably. Yes! I said quickly, underlining it with an embarrassing school-girl shriek.

The prime minister smiled. Well, she said. Nice to see you so excited.

My husband seemed confused by this turn of events. I'm not going to jail? he asked.

Dear, I said, try to keep up. Your little joy ride netted us exactly what we came for. I grinned. Beamed. It was, I'm sure, somewhat annoying to behold just how excited I was.

Come on, then, said the prime minister. Let's get going.

We all rose to our feet and went to the door. How are we going to go? I asked.

Let's walk, said the prime minister.

It's a long way, I said.

Doesn't matter, she said. We could all use the exercise.

I was doubtful. We won't get back before dark, I said.

You worry too much, said the prime minister. It's a gorgeous day. Just go along with it.

I wanted to object some more but she wasn't having it. She put up her hand and without a word conveyed, in her prime ministerial way, that she would not accept anymore objections. I still had reservations, but decided this was her country and her rules.

We began walking through grassy pastures, the same ones we had traversed earlier in the trailer of the guide's bicycle.

The sun was bright, but not too hot. A thin mist of clouds separated us from its full glare. The walls towered above us and wrapped around us. We walked from one enclosure to another, opening and closing gates as we went. I asked the prime minister how long she had held her post.

The lottery was two years ago, she said.

Lottery? I asked. Not an election?

We gave up elections a long time ago, she said. They tended to put in office people who only wanted the office.

Yes, I said. Isn't that the way it should be?

People who crave power often don't wield it for public good, she said. Our solution was to draft random people into positions of power.

The concept had a certain wacky appeal. But I saw problems with it.

What if, I asked, someone gets into power who doesn't know what they're doing?

That happens, of course, but then the population rallies to their aid and helps them be a better leader.

And that works?

Look at me, she said. I had never held office before. I was a complete novice when I was chosen. But I've grown in my position. With the help of my fellow citizens.

The grass under our feet was thick and lush. Very green. It swept across my soles with gratifying caresses, as though the land was happy to have us treading on it.

I have to admit, I said, this country does have its appealing aspects. What do you think? I asked my husband.

It's hot, he said.

That's all? I asked. Nothing else to add?

I'm hungry, too.

I rolled my eyes. My husband can be like a zombie sometimes. Doesn't speak more than a phrase or two. Contributes nothing to a conversation.

The prime minister addressed him with interest, either feigned or genuine. I wasn't sure which. I think, she said, you might be the poet in our trio. Isn't that true?

What? said my husband.

You speak very little. When you do speak, there is wonder and profundity in your words. Don't you see it?

I'm homesick, said my husband. I don't dislike this country, but it's not mine. You have no spirits.

Spirits? said the prime minister. Is that what you're looking for?

He talks to walls, I said. Back home. The walls talk back. But not here. I turned to my husband. Isn't that so? I asked.

By this time we all had a sheen of sweat on our faces. The heat of the afternoon had sneaked up on me, and I was not prepared for the discomfort. I rolled up my sleeves to allow some cooling.

Yes, said my husband. I don't think I knew how much I needed them before today.

Oh, said the prime minister, we have spirits, all right. They're all around. They probably just don't understand you and your ways. They don't know how to understand you. What I would suggest, if you don't mind my saying so, is that you should allow yourself to fall into them.

Fall into them? said my husband.

The prime minister nodded vigorously. Most assuredly, she said. You simply don't understand our ways. And why should you? You're not from here.

Fall? said my husband.

Here, said the prime minister. I'll show you. She put up her hands, indicating that we should stay where we were. We stopped and watched her walk a few dozen yards away from us. I put my hand up to shield my eyes from the sun.

The prime minister stopped walking when she came to a wall and turned around. She grinned at us as sheep flocked to her. Before long she was surrounded by them.

Then she held her hands up high and closed her eyes and let herself fall backward. My husband and I both expected her to stop at the wall, but she didn't. Instead, she went *through* the wall and fell to the ground. Only the bottoms of her legs remained on our side of the wall. The rest of her was out of view.

We looked at each other, my depressed husband and me, hardly believing what we just saw, and then we both ran for the gate. Sheep scattered before us. We careened through the gap in the wall and ran toward the prime minsters who was on her back, on the ground, looking at us as we ran.

Mind the gate, she said with barely a raised voice.

We skidded to a halt and ran back to the gate and closed it, then turned and ran to the prime minister, who had stood up and was dusting herself off as we approached.

How did you do that? said my husband.

Oh, said the prime minister. It's nothing.

Nothing? I said. You fell through the wall.

Yes I did. We can all go through walls if we want to. Even you.

My husband reacted like a school kid. Show me, show me! he said.

It takes some practice, said the prime minister.

You just said anyone can do it, I said.

Most assuredly, said the prime minister. Just like anyone can read. That doesn't mean you're born with the ability. You have to learn it.

I want to learn, said my husband.

I wanted him to quiet down. Why was he so excited about this? It had to be a trick. Some illusion of the eye. I went to the wall and examined it. Must be some kind of trick gate.

I ran my hand over the stones. They were rough with sharp edges. I looked for a seam, some kind of line in the wall, but found none.

A skeptic, huh? said the prime minister.

I'm still not sure I saw what I thought I saw, I said to her.

Do you want to learn? she asked.

How to fall through walls?

The prime minister nodded. I can teach you both.

My husband was right there. He held up his hand. Me, me, he said. I want to learn.

He was not only a school kid, he was the enthusiastic, over-achiever school kid.

All in good time, said the prime minister. There are things to consider.

Like what? I asked.

Like the fact that the wall took some of my spirit from me.

My husband's hand dropped down to his side. Took? he said.

You wondered why the wall did not talk, said the prime minister. Most of them *are* empty, as you surmised. It's because we in Slothin don't fall through them too much. If we make too many falls, we lose some of ourselves. Best to keep the walls pure, as it were. But it's okay to fall through once or twice a year, as I have just done for your delight. Wasn't it entertaining?

I nodded.

My husband seemed deflated, as though someone had taken away his balloon. I looked at him with a little bit of dismay. He seemed suddenly more immature than I had ever expected him to be.

Anyway, said the prime minister, I was only trying to demonstrate some of the peculiar details of our country. I would wager the entire value of Slothin that you have no such phenomenon in your own country.

Not that I'm aware of, I said.

The prime minister beamed. Onward, then, she said. On to the mausoleum.

We didn't go through any more walls. Instead we plodded along through the tall grass and opened and closed gates. I think we probably went through a good dozen or more. It became a meditative journey, each opening and closing a kind of mantra that got repeated a short time later.

I felt some of the excitement of the prime minster falling through the wall in my husband. It had made him more than a little happier about being here. He craved the supernatural in his life. I knew that. But I also sensed it was not quite enough for him. Falling through walls was not the same as talking to walls.

By the time we got to the mausoleum, the sun was low in the sky and I realized we would be going back in the dark. It didn't bother me. As long as we had the prime minister for a guide, I felt we would be safe.

Are there wolves around here? I asked.

The walls keep them out, said the prime minister. They can't scale them.

That's good.

We have to protect our sheep, she said. She entered the mausoleum and we walked through the twilit halls and came to Nionc Tigo's vault.

Here it is, said the prime minister. Now don't you feel ridiculous planning to crash into here with your excavator?

My husband nodded. Still don't know what got into me, he said.

She patted his hand. Don't worry about it. It brought us together. We got to know each other. Everything turned out for the best.

She retrieved a key from her pocket and placed it in the receptacle next to Nionc Tigo's vault and turned it. A drawer popped out of the wall and we stepped back to allow it to unroll completely. It was a little above my head so I couldn't peer inside, but the prime minister asked my husband to take a look.

He walked over and put his hands on the edge of the drawer and peered inside. I see some papers, he said.

Why don't you get them out? said the prime minister. My husband put his hand inside and scooped out several white stapled booklets. They tumbled to the floor. Each of them had a picture of a heavy machine on the cover.

I bent down and retrieved one of them and examined it. I flipped through the book. It was a set of instructions, written in Slothin, on how to use a bulldozer. I looked up at the prime minister.

These are operating manuals, I said.

The prime minister had a dreamy look in her eyes. Yes, she said. And they're pure poetry.

But I expected—something else, I said.

She saw the disappointment in my eyes and heard it in my voice. Oh dear, she said. You wanted her other writings.

Well, yes, I said. These aren't writings. These are—instruction manuals.

Ah, said the prime minister. You are not aware of Nionc Tigo's life work.

Life work?

My husband, meanwhile, had scooped out more of the manuals. There had to be close to a hundred of them.

These are great! he said. I *love* operating manuals.

It was true. My husband would read them for pleasure. He liked the organization of them. The way they conveyed information in a concise manner. They were his poetry books. I thought he was crazy to love them, but now, it seemed, others shared his adoration of them.

I'm afraid, said the prime minister, that you are not aware of Nionc Tigo's principle work.

It appears not, I said.

Nionc made her living by writing these manuals.

My husband brought some of them to me. There were not just manuals for heavy equipment. I saw manuals for food processors, cell phones, air conditioners, vacuum cleaners, microwave ovens, a complete menagerie of mechanical beasts that populated the world outside of Slothin. And they were written for dozens of different manufacturers. I recognized a lot of the names. They were completely familiar brand names of North American products. All very interesting, but I couldn't help wondering where the manuals for sheep herding, or wolf repelling, or stone building were. Not here. Those skills were part of the Slothin mind, I guessed. No need for manuals.

But none of these things exist in Slothin, I said to the prime minister as I held up a sheaf of the manuals. They were all on bright white paper printed with very correct looking black ink. No frills. A severe design sense, as though they had all been produced in the same shop.

The prime minister nodded. Nionc Tigo thought of them as fanciful stories, her books for the makers of these products. She worked very quickly, you see, and the manufacturers, once they found this out, they sent her pictures of the product and she produced the most beautiful manuals for them. She told me once that it is a neglected genre, operating manuals. For many people, such books are the most important and useful pieces of literature they will ever read.

How could she know about these devices? I asked. She never used them.

Sometimes the manufacturers sent prototypes of the contraptions.

Sometimes?

Often she worked only from the descriptions that the manufacturers would send. It was usually sufficient. The builders of the devices were never disappointed. You seem very interested in the process.

The process, I said, is fascinating.

It is the product that is important, though, said the prime minister. The finished work, don't you think?

I suppose so, I said, but these books are all written in English.

Oh yes, said the prime minister. Nionc Tigo was fluent in English. Many of us in Slothin are.

So I've noticed, I said. But she wrote her other works in Slothin.

The prime minister looked puzzled. Yes, of course.

And some of those are hidden somewhere else?

Not hidden, said the prime minister. I would say more that they are stored away for safekeeping.

I heard that some of them were considered dangerous to Slothin, I said.

Don't you know, said the prime minister, that it is dangerous to believe everything you hear? Those other works are for her fellow country people. She used the Slothin language to express Slothin views and to communicate with Slothin people. How could it be otherwise?

I was still wrapping my mind around the fact that Slothinites, or, at least one Slothinite, the prime minister, believed one of the most important literary figures in the world did her major work in the genre of operating manual.

I am speechless before this volume of work, I said.

Why don't you sit down for a bit and look through some of them, said the prime minister. I think you'll be pleasantly surprised.

My husband was already ahead of us. He had found a bench a short distance away and was engrossed in a thick manual describing the configuration and proper operating procedures for a train locomotive. He was alternately laughing and crying. This is fantastic, he said. So good. So true to life.

I was mystified by his reaction. How could a manual of instructions cause so much emotional reaction?

The prime minister saw my puzzlement. Just pick one up, she said, and start reading. You'll understand soon enough.

She held a few of them out to me. I sighed and picked one at random. It was for a digital recording device. A slim volume. I picked it on purpose.

I didn't want to spend a lot of time with it. I found a cushiony bench and sat down and began reading.

It is difficult to describe just how sublime the experience was. Surely the setting had something to do with it. A mausoleum invites a certain reverent frame of mind. It is not unlike the reading room of a large and quit library in that sense.

I inhaled the ominous silence.

I blocked out the sound of my husband's laughter. It was good to hear, but I had other matters to attend to. I had to completely alter my view of Nionc Tigo and her life's work. I took in a deep breath and gave my whole attention to the work at hand. I flipped the page and began reading.

And was transported.

Machines are the magicians of our age. They transform with buttons and beeps as a traditional magician might use sleight of hand and magic words. They are the hocus pocus and the abracadabra of modern life. Most people don't know how they work. Most people don't care. They only care that they *do* work. The manuals that they come with, mostly unread—like most great literature—didn't have to be dry and boring. Nionc Tigo proved that with the very first one of hers I read.

The manual operated on two levels. It described the use and function of the recorder, but it also, beneath the surface, told a story about the need for words, about the human requirement for keeping things in the form of a record. We are hoarders, all of us. We save things, snippets of speech and music, the words that usually fly away into nothing are there to be kept by this device.

Nionc Tigo, in bringing to life this inanimate object, brought a poetry and joy to the form. It was like reading an epic poem. I was completely and instantly enthralled and read through the thing without stopping.

When I finished I had the urge to flip to the first page and read it again, but before doing so I looked up. My husband stood next to me. Really something, wasn't it? he asked.

Yes, I said. It is one of the most beautiful things I have ever read in my life.

A story and an education. Both. Doesn't get much better.

I nodded. Where's the prime minister? I asked.

She went back to her house.

We're stuck here? I asked.

I wouldn't call it stuck. We have this amazing library. It'll keep us busy. She said she'd be back with some food in a while.

I looked through the pile of manuals. I think I'm ready for something bigger, I said. Meatier.

He fished a thick one out of the pile. It showed a drawing of a construction crane on the cover. You might like this one, he said.

I took it from him and sat back down and began reading. Once again, I was captivated by Nionc Tigo's prose and her view of the world. I learned how to operate a construction crane, but more than that, I learned something of the human need to build things. It was eerie, how she inhabited the world of construction cranes. More so since she most likely never saw one, much less operated one.

I read through the manual in the waning light while my husband read others. He dipped into manuals on cell phones, string trimmers, printers, and dump-trucks.

When I finished my crane manual, I looked up at my husband. An hour or so had passed since the prime minister left us.

She's not coming back for us, I said.

I'm beginning to think you're right, he said.

Must be part of our punishment, to leave us here in the mausoleum all night.

I miss the ocean, he said.

I thought you missed the spirits in the walls?

That too. But the ocean more. The sound of it gets into your head so you want it there all the time.

A house by the sea?

That's what we have, he said. It's nice.

The air had that grainy oatmeal quality that turns everything gray and mealy. A chill descended on us. I think we're going to spend the night here, I said, unless we want to brave the walls out there and walk back. It's like a maze, though. We could get lost pretty easily.

Let's put our benches together, he said.

We pushed them so they formed a wider platform. We both stretched out on the benches, our sides touching each other. Don't get any ideas, I said. It's too cold for anything like that.

He laughed. I wouldn't want to have creepy sex, he said. I mean, this is a mausoleum. Dead people all around.

There's always dead people around. Or, at least, dead creatures of one kind or another. The world is covered in dead people. We came to this country to find the literary remains of a dead person.

Since you put it that way, he said. That makes it all better.

I elbowed him in the ribs. He said ouch a little too loudly, like I had really hurt him.

Such a big strong man, I said.

At your service, he said.

We were quiet for a few moments. The halls of the mausoleum were dark and forbidding. They seemed to stretch out into an infinity of nothingness.

You know the crazy thing? I said.

What?

Nionc Tigo is the real translator here. All these manuals are in English, and English is not her native tongue. She learned it and then she made a living by employing it.

Just like you with all your languages, he said.

I rolled over on my side and moved closer to him. He wrapped his arms around me and pressed his chest against my back. I don't know if I ever felt more cared for. Such a simple gesture on his part, to hold me without me asking.

I waited for our breathing to synchronize. What made you crash through those walls? I asked.

He didn't stiffen or pull away. I noted this without saying anything. It was as though we were in a different mode of being with each other.

I wanted to get to Nionc Tigo's works.

No, I said. Really. Don't say it was for me. Tell me what was really happening.

He took two breaths. I felt him sorting through the detritus in his brain. It was as though he was raking away leaves to find the kernel of truth underneath. Truth in the form of something other than more leaves.

I often had the feeling my husband was buried under burdens of fluff and extraneous baggage. His job was to sweep that foreign matter away. Sometimes he succeeded, more often he didn't.

This land, he said, is so strange. It feels locked up by the stone walls. I wanted to release it to the wild.

Really? I asked. Is that really it?

Far as I can tell.

That's not what it seemed like. It seemed like you were going a little crazy.

Does that scare you? he asked.

Not really. Even if you went insane, I don't think you'd be dangerous. A pain in the ass, but not dangerous.

He laughed. You've thought about these things?

Of course, I said. I think about the possibility of catastrophe all the time. It's what keeps me young.

We both felt the night closing in on us. I was shivering, despite being wrapped in his arms. The sun was long gone. We heard noises outside. Rustlings and brushings against the doors and walls.

Are those wolves? I asked.

Not likely, he said. Probably our imaginations.

We can't both be imagining strange noises.

I'll go check, he said.

I put my arm on his thigh. No, I said. Don't go. Stay.

He relaxed. Okay, he said.

We both dozed soon after that. I dreamed of him operating excavators. I don't know what he dreamed of. I woke up several times in the night. He had rolled away so I hugged him from behind.

The mausoleum got warmer. I suppose our body heat was trapped in the building. When dawn broke we watched the sun rise, silently. Something about the night seemed bigger than us. It was as though we were passengers on some strange vessel that had moved over the landscape.

You think the prime minister will come back for us? I asked.

Maybe she forgot about us, said my husband.

I'm hungry, I said. I don't think I want to wait for her. Let's get going.

We opened the door of the mausoleum. What about the manuals? he asked.

They were still strewn about the floor, where we had left them the night before. I thought about taking them with me, but they would be too inconvenient to carry. Leave them, I said.

On the floor, like that? he said.

I saw his point. We gathered them up into neat piles and placed them back in the vault. Then we left the mausoleum and waded through the grass. Sheep flocked around us, as though we would feed them.

We got nothing, I said.

Lamb chops sound pretty good about now, said my husband.

You the big bad wolf? I asked.

Something like that, he said.

He lunged at some of the sheep. They scattered, then regrouped and came back to us. I shooed them away but they wouldn't stay shooed.

We came to a stone wall. This the way to go? I asked.

My husband looked around, as though he could gauge the landscape and tell where we were. I don't think he was trying to be funny, but I couldn't help laughing. You a master tracker now? I asked. You have a map of Slothin in your head?

Not exactly, he said. Just trying to get the measure of the land.

Funny. Let's walk through the gate. Maybe something will trigger our memories.

We pulled the big wooden gate open and stepped through the threshold. Sheep came up to us, making baaa noises.

I was sick of sheep already. I could never live in Slothin for long. The sheep would make me crazy. They were always *there* in your face. Coming up to you. Little wool factories. Not that that was a bad thing, but still. They turned grass into wool. I got it.

Where do you think all the wool goes? I asked my husband.

He was busy wading through a flock of them and turned back to me.

What? he asked.

The wool, I said. There's so much of it. What happens to it?

They must export it, he said. Didn't you say the sheep shearers invade the country?

Yes, I said. They turn the sheep into giant naked rats.

Rats?

That's what Nionc Tigo said in her book on sheep. She was creeped out in the fall when all the sheep became rats.

That's a poet's eye for you, he said.

I pushed through the flock that had gathered around me. The sheep bumped out of my way, parting as though they were waves and I was a boat.

We trudged over the grass, not having any idea if we were going in any direction that meant anything. The walls were so high we couldn't see past them to try to find the skyline of the city.

We got to the other side of the stone enclosure and found another gate and went through that. Some enclosures had only one other gate, so the path was obvious, but others had gates on three sides, or even four sides. Some had two gates on a side and each one led to a different enclosure. After we went through half a dozen gates I stopped my husband. We have no idea where we're going, I said.

I know, said my husband, but I'm hungry and I want to get *somewhere* we can eat something.

But that's my point. We don't know where we're going.

Better, he said, to keep moving than to stay in one place.

We could be going away from the city, I said.

And we could be getting closer, he said.

I sighed. I wish we would find some *people,* I said. A native could set us on the right path.

Look, he said, there's the sun. He pointed to it hovering above the horizon.

Yeah, so?

The city is south of the Mausoleum.

You sure about that?

He nodded. I wasn't sure he knew what he was talking about, but I didn't tell him that. We keep the sun to our left, he said, and we'll be getting closer to the city. Simple.

Unless we've already gone off course, I said. Any spirits in the walls telling you anything?

No, he said. The walls are completely vacant.

I felt like I wanted to stop and have a good long pout. I felt like a two year old. There were so many better things to be doing than what I was doing here. I wanted to be at home with an esoteric text in a strange language, turning it into English. I wanted a simple life and this was not simple.

A flock of pelicans flew overhead. My husband cried out and pointed. See those? he asked.

I see them, I said, not caring a whit for them.

Pelicans usually go to water.

Yeah. So?

The city has water.

Ah. So, I said. We follow the pelicans?

Yup. He beamed, like he had just eaten a particularly delicious meal.

We altered our course somewhat, trying to follow the line of the pelicans. They had disappeared behind one of the stone walls, but we kept the general orientation of them in mind. We went through a few more gates until we came to a demolished wall. The stones had been dislodged from the structure of the wall and were scattered on the grass in random piles.

This looks like your work, I said to my husband.

Yes, yes! he said. This is where I crashed into the wall with the excavator.

So we must be close, I said.

Very close, he said.

We scrambled over the rubble and saw another wrecked wall. Funny, I said, that no one's out here fixing it.

They're not in a hurry in this country, said my husband. They take things easily. Someone will get to this eventually.

I don't know where he got that idea. I don't know why he thought he knew the character of this country. But I also did not care. I wanted some breakfast, too.

How many walls did you demolish? I asked.

Not sure, he said. Something like five or six. Maybe seven.

We've gone through five, so we must be close.

Yeah, he said.

I was getting tired of climbing over rubble, but the gates were not operating anymore, since they had been smashed by the excavator my husband so expertly operated. I climbed up on a pile of rocks that had been crushed to rubble by the treads of the excavator.

At the summit, I finally glimpsed the top of our hotel, floating, as it were, above the line of a wall just a few cells over.

We regained some sense of purpose and urgency, then, and doubled our speed. We ran hand in hand on the grass, stepped lively over the last two remaining piles and broke into open land. The city of Slothin lay before us, like a miniature doll house city, or the tiny figures on top of a wedding cake.

We ran and laughed, like we were children at a birthday party where they were about to hand out dishes of ice cream.

But as we ran, something started to bother me about where we were running *to*. Wait a minute, I said. I slowed down. My husband's hand tugged at mine as he kept going, but soon he slowed down too.

What is it? he asked.

Where is everybody?

What?

Do you see anyone?

He looked away from me. We were both breathing hard. I was thirsty, as well as hungry. I wanted a glass of water more than I wanted a plate of food.

A silence like a weight of cotton was on us and the city. We saw no activity. No one in the streets. Nothing at the train station. No activity visible through the windows of any of the buildings.

This is awfully strange, I said. Where's the guy with the bicycle? Where's the prime minister?

We walked down the main street and entered our hotel building. The lobby was empty. No one behind the desk. We climbed the stairs and came to our room. Our key worked. No reason to think it might not, but things were so strange that even a simple thing like a key might display odd tendencies. At least, that's what I felt. I don't know what my husband thought. At first.

As soon as we got in the room he took my hand and moved toward the bedroom. I recognized what he was up to.

What? I asked. The end of the world got you excited?

It's not the end of the world, he said. Just the world arranging for our privacy.

We had privacy last night, I said. We don't need everyone to go away just so we can have alone time.

We sat on the edge of the bed and moved close to each other. I put my arms around him, so familiar and welcome. His hands roamed my body.

We soon got under the covers and lost our clothes. The next spell of time seemed to go on forever and, simultaneously, to not go on long enough. We didn't care about the outside world or that everyone in the city seemed to have vaporized.

As the sun beat down on the window, we lay next to each other, him with his arm under my neck and around my shoulder. Me with my hand on his chest and my leg hooked over his belly.

A certain amount of sweat scented our reverie. It smelled strong and right, as though we had exerted ourselves in a good cause.

You don't seem the least bit worried about everyone gone, I said.

I'm relieved.

Why relieved?

There are no spirits in this city, he said. This country. Now that the people are gone, it makes sense. No people, no spirits. The equation balances.

Well, I said, I guess it's nice that there's balance, but it's still strange, isn't it? The prime minister takes us to a mausoleum, and then disappears along with everyone else.

He shrugged. The motion jostled my head. I adjusted myself on the pillow to allow a little more room between us.

So, I said, your response is: *whatever?*

More or less, he said. What do we have invested in this place, really? We'll remember it for this afternoon. That's it.

I moved even farther away from him. I don't know if he noticed or not.

Time to leave, he said, don't you think? You found out about your poet. She wrote instruction manuals. Big let down. Now let's go home.

We only just got here, I said.

But there's nothing here now. Sheep and walls. That's it. Not even people anymore.

I slid a little farther away, slipped my leg off him and lay shivering next to him, no skin contact between us at all.

I don't think I'm ready to leave, I said. Not yet. I have to find out what happened to everyone.

This place isn't even real, he said. It never was. From the beginning. You said so yourself. It lives in the space between two other countries. It's a border county. A *border* place. We don't have to stay here anymore. It's like an old house that everyone has moved out of and no one wants to buy. Best thing to do is let the elements reclaim it.

Bulldoze it? I asked.

He considered this, even though I had not offered it as anything plausible. He didn't say anything as he thought it through.

I could tell he wanted to do the job. Plow his excavator through every building. Turn the whole county to rubble.

I was *kidding*, I said.

I know, he said, but it has its advantages.

What advantages?

Puts this country in its place. What kind of country has no sprits? What kind of country has no vices in the walls?

I pushed the covers off me and got up and put my clothes back on. He looked at me wistfully, like he couldn't understand why I would break our reverie. It was so—something. Was he really so blind to the world that he couldn't see how upset I was?

Where you going? he asked.

I'm going to find out what happened to the people.

They were never here, he said.

What?

Think about it, he said. People don't just disappear, I'll give you that. But we interacted with them, or thought we did. So we think they must have been here to begin with. Well, maybe not. Maybe it was all in our imagination.

Your imagination, maybe.

And yours too.

I don't have an imagination, I said. That's your department.

He got out of bed and began putting on his clothes. The smell in the room suddenly seemed rank and vile. Did we really just make love? I wasn't sure anymore. We had been close, but now we were separate again, as though we had to be apart, emotionally, to remain in Slothin.

Where you going? I asked.

I'm getting out of here, he said.

The trains probably aren't running.

I'll walk.

I laughed. You're going to walk out of Slothin? I asked.

Yes. He pushed his hand through his hair, which needed it. It looked like something a cat might have dug up and brought into the house.

I don't want to leave yet, I said.

You don't have to, he said. I'll leave the light on for you.

At home?

At home.

I felt awkward, like something had changed between us, something ir-revocable. This is all wrong, I said.

That's why I'm leaving.

You aren't going to wait for me?

Wait for *what?*

I want to find her papers. The ones they found in the nephew's attic.

They're nothing, he said. No one in this country thinks anything of them. They think they're just scribbles.

Scribbles are literature, I said. All literature comes from scribbles.

He looked to the side, as if there was something fascinating in the space where the wall met the floor. He scratched the side of his head.

One day, he said.

One day?

I'll stay another twenty four hours, then I'm leaving. It's suffocating here. I can't stand the emptiness.

But you'll stay for me.

Yes.

I don't know if I should be relieved or annoyed.

Try grateful, he said.

I threw a pillow at him. He ducked. The pillow sailed past him and through the open window. We both went to the window and looked down. The pillow lay on the sidewalk below us like a tiny marshmallow.

Huh, said my husband.

We should go get that, I said.

We?

I pushed him toward the window. He withstood my assault and put out his hands so they grabbed the window frame. I kept pushing, though, as if I could put him through the window to join the pillow far below.

His eyes were wide. He wanted to strike me. I could see it. He worked hard to keep from doing so, but it was there, the urge.

I don't know why I wanted to push him. I didn't truly wish him to fall the seven stories to the ground below, as Nionc Tigo's nephew had done, but in the moment, I didn't question my motives, I only succumbed to their power.

I had my hands on my husband's chest and I believed that if I exerted enough pressure I could push his ribs far into his body, maybe crush his lungs and heart. We held that position for some time. Had come to a kind of equilibrium.

What's wrong with you, said my husband. More of a statement than a question, as if saying we both understood there was *something* wrong with me, we just had to discover what exactly it was.

I don't know, I said. Should we sit down and discuss it?

We didn't discuss it. My husband rallied his strength and adjusted his legs so one foot was flat against the wall below the window and he pushed back on my hands.

The balance of power shifted so that our combined center of gravity was no longer over the window frame but rather a foot or so into the room. This allowed him to release his grip from the frame and bring his hands around and grab my arms and pull them—gently, I'll give him that—away from his chest.

I stopped pushing against him and let my arms drop to my sides. We stood looking at each other. His eyes were no longer ablaze with buried violence. I think I detected something like sorrow. Or maybe pity. I covered my own eyes with my hands, feeling shame burn through me.

I'm sorry, I said. I don't know what happened there.

You want me dead? he asked. This time it was a question. He really wanted to know.

Of course I didn't want him dead. What I wanted was some kind of resolution to the mystery of the missing Slothinites. I couldn't exactly explain why that seemed to mean, in my mind, that I needed to put my husband in danger.

I think I want to jump out of that window, I said.

He moved to block the open window. It was a tiny move, almost imperceptible, but I saw it. He was worried about me. He didn't think what I said was completely ridiculous. He thought it worthy of paying attention to and even of making provisions for its possibility.

My thoughts, upon seeing that motion, were a jumble. I appreciated his concern for me, but resented him thinking that I could actually be suicidal. If he thought that was possible of me, then he must have thought I was unstable. No one wants to think their spouse thinks them unstable.

I dropped my hands and looked at him. We should go get that pillow, I said.

Who cares about the pillow?

We'll get charged for it.

There's no one here, he said, to charge us.

Nevertheless, I said.

I tried to smile at him. He didn't try to smile back. I rose from the bed and went to the door and down the stairs. I hoped he would follow me, but that didn't happen.

I kept going alone and stepped out onto the sidewalk and found the pillow. I looked up. My husband looked down from the open window and waved. I waved back, but I still felt deep shame for what I had done to him. I couldn't look at him for more than a second or two.

I picked up the pillow and tucked it under my arm and went back into the lobby. I noticed the young man's bicycle had been parked inside. The two-person trailer was still attached to it. It felt like it was waiting for passengers, even though the driver was nowhere to be seen.

I had every intention of going upstairs back to our room, but the bicycle was a distraction. I stopped and examined it. Like the rest of Slothin, it was poised. For what, I couldn't say.

I considered getting on the driver's seat, but elected to slip into the passenger seat instead. It was very comfortable.

I felt the immensity of the lobby over me, the walls surrounding me on all sides. The feeling of Slothin extending into the infinity of space.

Such odd thoughts, for me. I was not a cosmic thinker. I knew about words and grammar. I waited there for a long time. Probably a good fifteen or twenty minutes.

I knew my husband would come down, eventually. While I waited, I imagined what life would be like without him. I wouldn't have to endure his talks with the walls. I wouldn't have to think about him getting crushed under one of his earth movers. Life would be easier. Less stressful.

I wondered if Slothin was teaching me a lesson. Was I learning to be alone by being here, with all the people gone? My husband was having a hard time in a country that seemed to harbor no spirits. Now I was having a hard time in a country that also seemed to harbor no people.

I leaned back in the seat and let my mind drift.

I think I must have fallen asleep. A few minutes later, or so it seemed to me, I woke with a start and had to reconnect with the world. I built the edifice of my time in Slothin, slowly piecing the elements together until I got a sense of where I was again.

The lobby was darker than I expected. Where was my husband? I got out of the bicycle trailer and walked up the stairs to our room. The door was open, but no spouse inside.

I went back downstairs and out the lobby door and into the streets. Empty, as before. I called out to my husband. My voice was tiny, even in the minuscule metropolis of tiny Slothin. The wind grabbed my words and seemed to hurl them into the sky.

Be careful what you wish for.

The Slothin language, I recalled, had no word for lonely, so I was experiencing a state of being which Slothin did not acknowledge.

This was not what I had expected when I came to the country. I knew it was sparsely populated, of course, but I didn't expect not to see anyone at all. I looked out the window. Did my husband go to the shack where the excavator was? I strained my neck around the edge of the window frame but could not see it from that angle.

The edifices of Slothin's buildings rose up around me. They seemed to reach for the sky in their puny way. I sighed and removed myself from the window and went back down to street level.

I walked the few blocks it took to get to the shack. No one was inside. I walked through the shack and out to the back yard where the excavator had been earlier. Still no husband.

The sky had clouded over. It felt like rain might be approaching, but I didn't know the weather conditions in this part of the world, so could not be sure.

I climbed up on the wall, the one that my husband had crashed through only yesterday. I tried to think how Nionc Tigo might have dealt with this emptiness. She was the bard of Slothin, after all. She knew all its nooks and crannies.

Or so I imagined. I looked out on the sheep that populated the cells. They looked back at me, some of them. Others seemed much more interested in the grass they were eating.

The excavator was cold and dead. Like it didn't even want to power up.

I did have a description for the location of the manuscripts. I had found it during my online research before coming to Slothin. It might be genuine, and it might not. It seemed now was as good a time as any to find out. I pulled out some notes from my pocket.

Slothin did not display street signs on the corners of its thoroughfares, but it was small enough that the address might make some sense to me. The houses did not have numbers, either. It was more of a description kind of thing.

I looked at the description. It indicated a red house. There were many red houses in town. It also seemed to say it was next to a white house and beside one of the walls. That seemed pretty specific.

I took the address with me and began walking the streets of Slothin, staying on the perimeter since it would have to be there if it was near a wall.

I heard sheep bleating from the other side of the walls. There were no people sounds, but sheep filled the air. It was an eerie feeling, as though the people were ghosts speaking in sheep.

Animals, of course, have a language of sorts, just as humans do, though perhaps not as sophisticated. I have learned some animal languages. Dog and cat are actually pretty easy. Domesticated animals are so much like us that their language has evolved with ours.

Wild animals, especially birds, are harder to decipher. Their meanings are difficult for me to discern. This doesn't bother me. Few people want translation of dog, cat, bear, or bird.

But to hear the sheep in this empty city made me want to understand them. They vocalized quite a bit as I walked, as though they knew I was there. As though they knew everyone else was gone. I discerned a melancholy quality to their bleating. Was it possible?

In the far distance, I heard dogs barking. They wanted to herd the sheep, I suppose. Or maybe they were warning of wolves?

I let the few sounds around me wash over my consciousness. I passed houses as I went. I soon fell into a pleasant kind of reverie as I explored the dark heart of Slothin.

This is what was left after everyone was gone. Nothing but empty buildings with nothing to say. Buildings had their languages, too. The creaks and cracks and tiny sparks of sound: they were expressing the house's way of being in the world, which is all language is. Language comes from the architecture of the body that enunciates it. And houses had an architecture.

I went into some of the red houses. Each time I pushed open a door, I felt trepidation, as though I might encounter the *one* house remaining that had people in it.

But that never happened. I climbed up into attics and looked around. Most Slothin people had a lot of stuff in their attics. Boxes and boxes. I would search around a little, open a few boxes here and there, just to see if I could find Nionc Tingo's manuscripts. Then I would descend the stairs, leave the house, and find another red one.

I didn't do an actual count, but I estimate I entered and looked around in about twenty houses. It sounds easy, but it soon got to be quite tiring. And tedious.

I was prepared to admit defeat, when a tiny house presented itself to my gaze. It sat at the end of cul-de-sac, flanked by two other tiny houses. Really, all three of them were big enough for a family of one. If such a person can be considered a family.

I went into the tiny red one in the middle and found myself in a one room building. The kitchen area, if it could be called such, occupied a tiny corner. The sleeping area was above me, accessed by a short ladder. There were cupboards arranged around the bed at the top.

Cupboards.

Strange to have them there. I climbed up to the sleeping area and stood on the bed and opened one of the cupboard doors. Nothing but tools. A hammer, a screwdriver. Some nails and tape. I opened another door, not expecting anything at all, but was rewarded with a stack of papers.

As I reached in to retrieve the stack, a scent of smoke invaded my nostrils. I pulled down a few pages of the stack and looked at them. They were a hodgepodge of formats: longhand in ink, typewritten, photocopied, and printed in pencil.

I rapidly went through the pages, looking for names. The writing was in Slothin, but as I scanned them I was able to translate them well enough to realize I had found what I was looking for. These were the lost works of Nionc Tigo. I pulled out more pages and riffled through them.

I could not immediately discern any kind of sense to them, but I preserved the stack in order, thinking that might make a difference. Perhaps the disparate formats had some rhyme or reason to them and I didn't want to upset that.

I pulled out more and more stacks of papers. They began to fill up the tiny house. I reached into the space and found more of them and pulled them out until the cupboard was empty.

I looked around the rest of the little house. I pulled open a few more cupboard doors, but found nothing of interest behind them. By this time I was sweating and the smell of smoke was beginning to make me cough. I thought I had rustled up some dust while I was pulling out the stacks of paper. The dust must have had some kind of burnt aspect to it.

I ran my sleeve over my nose. My eyes were watering. Whatever the smell was, it had a burning quality to it. I was having an allergic reaction and this was not my usual response. Only then did I think to step away from Tigo's collected works and investigate further.

I stepped outside and was greeted with a frightening sight: great columns of thick white smoke billowed up out of the landscape and reached as high as my eye could see. Slothin and environs was burning up.

I think I stared at the smoke for a long time, perhaps two or three minutes. My response was completely counterproductive, of course, but I didn't know what else to do. The fires were burning in all directions. Everywhere I looked smoke filled the sky. As far as I could tell, the fires were not in the city of Slothin, but they certainly were gobbling up the countryside.

Was this why everyone had left? They knew the fires were coming?

That couldn't be. Wouldn't someone have told us? Wouldn't the prime minister have helped us evacuate, rather than leave us in the mausoleum overnight only to be threatened with death the next day?

I didn't know how to understand the Slothin way of thinking. I looked around the house and found a garden hose attached to a faucet. Whoever had this house kept a garden. The garden was only a patch of weeds now, but it appeared it had been someone's pride and joy at some point.

I turned on the faucet and water gurgled and gushed through the house in spurts. It rattled in my hand, and eventually brown water shot out of the end of the hose.

I put my finger over the opening, creating a spray and turned the plume onto the house. I arced the water high so it fell like rain. The sound of the water on the house soothed my spirits.

I gave the house a good soaking. It seemed to like it. It wore the water like a second skin, some of the moisture not falling away. I didn't even know how that was possible, but I didn't care. Slothin had mysteries to it.

I heard sheep in the distance. Were they being burned alive? Possibly. The sounds were filled with fright, even dread. I blocked them out. Too painful.

I think it was as I turned the hose to the grounds that I began to accept the inevitable end of my life. Surely this watering was only a stop gap measure. There was no way I could hold back the tide of smoke and flames that was evidently intent on coming my way.

The fires appeared to be leaping the natural breaks of the stone walls. Smoke was getting thicker and my eyes were stinging even more. I went back inside the little house. My only hope was that the fire would sweep past the house and its grounds and continue on its way. But that felt like a futile hope. I knew that fires had their own lives, they went about their consuming activities with no regard to what people wanted.

I sat with the works of Nionc Tigo.

I had spent most of my life translating the words of others. I never had any complaint before this. It was a good life. It was challenging and absorbing and I felt like I was doing some good in the world by bringing an understanding between people with differing languages and differing ways of looking at the world.

And now it seemed the end was near and I was left sitting next to a stack of papers that needed translation.

Or so I thought.

So I *wanted* to think.

The house was getting warmer and the air was getting murkier. Flakes of material floated in the space outside the tiny windows of the house.

I soaked a cloth in some water and put it over my face. That brought some relief, but not a lot. It was not going to filter out all the impurities in the air.

I supposed I was going to die of asphyxiation before I was going to be burned to oblivion. I considered the sequence of events that would lead to my demise.

First I would be overcome with coughing fits. My breathing would become labored and difficult. I would try to push away the smoke with my hands, desperately, knowing it was futile, but also knowing I would not stop trying.

I would not go down easily. I would fight the end for as long as I could.

I think I would also begin to panic. Who wouldn't? I might run around in a fit of futile energy, maybe expend what little I had left. My lungs would burn. My vision would cloud over. My skin might begin to cook. Smoke would hurt my eyes. I would hunker down, maybe curl up into a fetal position. Try to cover my nostrils, all the while knowing it wouldn't help, not in the long run.

I think I would hold onto the collected works of Nionc Tigo, as well. There was no way to protect them completely. No way to preserve them from the flames.

The foremost voice of her people was going to be extinguished and there was nothing I could do about it. If I had more time, I could have photographed each page and emailed them to some safe server, but, in any case, I did not have my camera with me and Slothin did not have wifi.

A roaring seemed to fill the sky, now. It was congruent with the smoke and flames. It was as though nothing else was in the world. I found myself wishing Slothin houses had fridges. Then I could have stuffed the collected works of Nionc Tigo to the fridge. I had read that in fires, the fridge will often survive, and the contents will be left untouched by the flames.

I didn't know if that was true, but it might have been. In the end, I put her papers in a pile and put myself over the papers. I stretched out so that they were under my chest and belly. I thought that I might protect them from the flames.

Then I waited. Slothin, the country, crackled all around me. I found myself thinking of the sheep. Did they get cooked in the fields? They must have been. there was no way for them to escape. I wasn't sure if the exterior of the house was getting wrapped in flames. It had to be, I suppose. There was no where else for the flames to go.

As I listened to the world crackle around me, I heard the sound of windows breaking, probably from the heat? I didn't know.

The shards fell near me. They sprinkled over the floor. It made me tighten my grip on Nionc Tigo's papers. The broken window invited in even more smoke and heat. My hair felt like it was about to be singed off. Then I heard the sound of wings in the air. They rustled over me and I looked up, trying to see something through the smoke, half believing I was hallucinating. It was difficult to see anything, but eventually I did discern a crow, perched up high on a beam, or what looked like it might be a beam.

The crow cawed once, then descended through the air, wings spread wide, and landed near me and began pecking at something on the floor. Some metal ring.

The crow was no more than three feet away from me. I released my grip on Nionc Tigo's works and went over to see what the crow was about. It hopped two steps away from me, but watched as I fumbled with the ring before I realized it was attached to a hinged door.

I scrambled to lift up the door, all the while hacking my lungs out. The door swung open and landed flat on the floor. I didn't know what was in the opening, but I didn't care. It would be my salvation, wouldn't it? Or it could be.

The crow didn't hesitate. It flew into the dark interior of whatever was there. I determined to follow it immediately, but hesitated. Only for a second. I thought of the worth of my life. I thought that if I survived it would mean nothing if I didn't also save Nionc Tigo, if only by the proxy of her work.

I scrambled on all fours to the pile of her papers and pushed them to the opening. They fell in a flutter down into—something. I wasn't yet sure what. I took one last bleary-eyed look around the area where her papers had been stacked, saw nothing more, and put my feet into the opening.

I felt no stairs or ladder. Was this a drop to death? What did it matter? Staying up here was certain death. I fumbled for a ring on the inside of the lid. There was none, but a rope presented itself helpfully. I pulled on the rope, swung the door up so it was about to fall, then closed my eyes and dropped down.

I held onto the rope so the door would shut above me. It did so, but I was still in free fall. For one panicked instant, I thought I would end up miles down with a broken body. At least it would be a quick end. Or so I thought. Hoped, even.

But I didn't keep going. My fall was broken by an unexpected softness. A mattress? Some straw? I wasn't sure. It felt like some kind of fabric.

Also, there were sheets of paper everywhere. Nionc Tigo's works. I had thought to bend my knees as I went down. That might have saved me from broken leg or a turned ankle. No way to tell for sure, but I was grateful not have any real pain anywhere in my body.

Except for my lungs, which were still working to expel the smoke it had encountered in the house. It was very dark in the hole. Cellar? I wasn't sure. I wondered if all Slothin houses were equipped with such rooms. The crow cawed.

Thank you, I said to it. You saved my life. For now.

It cawed again. I wondered if it was going to be inclined to attack me, but decided that since I was not food or a threat, it was most likely going to leave me alone. At least I hoped it would.

There were earthy smells around me. Which is what I would have expected. Probably lots of spiders and other creepy things lived down here.

My chest continued to spasm as my lungs worked to rid themselves of smoke particles. I could tell, though, that very little of the smoke had followed me into this space. I put out my hand and touched bare earth. It was soft and wet.

Still so dark, but my eyes were adjusting to it and I saw that there was a slight illumination, as though the ground held some kind of glowing objects. Maybe luminescent rocks? It was possible, I supposed.

The crow hopped on the ground and tore into some of the pages of Nionc Tigo's unpublished and untranslated papers. I reached for the sound and was rewarded with a sharp jab to my hand. The crow didn't like me crowding it. Fine. But don't rip up the dead woman's pages. That's all that's left of her.

Come on, crow, I said. You saved my life but that doesn't give you the right to tear into me. She cawed several times. The sound was close to deafening in the confines of this cellar. My eyes were still adjusting. I felt my surroundings resolve out of the chaos of the grayness, like floating oatmeal, into something more coherent.

It was also cold down here. I was shivering and had wrapped my arms around my shoulders without even being conscious of it.

How long you think we should stay here? I asked the crow. I could just barely make out its shape in the dim glow of the walls. It tilted its head at me and seemed to want to attack me again. I held up my hand. I'm not looking for a fight, I said.

It cawed at me several more times, then backed away, turned around, and—disappeared.

I was immediately bereft and lonely. The only other creature in Slothin that would have anything to do with me, and it was gone. Where did it go?

I put my hand out in the open space, trying to find it again, but it was no use whatsoever. It appeared to have melted into the walls. Now I didn't have any guide at all. I assumed it would start pecking at the door above us when the time was right and I would know to come out of the hole, but now I was on my own.

I wondered if the crow was even real. Did I hallucinate it? If I did, then I must also have hallucinated the cut on my hand. It wasn't bleeding a great deal, but there was some flow from it.

The wound was as real as anything else in the world. If I doubted my wound, then I would have to doubt Slothin, the hole, the fire, the smoke, and the glowing walls. That was too much doubt by a long shot.

I dragged myself along the floor—which appeared to be made of wooden planks laid side by side—and even though I expected to encounter the far wall, I kept going into the darkness and felt the way open up. There was no wall.

I was in a tunnel, of sorts. Some kind of route through the earth. I never wanted to be in this position. That's what I thought at that moment. It wasn't that I couldn't be there, but only that I didn't want to be there.

Even ten minutes ago I couldn't have told you or myself that particular fact. I had no idea that the experience of being underground would have been so distasteful to me, but it was. The crow hopped ahead of me. I cawed, but its caws were getting muffled as it put distance between itself and me.

Nionc Tigo's papers were scattered in heaps behind me. Should I leave them? I didn't know. I couldn't take them with me. They were too un-wieldy. I had nothing to carry them in. I had come to Slothin looking for those very papers and now I had to leave them behind.

At least I had her instruction manuals.

I laughed to myself. An instruction manual for navigating this tunnel would have been very useful indeed.

After a couple of minutes more of contemplation, I decided that fol-lowing the crow was the best option. I could always come back for the pa-pers later. I called out to my savior.

Hey crow, I said, wait up. Don't go on too far without me. It isn't nice to leave me behind. I laughed as I said it. So absurd. Talking to a crow. I steeled myself for the possibility that it was going to talk back. It wouldn't have been out of the question, but it would have been startling. Crazy, even.

It didn't happen. I kept hopping. It extended its wings, once or twice, I think. At least, I heard rustling of wings.

The light was still not enough to illuminate very much. The tunnel opened up high above me. I was able to stand up and did so, stepping carefully. My feet were out of my view. The floor of the tunnel might just as well have been on another planet. Maybe it was. I didn't know.

As I walked, I wanted to keep my hands to myself, but instinctively I put them out so that they touched the walls and my fingertips became guides through the passageway. I imagined myself pushing back the tons of material around me, my fingertips holding the power to—well, do everything.

There was an inescapable feeling that I was lucky enough to have the power over the planet. None of it made sense, not to what my life was on the surface, but down here, in this strange new realm for me, it was as though I had acquired the power of a superwoman. I *was* that superwoman.

I listened for sounds in the earth. Maybe the earth had things to tell me. Maybe there was a language it wanted to impart to me. I was ready to take in that language. Ready to find the truth of it. Translate it to something I could understand.

But that didn't happen. I thought of my husband, so lost without the voices in the walls. I began to understand some of his pain. It was the pain of loneliness, but also of rejection. I was here. It didn't seem possible that the consequences of that would be—nothing. No communication, no meaning, no contact. The crow had long since gotten way ahead of me. So far ahead that there was no way to catch up. It knew so much more than me, but it wasn't interested in teaching me.

And why should it?

Ahead I saw a dim reddish glow, like a sunset had magically appeared in the tunnel. I walked toward it. Somewhere, way ahead, I heard the crow caw and flap its wings, as though it had room to rise.

I continued to walk forward, slightly stooped in the cramped space of the tunnel. A little bit of hope blossomed in my heart and I didn't tamp it down. Instead, I let it bloom bright and big. I wanted to have some hope, now, while it still meant something.

The glow in the distance became a stronger light as I approached. I also heard voices. Some of them familiar. They spoke in Slothin. I was sure I heard the prime minister, the kid on the bike, and the man from the shack. There were other voices as well, but I didn't know who they were.

The ceiling of the tunnel opened up even higher and I was able to stand straight and tall as I walked. This changed everything. It gave me a sense of purpose. It made me feel as though I belonged in this strange realm.

I called out to the light ahead. Hey, I shouted. It's me. What's going on?

No answer. It seemed as though they wanted to ignore me. The voices stopped. I stepped up my pace.

Hey! I shouted again. Louder this time. I wanted them to know I was there and I wanted them to acknowledge me.

I saw that the light was the entrance to a bigger room here in the tunnel. I burst through the opening, fully expecting to find the Slothins I knew sitting in a circle and discussing the pressing matters of the day. Or maybe the movies they had recently seen. The progress of their children. How the sheep were doing. The bums who hung around the train station. The price of cigarettes. The state of the produce at the local supermarket. How much better the rock walls looked in the evening light rather than the more harsh morning sun. How difficult it was to find a good pizza in Slothin. What to name the new lambs. How much easier it would be if there were microwave ovens in Slothin. Not to mention the desirability of awnings on the buildings when it got too hot in the afternoon. The state of tea culture in Slothin. The recognition that Slothin needed to expand its horizons. The tedium of tending sheep. The clean air over Slothin that allowed an amazing view of the stars at night. The lack of children being born now that young people didn't want families like they used to in the old days. That crazy tourist who knocked over some of the walls. And wasn't it nice that the wolves seemed to be staying away this season? The possibility of Slothin fielding a soccer team for tournaments with other small countries. How much better the teachers in Slothin were than they were in other countries. The teachers at Slothin schools really *cared* about their pupils. Wasn't it true?

But my fevered imaginings proved nowhere near the truth. I burst through the entrance to the lighted room and found—nothing. No Slothinites conversing. No Slothinites at all. I must have imagined the voices.

Instead I found a room empty of people. There were a couple of chairs. Rudimentary things made of some salvaged wood, it looked like. The place was also a little cramped, but not too confining. I saw a trail of fresh bird droppings, so I knew the crow had been here. I hadn't imagined that.

There were several openings on the other side of the room. Tunnels that went who knew where. And who cared? If I went down one of them, wasn't I just going to be lost in a network of tunnels?

I sighed and plopped myself down in one of the chairs. It was too low. My knees stuck way up in the air. I looked around. The walls were studded with glowing stones, the source of the illumination I had seen. I looked overhead. There was an exit, similar to the one I had seen in Nionc Tigo's nephew's house. If I pushed that door open, where would I end up?

And how would I get to it? It looked to be about ten feet above the floor. No way I could reach it, obviously. Maybe if I stacked the chairs one on top of the other? But that wouldn't do. They wouldn't be stable enough.

What I needed was someone who could stand beneath the hatch and allow me to climb up on them and stand on their shoulders and push the hatch open. Simple. My husband would have been right for the job. Only he wasn't here.

I was tired and thirsty. My throat felt parched and my lungs still hurt. I was considering the possibility of going back the way I had come, to try to find my way back to Nionc Tigo's papers, when the earth started to shudder.

It was very subdued at first. I felt this very slight tremor, like one would expect to feel in a tiny earthquake. But then the tremors got a little more pronounced. The room trembled. The world around me started shaking and rattling. Dust fell from the ceiling in clouds. I didn't know what was happening, but I knew it wasn't good.

About that time, the sound of falling earth filled the room. More dust poured out of the exit doors. It looked like the tunnels were collapsing on themselves. I ran to the one I had come from, but there was too much material in the way. Mounds of earth filled the tunnel. All the tunnels leading from the room were blocked.

I heard the crow caw and caw behind me. I whirled around and saw it perched on the floor. It pumped its open beak in the air. It had out-flown the cave-ins and found this place as its refuge. It flew up to the ceiling and tried to find some perch on the overhead hatch, but there was none. It flapped its wings futilely against the ceiling, in full on panic mode.

Meanwhile, the dust from the cave-ins had invaded the little room that the crow and I occupied. My lungs and throat were newly irritated again. I coughed and hacked.

My eyes, as though remembering the previous irritation, were newly watered and stinging. I wanted only to get out of this room. The crow descended back to my level and began pecking at my shoes and ankles.

What? I said to the crow. You think I know what to do?

I looked around.

Well, the cave-ins had brought some new material into my sphere. Maybe I could do something with it?

I bent to my knees next to some of the dirt and pulled it towards me to the center of the room. That was easy enough. I pulled more over and began a pile in the center of the room, right under the escape hatch.

Hmmm. This might work.

I climbed over a big pile of dirt and braced myself against the wall and pushed with all my might. The dirt pile budged a little, then the top slid off, and me with it.

I ended up sprawled over the bulk of it, but what had been the top got pushed over toward the rest of my pile.

I kept moving dirt to the center of the pile. Before long I was making good progress. My accumulation of material grew from a few handfuls of dirt to a goodly pile of the stuff so that it afforded me a higher reach. Periodically I tested the height by standing on the top and reaching for the hatch.

I was getting closer, but not quite close enough, so I moved more dirt. I took off my shirt and used it as a carrying bag, filling it with soil and dumping the soil on top of the pile.

It was precarious. The soil was loose in places. As I climbed it, pieces gave way under my feet and I had to scramble to keep from falling. The crow seemed to have some sense in its head. It kept away from me and watched as I worked.

You could pitch in, I said to it. Just going to sit back and relax and let me do the work, huh? Then reap the rewards?

The crow tilted its head at me and cawed several times. I took that to mean I should get back to work, so I did.

It took probably an hour of labor I was unaccustomed to before I was able to stand on the top of a pile sufficiently stable enough to allow me to reach up and push the hatch open, which I did.

I sensed freedom beckoning, but that didn't last. The hatch moved maybe four or five inches, then stopped short. It hit something solid. I pushed it harder, to try to move whatever was holding it back. But it was not budging.

The crow saw the movement and immediately flew up to the opening. I let the hatch drop back to its fully closed position, wondering what my next move would be, when the crow raised such a ruckus of wing flapping and beak stabbing at my head and ears, that I almost toppled from my perch.

I caught myself by grabbing hold of the hatch and pushing it open again, just wide enough for the crow to slip through. It disappeared in an instant and I never felt so alone in my life. The only living creature sharing my problems was gone.

I stretched out on tiptoes to try to see where it had gone, but it was too dark. No light penetrated from above, which did not feel like a good thing at all. This was supposed to be my route to freedom and it appeared to be anything but.

I dropped the hatch again. It slammed shut with a sharp sound like the closing of a jail cell. I sat on my makeshift mountain of soil and shook with pain and panic.

My limbs were like rubber, especially my arms. I was covered in thick black dirt from head to toe. Soil had worked its way into my skin. I was stained with the earth and was just beginning to feel as though this was going to be my grave. A grave without a coffin.

I don't know how long I remained there, gathering my strength. It might have been five minutes, it might have been an hour. I felt like I was using my time to rejuvenate myself and find some strength in my own situation.

Never give up. Wasn't that what people said? I wondered if any of the people who claimed that as their motto were ever in a position similar to my own. Probably not.

Once I was able to stand up without wobbling, I tried to push the hatch up again. I listened to the noise it made as it stopped. Something massive was holding it back, that was clear. I reached my hand through the gap and felt for what might be there. My reach only went so far.

I felt some texture, like wood, but couldn't be sure. It might have been metal. Or something else. Only my fingertips touched it and then only momentarily as my legs again began to tremble and I had to ease back down.

The next half hour or so, I pulled up more dirt onto my mound. It seemed even harder than my first efforts. Infinitely harder. I was getting tired, even exhausted. I barely had the strength to push soil onto my shirt, then drag it up my mound and deposit it at the top.

I did this perhaps twenty more times, adding another foot or so to the mound. Then I climbed up to the top and pushed the hatch open as far as it would go. It thunked against whatever was holding it in place.

I felt some heat on my face as I moved my head as close to the opening as possible and tried to peer over the edge of frame.

There was very little light above the hatch. I saw dark shadowy shapes: long pieces of blackened wood, some tendrils of smoke rising into the air. I pushed against the hatch for all I was worth, but there was no movement at all. No budging. The door swung open half a foot then stopped dead.

Below me my feet began slipping on the mound. I grabbed the edge of the door frame, hoping to keep myself from falling, but my hands were too weak from all the dirt moving I had done. My arms trembled with the strain, and I managed to hold on for maybe five seconds before it was too much for me. I released my grip and tumbled down the mound to the bottom of the pile of dirt.

The crow returned. It perched on the edge of the frame and looked down at me, as though I was the most interesting thing imaginable. I told it to go find help. I cawed at me and its talons scrapped the wooden frame.

I can't get out, I said. I'm trapped here. Go find someone. Anyone.

The crow flew down to me. It was trailing a long length of string, very thin and pale brown in color. It looked like it was made of something like dental floss.

Where'd you get this? I asked the crow, half expecting it to answer me. It cawed and left the string at my hand. Then it hopped a couple of feet away from me, spread its wings, and flew back up to the gap where it disappeared into some world out there I didn't know anything about.

But wanted to.

I picked up the string and pulled on it. It was loose. I pulled some more and kept pulling until it tightened. Something was holding it in place way up the length of it. I had no idea how long it was, but it *felt* like it was something like miles and miles long. That wasn't possible. Was it?

My bones were aching and my muscles felt like they were made of jelly, but I pushed myself to get up and stood on my feet and braced myself against the bottom of my mound and pulled on the string for all I was worth. It held fast.

I climbed up the mound and stood on the top of it again and put my mouth to the gap and yelled for all I was worth, which wasn't much.

My throat was still rough and dry. I really needed something to drink. My voice came out small and raspy, as though forged in rust.

If someone was out there, they wouldn't have heard me. Couldn't have.

I did see that the string went on for some time. It glowed white against the black of the timbers. I put my hand through and tried to push some of the wood aside.

It didn't work. The weight of them was too much for me. Even if I wasn't weakened by my exertions, I think they would have been too much for me.

I felt numb and raw. The dread that I had been keeping at bay now filled me completely. I felt like I had no options left. I was going to die of dehydration in this crummy little room and there was nothing anyone could do about it.

I closed my eyes and wished for something to translate my world. I needed a transformation now more than I ever did before in my life.

The crow, as black as the wood, came back to me. It perched above me. What was that crow so interested in me? Why did it keep coming back to me?

I bunched up my end of the string and pushed it through the gap. Here, I said. Take it. I can't do anything with it.

The crow dipped its beak into the balled up mass of string and hopped over my head to the other side. The string trailed behind, as though leading to another corner of the rubble above me.

I tried to hook my eyes around the corner, but of course that was impossible.

You trying to tell me something new? I asked the crow. I heard a muffled caw from the other side, then the crow's beak tapping against the hatch, over by the hinges.

I ducked my head down and looked at the other edge of the wooden hatch. The hinges were made of metal, I could see that, and already knew it, but there was a weakness in them. The sleeve around the pins were rusted so badly that they looked as though they might be holding on by only a thin layer.

I put my finger on the rust and felt the metal give way. Not a lot, but enough to tell me it was weakened to the point where I might be able to—

—well, I didn't know. But something. I put my hand in my pockets, looking for something I could use to try to break the hinge open. I found nothing. And the room had nothing.

The mound held some rocks. I picked through a few of them. There were big ones and small ones. I wanted a good hefty one and after a few seconds of digging, retrieved one from the dirt.

I hefted it in my hand. It felt like it was maybe two pounds or so.

I braced myself and accelerated it in an upward direction to hit the hinge. A rattling good clang greeted me as it connected. I looked at the hinge and saw that it had been dented, a little, but nothing more. It wasn't any looser.

I slammed the rock against the hinge some more times, maybe a good dozen or so. The hinge was getting looser and looser all the time. It was secured by a few screws. I slammed the rock against the screw heads, hoping to see some progress there as well.

Dust fell from the ceiling and I was getting very tired. A few times my knuckles slammed up against the hatch and tore open. Blood flowed down my fingers. I didn't care. I should have cared. I should have stopped and tried to stop the bleeding but I was not interested in anything else except getting that hatch open.

My hands were dog tired. I could barely keep the rock above me, and my head was bent to the side so that my neck was hurting. I wanted so badly to be doing something else. To have the ability to do something else, but there *was* nothing else that mattered.

Eventually, after what I estimate was a good half hour or so, one of the hinges broke loose. The hatch sagged down, partway, and I gripped the edge of it and pulled it down further, twisting the other hinge as I worked the hatch for all I was worth, which, at that point, wasn't much.

But the other hinge was weak as well, and it finally came loose. I let the hatch fall to the mound and it slipped down the slope to the bottom. It had been keeping me here, stubbornly acting like a block to paradise, and now it looked like something pathetic and weak.

I did feel a sense of triumph, as though I had vanquished something much bigger, like a dragon, say, or some murderer that had been stalking me. But when I looked up and put my hands on the edge of the hole that now remained, I felt a new wave of despair.

I would have to lift my body up and into the frame if I was to escape, and I didn't think I had the strength. No, I *knew* I didn't have the strength. It wasn't there. My arms were rubbery, like they weren't even made of muscle and bone.

I did try to push some of the debris away that had been blocking the hatch from opening, but the various lengths of wood, crisscrossed one over the other, did not budge.

I put my head through the frame as far as it would go and I called out to the air above me. I yelled my husband's name and I yelled for the prime minister and even the guy on the bike.

My voice felt muffled. As though it did not travel more than a few feet. Maybe only a few inches. I wasn't sure. It was as though the debris that had been arranged over the hatch was a net, catching my words.

Then something happened which I cannot quite explain. I've thought about it many times since, tried to come up with some rational explanation, but it has always evaded me.

I began talking to the debris. Not in English. I reasoned that, being in Slothin, the wood could not understand my native language. So I talked to the timbers in Slothin. I told them they were handsome timbers. I explained to them that their attractiveness did not keep them being an annoyance.

I also explained to them that it would be in my interest for them to remove themselves from their obstructionist setting. If they were out of the way, it was entirely possible that I might be able to remove myself from my situation.

I would like to report that something magical happened then, but it did not. The timbers did not suddenly disappear. My path was not immediately made clear.

Instead, the crow returned.

With some friends.

Five or six crows in all. They stepped down through the tangle of timbers, cawing the whole time, and ended up not far from my head. We stared at one another. I was so tired I didn't have the wit to be scared of them. Any one of the birds could have leaned forward and pecked out one of my eyes. I wondered why they did not. It would have been great fun for them.

Or so I thought.

Instead they seemed able to simply watch me with some kind of glowing energy behind their eyes.

Listen, I said in Slothin. Go find someone. Anyone. I don't care. I need help. I would take an assassin right now to come and kill me, just so I don't have to be stuck in this awful place anymore.

The birds stepped back a few paces. I tried to look past them, to see what was above. All I could reasonably discern was a vague ceiling over me, and some diffuse light filtering through the dusty air. The timbers were blackened in spots. I assumed the fire had reached every part of Slothin, so the wood that had been the structure above the hatch must have been blackened by the fire as well.

Some of the crows shook themselves. For the first time, I noticed that they were covered in some kind of dust as well. Soot? It might have been.

I leaned closer to the them and put my hand up and stroked one of the bird's feathers. Black soot came off and stained my fingertips. I rubbed my fingers together.

The soot was gritty and greasy at the same time. As though I had put my hand into something I did not understand. How could it be both? The crow's beaks were not black. That was the next thing that came to mind. Instead, I saw that they were also covered with the soot.

Underneath, the beaks were yellow. Of maybe white. Ivory? Something dull.

My heart began beating with unaccustomed rapidity, as though I was on the verge of knowing something I could not know. Or did not want to know.

I grabbed one of the crows. It did not try to get away from me. It seemed to welcome the contact. I pulled it down from the edge of the hatch opening with both hands and held it close.

Its eyes were black. It weighed next to nothing, or seemed to. Hollow bones and weightless feathers. It stared at me with unblinking intensity. It was as though it wanted to consume me and was sizing me up for the kill.

It didn't try to extend its wings. They stayed safely tucked against its body, as though the wings were there to hold its body in place.

It was covered in black powder. The powder came off on my hands and filled the air.

Where did you get this? I asked the creature. The other crows were at the hatch frame, looking down at us. I rubbed powder off the bird in my hand. It was as though it had flown through smoke and the smoke had attached itself to the feathers. Underneath the powder, it looked like the bird was probably yellow, maybe whitish. A dove? I didn't know birds enough to identify it from its profile, but I did know enough that there were no white crows.

I sat down on the mound and put the bird in my lap. It continued to look into my eyes and it was starting to spook me a little. I never wanted to feel the moral pull of an animal's eyes. They had so much to accuse us of. People, I mean. It was as though they had to make us feel bad about ourselves.

I've never killed a bird, I told the creature in my hands. People save birds, I said.

I was thinking of those pictures I'd seen at oil spills, people bathing blackened birds in soapy water. Hundreds of people did this sort of thing all the time. Lots of people were moved to help helpless creatures. Didn't that count for something?

I found it was much easier to avoid the eyes. I looked to the feathers and wings. I looked to the tail. I began wiping the powder off the bird. It came off the feathers in dusty clumps.

I took to patting the feathers with my hand as firmly as I dared. The powder collected in the air around me. It smelled of burnt wood. I thought I identified something that reminded me of barbecue, but I couldn't be sure. Mostly it was just the smell of a forest fire. The way the aroma of destruction can come off the trees. It felt like this bird had done just that: flown through destruction and acquired this patina of death.

I patted the wings and tail. I put my palm out and the bird hopped up on it and allowed me to dust off its body. The color came out, gradually, as the powder, grit, and dust came off in clouds. Under the soot was a quite handsome creature. It stood in what I took to be a proud pose, as though it wanted to have its picture taken.

I would, if I had a camera, I said.

It extended its wings. Sooty grit had collected in the nooks and crannies of its body and the places where the fathers clumped together. I brushed them away as best I could.

When I thought I had done about as good as was possible, I lifted the creature up to the hatch frame. It cawed once or twice. Thanks? I wasn't sure.

How do you know crow? I asked it. If you aren't a crow?

I hopped back from the edge and another bird came forward, flew down to the mound and allowed me to pick it up and brush it off, exactly as I had done with the first. This one went faster, since I was no longer worried about hurting it and I had come to understand some of the intricacies of bird anatomy and where to look for the clumps of soot.

I finished in about five minutes or so. It was as regal and proud as the first one, and just as brightly colored. I imagined that without the soot, the birds were probably very beautiful indeed. My cleaning of them did not take them to their former glory. They were still a little dirty, as though they had been grayed out.

The rest of them were just as eager to be cleaned off. I did each one in turn. As I worked, the ones I had already cleaned remained, watching my actions.

There was something meditative and lovely about the whole interlude. I was no longer concerned for my safety. Maybe I should have been, but working to clean up the birds took all that away, as though I had found some kind of therapy in the middle of my terror. I didn't think of my husband or of my predicament. The only thing in the universe was the bird that needed cleaning.

The birds, on the other hand, displayed no such sentimentality, as far as I could see. When I had dusted off the last one, it joined its flock on the hatch frame, then they all, as one, hopped up through the tangle of timbers. I heard their talons click on the wood. They were already getting some of the black soot on their feathers again. It didn't seem to hurt their flying ability, though.

They got to the top of the pile, spread their wings, and took flight.

I watched them for as long as I could, which wasn't very long at all. In no time they were tiny dots in the little bit of sky I could see, and then they were gone, completely out of sight.

I don't think I had ever felt in more despair than I did at that moment. The only living things I had any contact with had abandoned me. Even worse, it appeared that the debris above me was just as impenetrable as I had imagined.

I sighed and slipped back down and sat on the mound I had constructed. The way above me was blocked. Maybe I could find a path back through the tunnels to some other room that was below something more accessible.

I cast my attention to the entrances of the tunnels. They were blocked by earth. It would take a lot to dig them out. I wasn't sure I had the strength. I was so hungry. And thirsty.

I was also beginning to feel dizziness. Probably from dehydration and fatigue. Not a good sign. I think I may also have hallucinated at that point. I remember the room shimmering and flowing around me, like it was made of colored smoke. That brought more anxiety to my heart. I felt as though I was going to drop from the stress.

None of Nionc Tigo's books ever mentioned this particular feature of Slothin life. I had no idea that fire swept over the landscape and people, evidently, retreated to their hidey holes to survive.

Time takes on a different texture in such situations. I thought that I was mopey and feeling sorry for myself for approximately five or ten minutes. But when I finally kicked myself (metaphorically) for being morose and useless, I lifted my head from its hanging position and looked up at the hatch frame and saw that the light had disappeared outside.

It was night already. A full day and more had passed. It was getting cold. A chilly breeze dropped frigid air from above and dumped it directly onto me. The entire universe, so it seemed to my sensibilities, had conspired to make me uncomfortable. I worked my way down the mound, attempting to find some warmth in the room.

It proved elusive. Soon I was shivering and my teeth were chattering. I thought at first it was at least as much from fear and the feeling of abandonment as it was from the cold, but soon the cold took over completely.

I tried calling out, again, bu my voice was a feeble thing. I called out in all the languages I knew, which is a considerable amount. I said *Help!* repeated in all its possible flavors. Even as my feeble voice attempted to call to the world I felt it was completely futile. But all I had was my languages. All I could conjure up was the voices of the world.

Then a peculiar thing happened.

We started talking in earnest. When I say we I mean me and the voices around me. It was as though my saying help in all those languages brought out the spirits in the ground. I was just barely conscious of the fact that I was probably hallucinating, but that didn't bother me at all. At that point, I *welcomed* the loopiness of my situation.

It seemed much more productive to be speaking with spooks than to be lamenting my abandoned state.

Here's what they told me, simultaneously, in a few dozen languages all at once: Go underground.

At first I had no idea how to take this. I was *already* underground, wasn't I? But the voices seemed to have wisdom. And more than wisdom, knowledge. Knowledge that I didn't have. I spoke back to the voices.

I spoke all the languages at once. The words came out in an incoherent mess. I felt all the languages in the words, but they were peculiar, an amalgamation of sounds and signifiers that coalesced into meaning, of a sort. Maybe it was anti-meaning. I couldn't tell for sure, but the voices seemed to respond. They urged me to look down.

Down?

I walked around the mound, careful to see where my feet trod. I circled the mound twice. The light was dim at the base of the mound. The rocks in the walls illuminated the space, but not as much as perhaps they should have. Or could have. Not as much as I wanted, in any case.

I shuffled my feet along the floor. What I was looking for was something to validate what the voices were saying. If they wanted me to go further down, there had to be a way to get down.

Didn't there?

On about my fourth circuit of the mound, when I was beginning to doubt myself and the voices, I kicked aside a rock that I had passed before and saw a tiny corner where the rock had been. It was the edge of another hatch. I fell to my knees and pushed away some of the mound.

Unfortunately, I was at the base of the mound, which meant that more material from above cascaded down and covered up the corner. I saw that exposing *this* hatch door was going to take some work. I had to move a big chunk of the mound over. Handful by handful.

I was still cold. And tired. That hadn't changed. But the prospect of something new, of perhaps some *escape* invigorated me to an extent I had not thought possible. I bent to my task immediately. My breath was visible as I worked. Dirt was everywhere. In piles all around me. Ground into my skin. My finger and handprints were colored with dirt. The fibers of my clothes were caked in dirt and mud. Some it was dried, some still damp. The voices urged me on. Told me to get even more dirt into my being. It was the only way.

I believed them. They spoke my languages. I was dimly aware that there could not be voices. The Earth did not speak in that manner. The voices had to be coming from me. But I didn't care. They were offering hope and hope was all I had at that point.

Eventually I had created a dent in the mound. It was as though a giant had taken a big bite out of a mound of chocolate. I brushed some dirt and pebbles off the hatch that had been exposed. It worked just like the other one I had gone through, an act which seemed so distant that I thought it might have occurred in the last century.

I lifted the handle. The door was heavy. Or I was weak. Or maybe both. I wasn't sure. I was able to lift it only a fraction of an inch. Impossibly bright light leaked through the tiny gaps I thus created. Piercing light. It stabbed my eyes and I dropped the hatch quickly. My heart was beating like crazy. I was unsure what to do next. Open the hatch and go down? Where would I be going?

I passed my tongue over my lips and tasted dirt. My lips were dry but the dirt was damp. About this time I heard a rumbling sound above me. At first I thought it was thunder. It sounded like thunder and the ground around me shook.

I didn't want to think about the ground shaking. That meant I might be in an earthquake, and here I was underground, completely vulnerable to the earth falling on me. I did not relish the thought of being buried.

The rumbling grew louder and the vibrations began to shake the debris above me, still visible through the hatch. Blackened timbers looked as though they were being tossed around up there. I stood between two realms, the dangerous one above, and the unknown one below. Full of light, but was it dangerous as well? I didn't know. I lifted the hatch once more.

This time I swung it up and over so it flopped back, revealing an entrance to a dazzling expanse of space. My eyes hurt from viewing it. I narrowed my eyelids to slits and shaded my eyes with my hands. Where was that light coming from?

A few pieces of wood fell from above. They hit the mound and slid down. One came close to me. Others collected at the bottom of the mound in a tangle of blackened wood. The wood filled the space in no time. I couldn't wait for my eyes to adjust any longer.

A phrase came to me: *Go toward the light.* I didn't know where it came from. It sounded like something someone would say to a dying person. Did I think I was dying? *Was* I dying?

Now I heard a loud crack, like a tree snapping in wind. I looked up and saw a jagged path break open the ceiling and lead away from the hatch frame. It was as though the ceiling was beginning to break up. Even more alarming, the ceiling seemed to bulge down toward me. Something very heavy was pushing down from the other side. The newly formed gap grew wider.

I thought I saw through the gap. The edge of a caterpillar tread presented itself to me, but by then I had already made my decision. I looked down and without even checking to make sure where was something there, I jumped into the light.

Air billowed my shirt sleeves and inflated my pant legs. Cool, refreshing air. The kind of air that you wanted to take in in big swallows and fill yourself up with.

Light was everywhere as well. A fleeting thought came to me. The caterpillar above me was probably operated by my husband. Maybe he was looking for me? I couldn't be sure, but wanted to think it was true.

I was falling. The sound of crashing, still high above me, was dim and distant now. I should have been afraid. After all, I didn't know what was going to meet me at the end of my fall. Was it something soft and resilient? Or just plain ground? Was I about to die?

Since you're reading this, you know I'm not dead. Dead people don't compose fantastic tales or even more fantastic memoirs. So there is no sense of doom for you reading this, impending or otherwise. For me, there was, but I didn't care. I was happy to be out of the vicinity of the mound. I was glad to have left the little room behind.

Tentatively, I put out my hands, to try to guide my fall. Air swept over my limbs. Those birds, the ones I had dusted off, came gliding up beside me, as though escorting me to my death. They cawed and flew in formation right along with my fall.

Now I thought maybe we were all falling to our doom. It was a liberating thought. It was as though we had no care in the world. I let the avalanche of words flow over me. All the words I knew in all the languages I had mastered.

They coursed over me with unaccustomed power. They opened the world to my heart. Or my heart opened up to them. I wasn't sure which. During that fall, it was as though my own consciousness had turned itself inside out and I was not so much a woman *falling* as I was a being unfolding.

The light I saw all around me penetrated me and peeled me open. I enfolded the light in my own being. As I did so, I began slowing down. I was able to manipulate the fall to some extent and slowed the rush of air over me.

Gradually, as my environment began to darken, the light was not so overwhelming. I was able to discern some details of my surroundings. There were clouds, as I might have expected. But there were also strange things floating in the air around me.

Sheep, for one. They had their legs extended in comical poses, as though they were unsure how to behave in this falling environment. They made noises at me. Did they think I could help them?

There were also buildings. Lots of them. They were unmoored from their foundations and seemed to incorporate a tiny town, existing on the air. Cloud town. I recognized some of the buildings: they were the ones we had encountered in the Slothin City. The hotel. Some of the houses.

I didn't see any people.

That was a disappointment. If I had seen some other folks floating on the void, I might have decided this whole thing was completely normal. After all, if I wasn't the only one, then others could share my bizarre experience.

In any case, I moved toward the buildings, loomed large, and swallowed them up. Now they were inside me. Felt good.

I grabbed up the sheep next.

Even better.

Soon I slowed down. The sensation of falling diminished to the point that I felt like I wasn't falling at all, merely floating in some unrecognized ether.

The spirit of the world supported me, but I was also lost. No moorings anywhere. The menagerie that I now contained seemed to fill every nook and cranny of my interior. It was as though my skull had been stuffed with material not my brain and my limbs were stuffed full of something other than bone and muscle. And in the midst of all of this, I managed to make contact with a familiar voice.

Not my husband's. No. He was still somewhere I couldn't comprehend, mostly because I couldn't comprehend exactly where I was *now*.

No, the voice I'm referring to is Nionc Tigo's.

It was child-like, in a way. But with a strange gravelly aspect to it, as though there were rocks between the lines. She talked about sheep, of course. That's how I knew it was her. She quoted one of her own paragraphs on sheep, from the book that first brought me to Slothin. She talked about her sheep, how the wool her sheep yielded made clothes for her and her family. How she had to do her scribbling between taking care of her sheep. Especially during lambing season, when every ewe, it seemed, brought forth her own lamb.

There was nothing but wonder in her voice. It was the voice of amusement and, more than that, the voice of knowledge and certainty. There was nothing in the world more important than sheep.

I asked her about the manuals.

Oh, those, she said. They were just to make a living.

Some people seem to think they are your most important contribution to literature.

She laughed. Manuals aren't literature.

My husband liked reading them. I think he thinks the ones you wrote about earth movers are classics of their kind.

I did try to make them a little more than just instructions, she said. You know, operating manuals, for people outside of Slothin, they are the stuff of life, aren't they? So many contraptions out there and how can anyone know how they all run? In Slothin we don't have that quite so much. We operate everything out in the open. We have levers and pulleys and gears and belts, but you see them. With your machines, it's all hidden away. You have shame invested in them, I think.

As she talked, I tried to take in her words, but it was difficult. The ground had risen up to meet my feet. I was lighting on some surface that I could not see. I didn't want to be blind. That would never do, but I also couldn't see how to look outside of myself.

You do have excavators, I said.

Well, she said with an air of gentle dismissal, there are some exceptions.

The people of Slothin, I said, they seem to love you.

She hesitated. You cannot love a dead woman, she said.

I think you can.

You can extoll, venerate, admire, and appreciate. All that, you can do. Anyone can do. Invest the memory with respect and gratitude. I will agree with all of that. But love? It's difficult. Love involves seeking the well-being of another. A dead person cannot have well-being.

She was a philosopher, it appeared. I did not know this. I cleared my throat. The air here, wherever here was, had a certain coarseness to it. As though I needed to filter it before breathing it. That felt dangerous. Not to mention uncomfortable.

Do you know where we are? I asked.

You're on a journey, she said.

Yes, but *where?*

So many questions, she said. I don't even know why I'm here. Did you bring me forward? You seem to know many languages. Maybe you know the language of death?

I did not mean to rouse you, I said. I did not know you would come back from the dead.

No one comes back from the dead, said Nionc Tigo.

In that case, I said, since I'm talking to you, am I now dead? Did I pass to this realm without noticing? Because if I'm dead, it slipped by me.

Did you think you would know if you were dead or not? It doesn't work that way.

Part of me wanted to pursue this line of conversation. I wanted to know. But part of me also had no intention of finding out the truth. It was too frightening to contemplate.

Instead, I cleared my throat. I found all your unpublished work, I said.

My nephew probably got all those, she said.

I think I found his house. I threw them down when the fire came.

Truly, she said, you need to go back to your own land. The land of machines that need instructions. Did you ever notice people don't have instruction manuals attached to them? The universe knows how to operate us without them. I used to think that was the most marvelous thing. I had never even considered it before I began composing the manuals that all of you need.

You do realize, I said, that most people who own the devices don't read the manuals? It's sad, but most people don't want to consult the instructions.

Ah, she said. They think they are like gods. Or the universe. They think they can do things they cannot do.

Something like that.

You seem to want to talk.

So do you.

I'm nothing but talk, now. Nothing but a voice in your head.

Actually, I said, you seem to be everywhere, not just my head.

You're alone.

Yes, I said. And I don't know where I am.

You mentioned that. Why don't you open yourself up to the world. Then you'll have an idea of your location.

I don't know how to do that.

Here, she said, let me.

I felt an insistent pressure on my entire body. It was as though I was wrapped in a blanket and someone was twisting the ends so that I was being squeezed, like a sausage. The sensation was not exactly *pleasant*, but neither was it distressing. In this strange world I was living in now, it felt exactly like what it should feel like. It was as though this was the sort of thing that should be happening.

Much later, I would see that the squeezing was just as odd and off-putting as it should have felt then, but I was immersed in the strangeness of it. Or, rather, the *wonder* of it, since it was telling me that I was still an entity. I was still a physical body that experienced pain, pressure, and any number of other sorts of sensations.

Still, the main sensation I was experiencing was the voice of Nionc Tigo.

Are you jumping out of your skin? she asked.

I think I jumped *into* my skin, I said.

She laughed. Yes. Of course. You're a translator, aren't you?

Yes, I said. I came to translate your work.

So I understand. How's it going?

I only just found the pages.

Ah. So you haven't actually looked at them? My fire subverted that?

Yes, I said. Only I didn't know it was your fire.

You shouldn't worry about your husband, she said. He's safe.

My husband? You know where he is?

Well, she said. Not exactly. But I know he's safe.

How can you know that? Do you even know where *I* am?

She laughed again. Nionc Tigo spent a lot of her time laughing, it seemed.

When you came to Slothin, she said, didn't it seem strange that we only had rail service in and out of the country?

I admit, I said, that it was odd. But different countries have different ways of doing things. That's normal.

She laughed again. It was beginning to get irritating.

So, she said, you are making the assertion that *odd* is *normal.* Do I understand you correctly?

In this case, yes.

When you go to foreign countries, you expect to see odd things.

Well, I said, sure. Who doesn't?

And yet, your own country is not odd.

That's because it's not foreign.

To *you* perhaps, but to a visitor it would be.

Nionc Tigo seemed to like word games and conundrums. I was not immune to the pleasures of such things myself. Anyone who plays around with language and words, as I do, can be susceptible to the lure of word play. But I was not in the mood right then.

Can you explain to me, I said, what exactly is going on in Slothin?

Here Nionc Tigo chose not to answer. A heavy silence descended between us. I was still falling. I still had strange sensations of being caught between worlds. Between many worlds. It was as though my identity had been extracted from me and strewn across the universe.

As I continued to fall and as Nionc Tigo continued to ignore me, I experienced the most profound sense of loss I had ever experienced in my life. It was as though my entire being had been ripped from my moorings and been tossed out with the stars. My identity sparkled in the sky, a million bits of light shining with some kind of intensity I could not fathom. I was a constellation. The biggest constellation ever, perhaps, but nothing more than a constellation.

It was a sobering realization. My essence had been translated into something completely foreign. I looked in wonder at the spectacle of it. I chose to believe nothing could unmoor me, but this was unmooring. This was an epic confrontation with metamorphosis on a grand scale. Below me, beneath the stars, I saw only emptiness.

But the stars themselves were adrift in a vast emptiness more profound than anything I could have imagined. And I didn't have to imagine it. It was happening to me. It was as real as anything real could be so called.

I don't know how long I drifted in that state of being, that state of knowing or unknowing, I'm still not sure which it was. My sense of time told me it was perhaps a few minutes. And yet, my sense of *time* insisted it was more like a few centuries, perhaps a few eons. I have had such feelings before. Not to that extreme, but I recall many times when I was immersed in a translation project, with the text before me, my reference books strewn around me, two computer screens displaying searches and my own translation in progress, the whole enterprise humming along like some Rube Goldberg contraption with my mind at the center of it, orchestrating the chaos into something approaching cohesion.

On such occasions, time did indeed seem to slip away from me. I was adrift in meaning and words, nothing but my mind coming to some kind of fruition with the texts bouncing off each other, meanings blooming out of nothing, then growing strong, or, sometimes, wilting and dying, other meanings springing up in their place. The whole give and take of translation was exhilarating. The edifices I built were sometimes long lasting, and other times so evanescent that only I knew they had been built at all, and then they faded or crumbled or melted and another edifice rose in its place.

Yes, becoming a constellation was rather like that. A translation project.

I'm sure, I said to Nionc Tigo after a few centuries, that we must have used some of your manuals at some time.

Very likely, she said. I made a lot of them. The countries outside of Slothin seemed to love them. At least, they were insatiable for them.

I have often thought, I said, that when there are too many instruction manuals in a place, then that place has become too complicated for human habitation.

Truly? asked Nionc Tigo. You have really had such thoughts?

She asked the question without malice, but I took her inquiry as a challenge to my honesty. Don't ask me why. I was in an altered state and cannot account for all of my actions or reactions. I felt my being fill with color and rage. The extent of my anger proceeded away from me like a cloud. It enveloped everything: my immediate surroundings, including Nionc Tigo, and the farthest reaches of the universe, all the way to the distant quasars that had been birthed at the beginning of the big bang.

I don't expect you to necessarily believe what I'm saying, I said. I can only tell you that those are the sensations that visited me at that time. It was as though I could encompass all of creation.

I felt thinned out.

Nionc Tigo noticed it immediately. Whoa, she said. Come back, sister. You're much too spread out. I don't know where you are.

It was true. She wasn't talking to me, she was addressing the general environment, the way one does when asking the universe *why me?* I saw that, and my anger softened. As it did, I shrunk back to a more manageable size.

You *do* know where you are, don't you? she asked me.

In Slothin, I said. Or, rather, under it, I guess. Something.

Think about it some more, she said.

I don't want to think about it.

She tapped one finger against her thumbnail, as though she wanted to turn it into a clock, the tapping emulating the ticking of a second hand. I liked that idea. I wanted it to happen. Turn the world into a clock and make time slip past me.

The world of Slothin was too strange for me. None of my skills were able to translate it into anything that meant something to me.

You know, said Nionc Tigo, you're not falling anymore. Have you noticed that?

I hadn't. But as soon as she said it, I looked around. The air was not moving past me. My feet were situated firmly on some hard surface, though I could not quite ascertain what that surface was. It pushed up against the soles of my feet in a satisfying manner.

I relished the sensation and wondered how it had escaped me until Nionc Tigo had mentioned it. Around me, the landscape was bright. So bright, that it obscured any features I might have seen.

The light suffused everything. It was a palpable thing, like the seaweed that might flutter in an ocean. It combed the space, turning it into something that felt alien. Even more alien than everything that had come before.

I'll leave you now, said Nionc Tigo.

No! I said. Don't go. I don't know where I am.

That's odd, because it's obvious where you are.

Not to me.

About this time the light began to dim, somewhat. The landscape behind the light asserted itself. I beheld a desert scene: bare rock and sand as far as I could see, all the way to the horizon. Some scrub plants here and there. Bushes and low squat trees. Everything was dry.

The air rose in shimmery waves of heat that made everything seem to undulate. I saw the wonder of it. How had Slothin transformed into this dead space? It was sheep and green hills and moisture and gentle breezes. A most agreeable environment. Why had it changed to this? I asked Nionc Tigo, but there was no answer.

Hey, I said to the air. Where are you? Don't leave me alone. Answer me.

Even as I said the words, I knew there would be no answer. Nionc Tigo was gone.

Here the sensation of loneliness enveloped me so completely that I think I lost my vision for a moment. The desert around me shimmered even more than the heat waves suggested they should, and my eyes grew moist and bleary, as though something or someone had dropped great gobs of water into them.

Or as though I was underwater. I needed all these odd sensations to come to some kind of conclusion. I needed some anchor for my experience. I could not go on like this for much longer.

I did close my eyes then. I still stood on my two feet. Still held my ground, as far as that went, but I was frightened of moving my feet. I did not want to lift them or shuffle through the sand.

Everything that had come before this was odd enough, but now the very thought of actually becoming ambulatory seemed the very height of peculiarity. I wanted to be a statue. That seemed the safest and sanest course of action. If I did not move, if I *could* not move, then all of this oddness could be ascribed to the environment, not me. Suddenly that seemed the most apt and agreeable thing that could possibly happen to me.

I let my breathing become very shallow. I held my limbs as still as I possibly could. I was so still that a crow, somewhere off in the distance, called out to me. I wanted to answer it, but did not. I opened my eyes and saw the dot of it in the sky. I called out several more times. It swooped down from the sky, became a bigger and bigger dot, until it acquired the profile of a good-sized bird and came gliding in directly at me.

I held my position.

I did not move.

The air over its wings rustled with undue and crushing sound. It was so loud that it seemed to wreck the environment around it. Then it abruptly pulled up, extended its talons, and lighted on my shoulder. It rustled its wings for several seconds and settled down into a crouch. Its talons gripped my shoulder. It cocked its head back and forth, and then it ran its beak over my ear and along my scalp. It was looking for something, I assumed, but I did not know what.

Hey, crow, I said. It didn't answer. I know some crow, I said, and cawed to it. It didn't answer that either. Any of your friends around? I asked.

The crow walked along my shoulder, over the back of my neck, and around to my other shoulder, where it took an interest in that side of my scalp.

It was at just that moment that I recalled a poem of Nionc Tigo's. The one with the crow flying around her skull. For the fifth or sixth time (so it seemed) in the last few minutes, my world twisted itself inside out again. I felt the blood drain from my face and head. I was so light-headed, in the course of an instant, that I had to sit down. I put my hand behind me, to support me as I fell.

The ground I touched wasn't exactly ground. It felt smooth, like marble. Cool. I sat and stretched my legs. There was no dirt here at all, only a smooth and inviting hard surface. It was as though rock had been softened very slightly. There was a little bit of give. Not enough to be pliant, but enough that I did not feel as though the surface was completely unyielding.

The crow, meanwhile, was feasting on my hair. It pulled at it, yanking out the roots.

Stop that, I said. You don't have permission to pull out my hair.

The crow stopped, momentarily, perhaps distracted by my voice, perhaps not. In any case, it did not stop its work for long. In a few more seconds it was at my hair again.

I recalled the crow in Nionc Tigo's poem. It flew through her brain matter, collecting bits and pieces of thought and emotions, like they were shiny trinkets.

When I told my husband about this poem, he was at first repelled, but after he thought about it for some time, he decided it was a good thing. He said it was a good description of a haunted person, someone who was possessed by a creature intent on filling up that person's personal space.

It reminds of the walls I talk to, he said. The walls don't have any life of their own. The voices there are voices from somewhere else, trapped in the walls.

I had never heard that explanation from him before, and I thought, on that day, that he was just being contrary. Or maybe a little loopy. He was a loopy person at times. He was in the world, but not of the world. It's what I liked about him, I suppose, but it was also what made him something different, something that the world did not understand.

But now, his words seemed to make sense.

I waved my hands over my head so the crow would get the message I was not okay with its rooting around in my hair. It got the message. It cawed sharply, twice, then rose up from my head in a splash of black wings, swishing air around loudly and unpleasantly.

The flow of air over my face felt wrong. I wanted the peace and serenity of no motion at all. It tried to land on my shoulder. I shrugged it away. It regrouped and extended its talons toward the side of my head.

I opened my mouth and shouted to it as loudly as I could. It backed away, hovered, flew in small circles, cawed to the world with undisguised irritation, which mirrored my own, then decided I won this round, and turned and flew up to the ivory sky, which meant it left in a quite pretty image of black against cream. I watched it shrink to a dot, then disappear.

At last. I put my head down on the smooth surface beneath me. I had some inkling that this was bone matter. I didn't want to believe it, though, so simply rejected the thought as some kind of errant flitting impulse.

A random firing of neurons. Didn't they happen all the time? The brain making connections or attempting connections when none were there? None that warranted paying attention to, at any rate.

I touched my head to the surface.

Then the connections no longer seemed random. I got a strange sensation, like I had done this before, touched skull to skull. My husband's skull. Certainly we had bumped heads on occasion, and other times had connected skull to skull under more agreeable circumstances. Didn't all couples? Wasn't the touching of head to head one of the benefits of intimacy?

That glancing contact was a kind of reminder that as a couple you were two separate people that had chosen to bump heads.

I laughed. Bump heads.

I lifted my own head from the surface, then let it drop again. Such a strange sensation. The sound was a dull thud. The pressure on my head was soft. And insistent. As though the surface wanted to contact me.

I wanted an instruction manual for this strange space. If this was the earth, it was a strange part of the earth. Nothing here to anchor the senses. Just off-white material as far as the eye could see.

Well, not quite as far. It looked like it rose up in the distance. In fact, all around, in all directions, it rose up. I was at the bottom of a bowl of material. Like the inside of a skull, with the bone curving up all around.

I was of two minds at that point. On the one hand, I knew exactly what was happening. On the other hand, I didn't want to believe what I knew. I didn't want to acknowledge to my own self that I was inside Nionc Tigo's skull.

For one thing, what did that even mean? Nionc Tigo was cremated. There was no skull anymore. In any case, I was too big to fit inside anyone's skull.

I couldn't deny my surroundings, however. I was in the interior of a large bone-white space that curved all around me. It was smooth like bone. Once, in what now seemed like several lifetimes removed from my present one, I took a biology class and handled a human skull. The bone of that skull felt exactly like the floor of my current environment. I saw absolutely no difference between them.

In fact, the sensation of running my hands over the floor here was exactly the sensation I remember from that time. If I closed my eyes, I could take myself back to that time with the skull in my hands.

I couldn't stay here forever. I had to get out. There were no tools here. I searched my pockets for something, anything, that would help me get out. I did have the key from the hotel room. It was, true to the rustic ways of Slothin, not a modern key card, but an old fashioned metal key. It had a serrated edge, like an old fashioned key usually had.

I took it out of my pocket and applied it to the material I stood at. At first I made no progress beyond a very slight scratching mark, hardly visible. More like writing than etching. But I applied more force to the key and pressed as hard as I could. Soon I was able to put a large scar into the material. It was difficult work. My thumb and fingers became sore very quickly and I had to stop frequently to stretch them.

Fine particles of bone began accumulating around the scar I made. I brushed them aside to reveal more of the scar. I pushed harder on the key, scraping through the top layer, until I got to the honeycomb material underneath the surface. There the going got easier. The bone was thinner and more easily broken through. I made rapid progress for a while, until I got through about three or four inches of material and reached the other side of what I still assumed was Nionc Tigo's skull.

Still unsure of the reality of my situation, I pulled the key back and examined it. It was scarred and the serrated edges were duller than when I had started. The bone material had worn down the metal edges of the key. The key was going to be less viable as a tool as I went on.

I sat back and considered my options. If I could make an opening big enough for me to fit through, then the key might just last long enough. I used it to scrape a circle on the surface, using the line I had just dug as a base. It was about a foot and a half wide. That was small, but I thought I would be able to squeeze through a hole of that size.

My thought was that I could scrape through the bone on several lengths along the circle. Then, when the key gave out, I thought I would have enough gouges that I could jump on the circle and break the parts between the gouges and punch the piece through, creating an opening for myself. It seemed barely plausible and I bent down to the task again, using the rapidly dulling key as my only tool.

Again, I lost track of time. I was digging and scraping for a long while. My vision blurred as I worked. Sweat ran down my forehead and into my eyes, stinging them.

At some point, I'm not sure how long, except that I had gouged out about three quarters of the scars I had intended to make, the crow came back. And not just one crow. It brought with it several of its own kind in a flock that was bent on doing me harm.

They swooped down at my head and face and attacked me with their beaks. I was so startled I put my hands up to my face. The key fell and clattered away. I didn't know where it went. I didn't much care, either, not at that moment. I covered my face with my hands. The crows pecked at my fingers and the back of my hand. I felt blood trickle down to my wrists.

I stood up and ran for all I was worth. I ran as fast and as hard as I could. Some of the crows scattered away, but lots of them still hovered around me, as though they wanted to take me apart.

Whether they wanted to or not, I couldn't tell for sure. They were doing a good job, though, of actually doing me harm. Some of their beaks got through my defenses and nipped at my forehead and cheeks. One grabbed my lip. I grabbed it right back, holding it in both hands and squeezing it long enough to feel its neck begin to break.

But I never got that far. As I held it, another crow swooped in and nipped at my nose. I released the first crow and pushed the second one away with my hands, which, by now, were streaked with blood. I knew I could not keep going this way. The birds were going to finish me if I didn't find a way to get them away from me.

I stopped and cawed to them.

There were three or four of them on me at that moment. One on my head, another on my shoulder, and another, unseen, attacking my back. All of them stopped what they were doing as soon as I cawed.

Well. I had their attention. What now?

I told them, as plainly as I could, in their crow language, that what they were doing to me was completely unacceptable.

Some of them took to the air and flew around me. I could see their black eyes on me. I stood my ground. They were not going to intimidate me no matter how many of them there were.

You don't want me digging a hole in Nionc Tigo's skull? I asked them in crow talk. Is that it?

No answer, but I was sure I was right. They only wanted to protect their benefactor. They didn't want a hole stuck in her head.

You know that Nionc Tigo is already dead? You know that, right?

The crows were not completely tamed, but they did seem to want to listen to me. They hovered or perched with much reduced movement. Eventually, the ones who were in the air lighted on the ground, the hard bone shell of Nionc Tigo's interior skull. And I kept talking.

I told them they could help Nionc Tigo and me by finding me help. Finding me a way to get me out of where I was. I understood they were like the thoughts of Nionc Tigo, but that wasn't enough for me to simply lie down quietly and pass into oblivion.

I still had a life I wanted to get back to. I still wanted to return to my husband and go back to our home, a place that was not nearly as strange as Slothin or Nionc Tigo's head.

I tried to make all this as plain as I possibly could to them. My crow was a little rusty, I'm sure. After all, I had not talked crow in a long time. Not since I was a child, probably, back when I thought crows had something to say.

They fool you. They seem like they're very bright, and, more than that, like they have something to say and want to say it. But that's an illusion. Like most animals, they are mostly motivated by finding and eating food.

Nothing else really matters to a crow. They have to find food constantly. All birds do. They probably think I'm some kind of food and are a little perplexed as to why I'm fighting my natural place in the world.

My talks with crows as a youngster convinced me that they were not really worth pursuing as conversational partners. I did not even realize it at the time, but I was working my skills as a translator. I kept that knowledge to myself and did not use those skills until much later.

Now, in Nionc Tigo's skull, as I tried to bring up vocabulary and grammar that they would understand, I discovered that crows actually do deserve some respect for their intelligence. They did seem to understand what I was saying. They grouped together and listened. I told them about my journey to this time and place. I told them, in as simple terms as I could, that they were nothing more than thoughts in a dead poet's head.

One of them asked me where her brain was.

This impressed me. That they would have a concept of the brain. That was higher order awareness, right there.

I told them I didn't know. The cremation process must have burned it out.

Then another crow asked me why, if that was true, that the skull wasn't turned to dust.

That stopped me. I blinked and looked around. The crows were so black against the smooth and curved surface of the skull. It was a breathtaking tableau, elemental in its simplicity, yet full of significance. Or so it seemed to me. Maybe it was just a pleasing juxtaposition of colors and textures.

I think, I said, that you, the crows, are Nionc Tigo's brain.

They held very still for some time. Were they processing this information? Trying to fit it into their lives as they knew it? Or were they simply waiting for me to elaborate? So many ways to interpret their lack of motion.

Think about it, I said. You don't have any food here, do you? All you see is the skull.

One of the crows stepped forward and looked up at me from the bone-white ground. It cawed a long sentence of considerable complexity. It told me the crows wanted me gone. I told it I was fully prepared to go. In fact, I was trying to get away when they attacked me. The crow would have none of it. You don't understand, it said. We want you dead.

Why? I asked.

We've listened to your ramblings. They are the thoughts and statements of a mad woman. We don't want a mad woman here among us. You can't seem to escape, so the best solution is for you to die. You can take care of that yourself, or we can arrange it for you.

I held my position for perhaps two or three seconds as the implications of the crow's words sunk into me. Then I turned and ran for all I was worth.

I heard the crows behind me rise in one flock of menacing wings and feathers and beaks. I increased my speed. The crows swooped down on me. I knew running was futile. I *knew* it, but I didn't care. Running was all I had. They, that is to say, several dozen of them, grabbed at my clothes with their talons.

I tried brushing a few of them off. Tried hitting them with my fists. I was in full panic mode. I flailed at the black shapes. They buzzed around me and floated in front of me. They seemed to be enjoying the torment they were inflicting. Adrenaline had flooded my system and everything was in overdrive. My legs worked hard, my heart pumped hard and my breathing came rapidly and as for my thoughts—

Well.

My thoughts were completely destructive. I wanted nothing more than to see each and every crow perish. Preferably by my own hand. I would have choked the life out of every single one if I could have done it.

But there were so many. They covered me like a coat of black feathers. Their talons pierced my clothing and gripped my skin and flesh. I felt like a pin cushion, but I didn't stop running until the skull beneath my feet magically receded from me.

I didn't, at first, know what was happening. My legs flailed in the air, treading on nothing. Then I knew. I was airborne. The crows had lifted me in the air by the power of all their wing beats. In a day of strange happenings, this was perhaps the most strange of all.

My arms were extended as far as they could go. Twenty crows gripped each arm. Other crows held up my legs and the rest of my body. They all beat their wings with purpose and strength. It was as though they wanted nothing more than to carry me off to—somewhere. I couldn't tell where. I almost didn't care where. Not at that moment.

I just wanted to make sure they had a good hold of me and were not going to drop me. Instantly, I changed my attitude from wanting to kill them to hoping they would be as strong and long-lived as possible. I wanted them to be the most healthy birds in existence. The most healthy birds that *ever* existed.

The skull receded from my view. The horizon line curved upward and we, the crows and I, were reciting the poem of Nionc Tigo.

At first I didn't notice it. Then it became clear. The crows were still talking in their own language. It was not as though they had suddenly acquired the ability to speak human language. But it was unmistakable. They belted out Nionc Tigo's words as they lifted me higher and higher.

The sky and the ground became exactly the same. I was inside an irregular sphere of material. The crows knew their Tigo. They went through much of her oeuvre without stumbling, or, as far as I could tell, missing any line of any poem. I added my voice to their chorus, all the while terrified that I was going to slip away from their hold and plummet to my death. The crows weren't going to keep carrying me, were they? Didn't animals lose interest in things pretty quickly if there was no food involved? Weren't they going to decide I was too boring and drop me? The thought was more than terrifying.

It brought me a kind of sublime peace, if you can imagine it. There really was nothing I could do. I could not, if the situation deteriorated to the point that I was going to drop from the crows, try to grab onto any of them and keep myself aloft. They were much too small, individually, to hold me up. Which meant that I was completely at their mercy.

The words of Nionc Tigo echoed in the chamber of the world that I had somehow found myself in. Was there anything that I could do to help myself? It seemed not.

We continued to ascend. I continued to pray for their grip to hold me. And eventually, as the extent of my place in the world became apparent, I fell asleep.

I dreamed of crows. A million of them. Each one had Nionc Tigo's face instead of a crow's face. They all stared at me and kept asking me questions, as though I knew the answers to anything. I didn't.

The dream lasted a long time. As the questions kept coming, I began to see the words floating in the air before me. Nionc Tigo's words. They imprinted themselves on pieces of paper that floated in the void around me.

The paper multiplied and the words stacked up. So much paper, so many words.

In the dream, I picked up one of the papers and examined it carefully. The words on the page did not stay still. Instead, they shimmered and glowed and trembled. It was as though they were animated from within and had the benefit of a special effects technician.

Soon they sprouted wings of their own and lifted off the page. The words continued to shimmer and glow. They cast their light over all the space around me. They filled my eyes with visions: globules of light and pulsing phosphenes of energy.

When I woke, I was no longer being carried aloft. The air around me was dark, as though I was in a place touched by dusk. My feet were buried under me in a painful manner and angle. I shifted myself from side to side, in an attempt to straighten myself out. My hands touched rough material around me.

It felt like straw or sticks. Maybe some other kind of plant. Also feathers. Some soft, some more rough. As my eyes adjusted to my surroundings, it became pretty clear that the crows had deposited me inside a fairly large nest.

Large enough to hold me, at least, with room left over. I freed my legs from under me and stood up, slowly and gingerly. The floor of the nest was rough and uneven. I fell over a couple of times as I tried to get my footing.

The material was uneven and had lots of empty spaces between the fibers. I had a time trying to keep myself from falling between those spaces. I walked across the nest to the edge and raised myself up on tiptoes and peered over the lip of the nest.

The white sky was still there. Nionc Tigo's words echoed in my own skull. They filled me up. I could hardly think of anything else but her poetry. No other thoughts entered my cranium. It was pure Nionc, a kind of other worldly mantra.

I looked down and saw a branch of a tree extend into space. So, the nest appeared to sit in a tree. And not a small one, either. I lifted myself as high as it seemed possible to go, and looked down the edge of the nest and saw a long stretch of bark-encrusted trunk. It went down and down and down. So far down that I couldn't see the end of it: it disappeared into a misty nothingness, giving me the sensation of being aloft in empty space, as though there was nothing holding me up.

That was starting to feel familiar.

Also, I missed the crows. Their blackness, more than anything else, perhaps. My bland surroundings, so misty and white, were an emptiness. It didn't fill me with hope for the future. But the crows. They were menacing, yes, but they also had power and life. They brought a sense of purpose to my very strange life here in the underworld beneath Slothin.

If that was where I was.

My legs were getting tried. I dropped down to my heels, then let go of the lip of the nest and retreated to the center of the fibrous flow. I pulled some feathers from here and there and piled them up on the floor of the

nest. My makeshift bed thus appointed as best as I could make it, I
stretched out on the feathers and tried to relax.

Nionc Tigo's words kept running through my head. She had written a
cycle of poems about crows. In them the crows had a life of their own with
their unique civilization and tribal affiliations and ways of living. They
worked together, sometimes, and opposed each other at other times. It was
a microcosm of the human universe.

Nionc Tigo used the crows to tell stories about universal human truths.
At least, that's what some of the critics said. I think Nionc Tigo was just
having fun imagining what crows might be like if they were like us. It was
her joke on humanity: we were nothing more than scavengers, digging
about in the effluvia of the world, trying to make a living, surviving as best
we can just like any other creature under the sun.

Now it seemed that I was one of those creatures, trapped in a nest I did
not make and did not know how to get out of. I pushed some of the nest
material out of my way. The ends of the sticks poked into my back, making
my experience here uncomfortable. I already missed flying. Missed the
crows lifting me up. The air flowing over my skin, the feeling of freedom,
despite the talons stuck in my skin, it all lifted me up, figuratively and
metaphorically.

Now I was just a lump of flesh in this nest. Were the crows going to
return and offer me a worm? Maybe more than one. Was I then required
to eat it? I shuddered, thinking about it.

Suddenly I wanted to crawl into the space between the fibers of the
material making up the nest. Maybe that would offer me some protection.

I pushed aside some of the straw and sticks, making room for me. I
crawled down into the space. If I couldn't climb out, maybe I could crawl
through.

I came to layers of papers. I tore them out. There were more layers underneath. I tore those out. They had typing on them. They looked like
Nionc Tigo's work, but by then I was sick of hearing about her and hearing

of any of her words. None of it mattered. It was all so much garbage. It should all have gone into the shredder.

Would that have been too much to ask? Maybe Nionc Tigo should never have published *anything,* much less her extended ode to crows. It seemed I had somehow taken in the life of the crows. My own life had become crow like. I was in a nest and I was rooting around for debris. Something. I wasn't sure.

Eventually I got through the nest and came out the bottom. I was careful not to fall. Instead, I eased myself out of the hole I had created and stood on the thick branch that supported the nest. The bark was rough. It afforded me numerous nooks and crannies that I could use to keep myself from falling. My feet anchored well on the rough surface.

I scurried toward the trunk, which twisted and writhed in the air, as though it had once been a snake that had been tortured by Nionc Tigo, and had been turned into a tree in mid-writhe.

I felt the snake's pain, which surprised me. I was not normally an empathic person. I held my hands outstretched from my body, as much to feel the freedom as to maintain my balance on the branch. I took tiny steps to keep myself from falling. The trunk was a long way off, but it was not an impossible distance.

All I had to do was keep taking tiny steps and I would get there in due course. The air around me was filled with insects. They buzzed and circled my head and body. They lighted on my ears and nose. Some tried to get into my eyes.

I kept my concentration as best I could. I did not try to swat at them and did not curse them. They were a part of my world and I accepted them. Fortunately, none were biting or stinging, as far as I could tell. They only wanted to be near me.

That was fine. I didn't need to shoo them away based on that. As long as they did not impede my progress, it was no matter to me.

Eventually, the trunk got close enough for me touch it. I reached out my hands, intending to fall forward a little and feel the relief of having something solid holding me up.

But that didn't happen. Just as my hands came close to the trunk, it slipped away from me. Just enough to be out of reach.

I caught myself from falling, then realized how strange it was that the trunk would do that. How could it?

I stepped forward again, and again the trunk receded from me. I looked down at the branch. Was it growing? I studied the branch at my feet for several seconds. I could not see evidence of it elongating, but how else to explain what had just happened to me?

I looked up at the trunk again. It stood silent and unmoving. I imagined it mocking me. Was that what it was doing? Did it know I was there? Did it have a beef with me?

The trunk and I held our respective grounds, as it were, high up in the air above the skull of Nionc Tigo.

I breathed deeply, like I was taking in all the air the tree pushed out. The tree, for its part, seemed to drink in all the carbon dioxide I could expel. We went on like that for some time. I liked the idea of our symbiosis. As we both took in gases and expelled other gases, I felt as though we were both in a Nionc Tigo farce. That was the whole story, wasn't it? Nionc Tigo was playing an elaborate joke on all of us. She wanted us to think she was a literary virtuoso, but it wasn't so at all. Nionc Tigo was a jokester.

Was she even dead?

The tree and I, we continued our little confrontation. It did not move, except for respiration and some rustling of leaves caused by the wind. It also rustled my clothes a little, made them flutter in the air. It was as though my outer skin was being perturbed. Like I was perturbing the tree? Perhaps.

I called out Nionc Tigo's name, breaking the silence in a way that I approved of. And I think the tree approved as well. It made noises. It began to sway in the wind. It creaked and snapped and squawked.

There was a kind of symphony to the noise, as though the wind was coming around to catch us all and lift us up with the spirit of melody.

I was sure I felt it in the tree as well: this sense of freedom that music can bring to a situation. I began to lose the sense that I was a poor and powerless player in this drama.

The syntax and grammar of the tree and its bark and flesh began to assert itself. I knew that the tree was going to move in a direction I could not anticipate, but I was beginning to understand the language of the tree. Or so I thought.

My skill at deciphering languages sometimes made me think I knew more than I actually knew. After all, it was completely possible the tree had no language whatsoever. It did not have need of communicating with language. What would it say? *Kind of nice being stuck in one place forever, isn't it? There's a lot of decisions we never have to make. Makes life very simple. I like that.*

Well. I may be too unkind to trees. It's entirely possible, I suppose, that they have an active social life and incredible conversations. *Possible.*

But not likely.

More of Nionc Tigo's jokes. I began to snap and creak and flutter, imitating the language of the tree. I translated some of Nionc Tigo's poems, some that I remembered, into tree-speak. It went over pretty well. The tree got silent in the poignant parts, and raucous in the energetic portions, responding to the recitation like a real audience.

I never would have thought it possible. The tree was merely a support for the nest, after all.

I shuffled my feet along as I spoke. I took very small steps forward. The tree began to answer me. I inched toward the trunk. The tree added verses to Nionc Tigo's poems. It had some poetic chops, did that tree. It laid down line upon line with resonance and oomph. It knew rhyme and iambs and imagery.

Lots of its imagery was about wind and leaves. That was okay. And birds. Lots of bird allusions. It didn't use the ground much, even though it was rooted in dirt. Something about darkness it didn't much care for. I wasn't going to try to explain it.

Then, as we got going together, me reciting, and the tree, as far as I could tell, improvising, some splits occurred in the body of the tree. They started slowly and imperceptibly. I didn't recognize them as damage to the structure at first. What I thought they were was the tree adding new sounds to our reading.

But then a tremendous gap opened up in the trunk, accompanied by an ear-splitting snapping sound, as though the universe had found a way to break in two. I stopped reciting Nionc Tigo poems. I didn't want to make things worse for the tree. But the tree didn't stop. It kept going, like it *needed* the poems. It *required* the sound of poetry to keep its life on an even keel. How could that be?

I called to the tree. Stop it! I said. Don't make more noise. Stop telling Nionc Tigo's poems. They are not helping you.

But the tree would not stop.

I put out my hands, palms flat, and eased my wrists down in tiny motions, trying to tell it to slow down, to stop. But that didn't help at all.

In fact, the cacophony of snaps and twists and (now) whistles and grinding and scraping and hissing only increased in power and sharpness. It was as though the tree wanted to pierce the air with its pent up sound, the emotion that Nionc Tigo had evoked in the tree.

I kept inching forward and finally came close enough to hug the trunk of the tree. I grabbed on and held it tight for as hard as I could. I half believed I could hold it secure and intact with the strength of my arms.

Futile, of course.

Even as I wrapped my arms around the tree, it kept splitting. A great gash opened up its entire length. My arms had to loosen to accommodate the movement of the trunk away from the gash. I tried to hold on as best I could, but it was no good. My arms spread out with the widening gash and I had to readjust my feet so I would not be toppled off the branch of the tree.

More splitting occurred. My brain went into overdrive trying to translate the sounds of the gashes. I could not. There was no discernible pattern to them at all. They were not the tree speaking, they were the tree disintegrating.

More snapping and splitting noises. I never knew what it meant to split the air with sound, but I was hearing it now. The atmosphere around me felt like something had taken the frozen air and broken it into two or more pieces. I had to get away from the noise: it was an assault.

Splinters of sound continued to fall out of the air, as though there were pockets of truth that had to be translated. I tried to snag them with my ears. Tried to find the inner beauty in their structure, but there was none. I couldn't see the structure of the thing. Couldn't comprehend what the air was telling me.

I expected the tree to fall. I began climbing down the trunk. Slowly, at first, gingerly. I had this crazy idea that if I was too reckless, I was going to disturb the tree and cause it to fall more quickly, or, perhaps, more devastatingly.

As I climbed down, I soon saw that that was a ridiculous view of the situation. The tree *was* dying. Nothing I did was going to make it worse.

So I increased my pace. The tree, luckily, was a meandering thing. It jutted to one side, then poked to another side, then bent this way and that.

The trunk was not a straight shot down to the ground, which would have defeated me. Instead, I was able to scamper down on its wandering trunk.

I stepped over the gap and grabbed onto the rough bark. My feet found good purchase all the way down. As I neared the ground, the tree began to move with ominous purpose. It was as though it had decided to tilt to one side.

The gash increased in width. More snaps and crackling. Grinding noises, as well. Not to mention scrapes and an odd and persistent knocking or drumming, like something was beating it from within.

I eased myself down to the ground at the foot of the tree. Roots had writhed out of the white bone like serpents rising out of a sea. The rounded exposed length of them did something to the pit of my stomach, as though they had some primeval hold on my emotions.

I clutched my belly, standing there under the dying tree. As the gash widened even more, the tree tipped to a point of no return. Gravity took over and pulled it the rest of the way down.

It snapped and popped as it went down. Splintered the air like a lightning bolt, and sent gusts of air out from its length.

It ended up lying in a pathetic caricature of death. Its top was supported by the branches which had been high up on its trunk. The remains of the trunk left standing, a small sharp blade of wood, displayed fresh flesh to the world. It was bright yellow and looked wet, sodden with sap and tree juices. They dripped down the length of the exposed gash.

The tree did not groan or moan about its fate. It was still alive, even though it had fallen. The trees still thirsted for sunlight and the liquids still pulsed along its prone length, but we both knew its days were numbered. It no longer had a voice. Not snapping or creaking or squeaking.

I dredged up yet another Nionc Tigo poem, this one about the death of language, and I tried to translate it into terms the tree would understand. I used all the skills of my trade. I evoked a world of lost trees and the giant heart of trees. Nionc Tigo could pull anything out of the air. Even a eulogy for a tree.

The tree did not respond. Not audibly, at least, but I felt its power. It was *present* as only such a beast could be present.

I stayed with the tree for some time. How long I could not say for sure, but it felt like days more than hours. Maybe even weeks. I slept next to the tree and during my waking hours I maintained contact with the tree. I drank from its exposed gash, drawing whatever energy I could from its liquid with my tongue.

I ate some of its leaves. It was, surprisingly, not at all bitter, as I had expected. The leaves tasted like carrots and cinnamon. Not a particularly inspired combination of flavors, but not too difficult to get down, either.

I worked to get the roots up and out of the ground. There was more moisture in those roots. I drank from them as well, I fashioned a stand using roots where I put pieces of the tree that I had broken off and upended. Under the stand I placed a bowl that I had made by taking a burl of bark from the tree.

I learned quite soon that this was no ordinary tree. It had properties no tree I knew of possessed. I felt the spirit of Nionc Tigo around me, telling me how to turn the dying tree into something that could help me.

The days were not marked by sunups or sundowns. I saw no astronomical objects of any kind. This did not trouble me, but it did mean that time stretched out for an indeterminate length. I marked the days by my thirst and hunger. And by my waste products. I moved my bowels approximately every day or so, so that was how I knew a day had passed.

The tree, on the other hand, took a long time dying. Are trees immortal? If undisturbed, would they live forever? It seems possible. Trees die by accident, or deliberate intent, or fire and so on. They die if the ground moves beneath them and they topple. The wind blows them down. But I've never heard of a tree dying of old age. It must happen, I suppose, but when? A thousand years? Ten thousand?

My tree, for that is how I came to think of it, groaned with diminished energy. It snapped and creaked as its pieces settled, or shifted slightly, or moved in a strange way.

We never came to an understanding, the tree and I. It didn't know me and I don't think I really knew it. It had stories to tell, I was sure, but its extended death bed reveries were not to my liking at all. After all, the tree had lived in a wilderness of color and form. The only thing around it was white bone material and air. Nothing there to tell stories about.

I found myself wishing the tree would hurry up and lose consciousness. Was it too much to ask that it disappear from my view? My initial feelings of tenderness gave way to irritation and impatience on a grand scale.

I knew if I had had the proper tools, an ax or a saw, I would have taken it to pieces. Even as I drank its moisture, I cursed its stubborn longevity and insistence on remaining part of existence. The crows, I noticed, stayed away from the dying thing. They were wary of the monolith, unsure how to approach it or me, I suppose. The tree, in that strange place between living and dying, occupied a twilight zone they were not prepared to enter.

And me? Why was I so attached to this tree?

I can look back now and soberly assess the situation and tell you that it was the only gnarly thing in my universe at that time and, as such, demanded my attention as nothing else could. But that would be disingenuous. I had no such thoughts at the time. All I knew was that I didn't want to separate myself from that tree because I thought it would keep me alive.

That's all. It was my means of survival in the strangest environment I had ever found myself stuck in. I lost all sympathy for the tree in the first two or three days. After that, I wanted it to yield up more of its bounty. I wanted more moisture from it, and more leaves.

The bark was not tasty and the flesh was too fibrous. The twigs I could tolerate in very small bites. The leaves were good, but the tree did not have an infinite supply of them. What tree, outside of fantasy and imagination, does?

Furthermore, the leaves were beginning to wilt around the edges. They weren't getting their share of nutrients and they were dying. But *slowly.* The slow thing was maddening. I estimated, from how many leaves remained, that I had about a month of food from the tree.

The moisture was more difficult to estimate. It might have been a long time, and it might not have. I had no experience with drinking from a tree and could not make that estimate. It didn't matter, however. All I wanted was something to tell me I had not made a mistake by staying with the tree.

Perhaps I had kept myself from achieving an escape from here. By staying with the dying tree, had I sabotaged my own survival?

Such questions as this haunted me as I clung to the tree. I spent my days chewing on its leaves and murmuring comforting words as I uprooted it. The bone material was surprisingly easy to break off. It was not quite the consistency of styrofoam, but close enough that I could grab onto pieces of it and break off chunks with little effort. I tossed them aside into piles as I dug deeper and deeper in an attempt to pull out all the bits of root that it was possible to find.

Beneath the smooth surface of bone, the structure was like stilled foam. Bubbles of air trapped in a honeycomb of bone. The piles of broken off pieces grew as I tunneled deeper and deeper.

As the days dragged on, the stump of the tree grew more and more unstable due to me pulling out so much of the root system. Eventually the stump fell over, just as the majority of the trunk had fallen earlier with the split. I felt no remorse or sorrow for the tree at that point. The irritation had set in completely and I was only too glad to help it on its way.

I slept sporadically, with no way of telling how long I had been asleep each time I woke and saw that my environment had changed very little from when I had drifted to sleep. This was soul killing in itself. I died a little each time I opened my eyes and *nothing had changed.*

But I tried not to dwell on it. As I continued my work of excavating the tree, I had built a particularly large pit around where it had been rooted. The pit extended down for some considerable distance.

I fashioned steps in the material to make it easy for me to descend and ascend. There was something comforting about the pit. It reminded me of when I was a child and build forts with couch cushions. Did every child do such things? It seemed reasonable to think so.

The comfort of walls built of one's own hands. The feeling of protection. Everyone wanted that. The illusion of safety, after all, was something most living things craved. There was no true safety, not really, but the illusion was something we could all agree upon. Perhaps the only fantasy everyone had a part in.

I took to spending more and more time in the pit. I followed every little bit of the root, every tiny fibrous length of it. It extended into the bone material in all directions.

Some of the tiniest roots went through the material like a vein of ore goes through rock. It made the bone richer, more complex. I never thought I would dig around the ground, but here I was, tossing up chunks of white bone as I followed single strands of root into oblivion.

Sometimes I thought of my husband and his earth movers. I don't think I ever understood his occupation before my time with the tree. I thought what he did he did simply for the income, but there had to be a satisfaction to altering one's environment, and with his earth movers, that's what he did every time he went to work. He didn't hear the voices in the earth, but he must have heard some kind of siren call there, some sort of calling? I resolved to talk to him about it when we met again.

If we met again.

It took me a long time to face the fact that my life may have come to its stasis. It was entirely possible that I was never going to get out of this situation.

The thought made me feel desolate and dead. So I didn't have the thought too often. Much easier and, paradoxically, *saner* to spend my time excavating. I made little rooms in the pit. Places I could retreat to and feel as comfortable and snug as a bug.

There was heat from the bone. It enveloped me and kept me warm and cozy. When I emerged from the excavation to see to the tree in all its broken humility, I no longer felt pity. I spit on the tree and screamed at it to hurry up its dying.

Then I felt remorse and shame. How could I do such a thing? At those times, I fell to my knees and wrapped my arms around the tree and sobbed and said I was sorry. I didn't mean to add to its hurt.

The thing is, I couldn't leave the tree. As much as I wanted to, it had a hold on me. Its dissipating energy was not enough to release me from its power to hold me.

I felt like one of those dogs that stays with its dead owner for days or weeks. It neglects its own health, refuses to go hunting or find food, keeps other animals at bay, and the owner is *dead*. But it doesn't matter to the dog. Its instinct is to protect and it doesn't have the brains to know there's nothing to protect anymore.

I was like that dog. I wanted to stay with the tree until it lost all possibility of consciousness. Even though it was dead.

Once I finished eating the leaves, and once I got all the moisture that I could out of the flesh, the tree reminded me of a skeleton: dried out and stark without flesh.

The mind can make connections out of unconnected events. Sometimes that can be a kind of genius. Other times its nothing more than delusion. Even now, thinking back on those events, I'm not always sure of which it was at the time. I remember thinking the tree had finally given up the ghost. At least as best I could determine.

I also remember a light shining throughout the atmosphere. It was not like the light in the tunnel, and then again, not like the light from a sunny day.

It suffused everything, and it was very subtle, as though it wanted to hint at some form of enlightenment, but not be too direct about it. I looked up from the tree, aware that I gave the impression of an animal looking up from a meal and begging for more.

The sky above me was still blurry, suggesting, rather than revealing, the bony surface beyond. The light did nothing to reveal the surface, but it lit up the air as though the individual molecules were all fireflies.

The shifting allegiances of the atoms got me interested even more. How could all those molecules work together? They had nothing to do with one another.

As I stared up at the sky, the crows circled way overhead. They, too, were illuminated by this new and strange light. They, too, found it easy to look for the sources.

That is what they were doing, I was sure of it. They had the exact same curiosity I did. To seek and understand the language of the world, whatever the world happened to be at that moment. Everything has a language. Sometimes it's temporary. Other times it's permanent. My whole life has been distinguishing the temporary from the permanent.

And now I was in a strange environment. Perhaps the strangest. And I didn't know if the language of the place was a visitor or a long term resident.

The trails of the crows imprinted themselves on my eye. It was as though someone had taken a pen and written on my retina. I wanted to find meaning in those scrawls and took the next few minutes to do so.

I studied the loops and whorls. I bared my soul to the sky, if I might be so dramatic. I brought all my years of experience, indeed, *expertise*, to bear on the subject at hand. My only means of determining meaning was my own mind and the history attendant on it.

I opened my mouth to speak. The words of dozens of languages poured out of me. It was as though I was releasing them all to the wild. It didn't matter that I didn't know the nature of this wild, not really. It didn't even matter that words are not wild.

Words are tamed objects, the corralling of sound from lips, teeth, and tongue. What mattered was that all of those words were exiting my domain and entering the domain of Nionc Tigo.

And then, just a few minutes later, all meaning was gone from those words. I no longer understood any other language except my own.

It was a strange sensation, not to have the comfort of words in me. Learning other languages is not like riding a bike. You can forget. People do forget. All the time they forget. People who had a certain language as children, no longer have that language as adults. People who learn a language from visiting a country in their teens, will not have that language twenty years later if they don't use it in the meantime.

So I knew it was possible.

I just never thought it would happen to *me* since I was the genius at languages. It was my thing.

Which I no longer had. The tree at my feet was not silent. It made tiny noises. I no longer knew what those noises meant. It was nothing but an insult to the air, and I found it annoying. I wished the tree would simply release its sounds and quit being heard. Was that so difficult to do?

I undertook to bury the tree. That was important, wasn't it? The tree was dead and gone. It needed to be put under the ground, or, at least, what passed for ground in this place.

I began placing the chunks of bone over the tree. I took a good couple of hours doing so. The light still streamed over me and around me. The bone chunks were not enough to cover the tree, so I had to excavate even more pieces to complete the task. This took some more time and effort. By the end of my endeavors, the tree was under a pile of pieces of bone. It looked like a styrofoam factory had broken open and spilled its contents everywhere.

But the important thing was that the tree was out of sight. I felt incredible relief. I turned from the mountain of bone pieces that I had built up to epic proportions, and began walking away.

I felt empty. The only living thing that would have anything to do with me anymore was gone. I was alone and suddenly realized I was not only hungry but thirsty as well. My footsteps rung against the ground. I picked up sounds from the air around me: sparks of noise, clicks here and there, a hissing, some snaps and breaks, as though fingers were clicking one against the other.

All these noises, which I would once have considered elements of a language, made me think only of chaos. There was no meaning in these sounds. Never had been. That I could once have thought they did indicated a kind of delusion that might pass for insanity.

So I began to see that translation was a skill, but also a way of being crazy in the world. Too much translation brought meaning to things that had no meaning.

And yet.

There was meaning. Had to be. I looked down at the material I was walking on. The color was shifting. This was fascinating to me, because I saw no reason for it. There was not meaning in the ground, was there? It was just ground. Bone, in this case, but nothing more, really, than something to put my feet on.

It was turning darker. Still off white, but now with a tinge of green to it. Not a fresh and vibrant green like foliage. More of a dark green, the kind one sees in certain varieties of mold. It was not pleasant to look at, but I could not move my eyes from it.

I tried looking up, but could not. My eyes would not move from the tableau of color now spread out around me.

As I continued walking, the stain, for that is what it resembled, only grew darker. The green took away all the white and as it did, the texture of the ground changed as well. It softened. Before long, I was walking not on bone, but on what felt like dirt. Ground. My feet sunk into the dirt. Not enough to impede my progress, but enough to let me know that I was on a yielding surface, one that wanted to cushion my way. I was ecstatic. It was as though I had come home after a voyage of years.

I tried to quicken my pace. Wanted to do so with all my might, but I was too tired. My legs dragged. My feet dragged. Indeed, my entire being seemed to drag. If I let it, I felt like my soul could have slipped out of my body and entered the ground I was traversing.

I fought to keep that from happening. I didn't know where I was going, only that movement seemed most imperative. If I stopped I didn't know what was going to happen, but it seemed likely that I would have sunk into the ground and never gotten back out.

A sense of panic touched me then. I did not let it overwhelm me, but I also could not banish it completely. Given that, I decided to keep it close to me, so I could, with effort, keep it tame. I seized it and held it in my heart. The muscles there contracted, as a way of telling panic that I was in control.

It could try to leak out of my heart and invade my body via my blood stream, but that wasn't going to happen. I clamped down on it. I held it tight, like a wrestler with his foot on the neck of his opponent. It was an exhilarating image, one that I could relate to and wanted to hold onto.

All the while I kept walking. I never worried about where I was walking to. It felt as though my entire purpose in being was to get to a place where I could leave this wonderland behind.

It was wonderful being here, but not in a good way. The wonders I saw were constraints on my sanity. There's no other way to put it. My translation skills had kicked into overdrive. I was so deprived of information and context that I took to trying to understand everything around me as code for something else.

The universal constraints on language meant nothing to me anymore. It was all open and free. Words seemed to float up out of the void and fill the air. It was as though I was seeing clouds of letters and words everywhere.

In one sense, it didn't even matter if the clouds actually were representations of the tics of language. All the energy around me pointed to that as reality.

My walking continued for an unspecified length of time. Again, my perceptions were so skewed that there was no way I could ever say accurately how long I was in this underworld.

As I walked, I saw protuberances around me. The bone-shell ground erupted in bulbs of material, as though it wanted to mushroom into something else. It reminded me of some of the rocks along the shore of the ocean at Seagull Cove. I half expected the surf to come sliding in and closing around the protuberances, but that didn't happen. There was no water here. I was in a desert, of sorts. A desert that had no sand or sun, but was a desert nonetheless, with absolutely no moisture of any kind.

The bulbs and bumps populated the bone like groups of tumors. They also, as I walked, increased in density so that I was dodging them and having to squeeze my way through them in spots. As I did so, I felt their smoothness.

It was like sliding past polished marble. I let my hand fall on the surface and move across it. In other places, the objects, which I suppose I needed to call stalagmites, were more widely separated and I was able to come to several clearings where I stood and took in my surroundings.

The growths rose to enormous heights. I craned my neck to see where they ended up. They looked like they were taller than the tallest trees I had ever seen on the coast back home, some of which rose to hundreds of feet.

These bony white protuberances were higher than that. On some of the tops, I thought I saw nests. Huge nests that reminded me of raptor dwellings: great round bowls made of sticks and branches. But I couldn't be sure. I thought it might be an illusion brought on by my addled brain.

Still. There was a certain comfort in being in a forest again, even though the ground was not springy like a real forest. And even though the trees were not trees at all.

I sat in one of the clearings with my knees raised up to my chest and my arms around my shins, holding myself close in. The power of forests, whatever their constituent parts, comes out in the landscape and makes me want to protect myself. You can't trust power. It is always susceptible to corruption and corruption usually means that you are at risk.

My thoughts whirled around these ideas for some time. I wanted to love this forest, but could not. I could tolerate it if I had to, but it was easier to watch it from afar.

I think several days worth of time passed for me. I didn't sit huddled the whole time. I stretched out a couple of times to sleep, and I walked the clearing, endless circles of walking, trying to find some meaning in the forest around me.

I was pretty sure that as time went on, the stalagmites grew. When I looked up at the tops of them, they seemed to waver in the sky at a taller point. The nests I thought I saw were smaller as well. A true vision, or illusion? I was having great difficulty distinguishing one from the other.

Eventually, as the growths kept getting bigger, I realized that they were also getting wider and would, at some point, get wide enough to erase the clearing I was in. That troubled me. It meant I would no longer have a sanctuary. I determined that I would go through the forest, to whatever was on the other side.

My next few days worth of walking were the most difficult of all. I had to climb over strange growths, and scamper around others. The stalagmites were fusing in places, as though two trees had decided to merge into one.

I heard the crashing of the material as they meshed, the cells coming together and holding hands, loudly. I was able to punch through some of the growths. It was the same material that I saw where the tree had fallen and died, but it was—somehow—more inviting to me in this guise. It was as though it had decided to wrap itself around me and make itself part of my surroundings because it loved me. It wanted only the best for me.

At first I resisted this invitation from the bone forest. This was something I had to get through, not something that benefited me by being my friend or intimate.

So I kept walking. But the bones still pressed themselves upon me. Or around me. Something. It wasn't just their physical presence. There was also the fact that they were emotionally there for me. As though they wanted to wrap me up and keep me safe.

Was I so pathetic that I needed to be cared for like a little girl? I didn't know. Not for sure. But it seemed possible. Maybe I had regressed to childhood. In this place, anything was possible. I had lost my sense of time. It was as though I *was* a child again, attempting to understand language. I felt like I no longer even had English for my own self. There was no real language. It was all just empty meanings floating about in the ether.

And the bones kept crowding me. I squeezed between them. I looked for clearings ahead. They, at least, were places I could take stock of myself and my surroundings. Try to come to some sort understanding of my environment.

It took me a while, therefore, to sense the liquid gathering at my feet. It wasn't until the level had risen above my shoes and began lapping at my ankles that the sensation of being wet actually caused me to look down and observe a most curious thing: sea water was collecting at the bottom of the world. My world. The bone world. It was rising, slowly, but rising nevertheless. And I could tell it was sea water from the consistency and color.

Several emotions went through me then. I loved that this reminder of my home had found its way to this strange place. It made me think there was a possibility that I would come to a place that meant something to me. I also felt a sense of emptiness and dread. If the water kept rising, it was going to put me in peril.

I didn't worry about that. At least not too much. I wanted to get through the forest and see what was on the other side. An ocean, perhaps. Or, at least, a sea, which amounted to the same thing.

The smell of seaweed, faintly rich and rotten, entered my nostrils and snaked into my brain. My mouth watered, even though I have never particularly cared for seaweed as a food. It didn't matter. It was all a reminder of home.

I remembered walking the beach after a storm, great tubes of kelp washed up on the sand, and smelling that odor. It put me in mind of long walks on the beach. Sometimes at sunset, sometimes with my husband.

The path ahead was getting more and more difficult to see clearly. The water had risen to my knees and was showing no signs of stopping. It was cold and many tiny creatures floated in it.

The foam rose up around me as well. Some of it was thick and fluffy. Some of it was flat and floated on the surface of the water. All of it was broken by the stalagmites.

I don't think I was going to die. At least, that was not in my thinking at the time. For all I knew, I was already dead and this was hell. It certainly couldn't have been heaven. I knew that for sure. But hell, sure. It was crazy enough for that place.

My feet were getting numb, which meant I was cut off from the only world I had. It was as though my body ended at mid-thigh and I was floating on the water. Or flying. It was hard to tell for sure.

I reached out, with my mind, for Nionc Tigo's voice, but it wasn't there anymore. She had deserted me a long time ago, but I thought now, with the world changing so quickly, she might return to me.

Alas, it did not happen. The water rose so quickly that it lifted me up. I was floating on it. The stalagmites of bone surrounded me as white rocky islands might float in the ocean at Seagull Cove. We called them sea stacks. These were like that, only the sea stacks back home weren't bone-colored. They were gray and black, and craggy. The water was rising so quickly that I reached out for some of the bone stacks, hoping to gain stability for myself.

The crows were making a new ruckus. They came out of the sky in black swirls and circled around my head, cawing all the while.

I was struggling to stay afloat. My swimming skills were less than stellar. I hung onto the stalagmites for support. My legs kicked beneath me, under the surface. I had this premonition that things were going to be decidedly different from now on. If the water kept rising, then the white bone sea stacks were going to disappear and I would have nothing to hold onto any more. I would be adrift in the open sea with no life jacket and would get very tired of treading water very quickly.

My legs thought they were operating a bicycle, or perhaps more properly, a unicycle. I got the two objects mixed up and there was no reason for the mix up. I told myself in as clearly and distinctly a way as I possibly could that one of them had two wheels and the other had one wheel. Completely different.

I convinced myself of the difference, briefly, but it was still a fight to keep the distinction clear in my mind. I thought that if I could keep the difference as clear as possible, then I would be able to explain it to others. The impulse came from my years of translating. I knew that translation was nothing more than explaining a text in one language to people who knew another language. Lazy people, as my husband was fond of saying. I catered to lazy people.

But my skills were deteriorating. I tried, as I faltered there on the surface, to try to remember words in other languages. Tried to remember the *names* of other languages and I was having difficulty. I was not so far gone, mentally, to be incognizant of my situation, but I was gone enough to know that I was going.

I let my mind drift, trying to latch onto something familiar, but words were suddenly strange objects. I could see them, in my mind's eye, the curves and struts of the letters, but they meant nothing.

I put the thought out of my mind and concentrated on survival. That was the imperative here, wasn't it? To survive at all costs. Wasn't that the point of life?

I didn't know anymore. The sea, which had been calm, suddenly grew choppy and treacherous. I tried to put myself close to one of the sea stacks, but by this time there were only a few left. The water had risen to submerge most of them and only a few points were visible around me, like rotted teeth floating on the surface of the water. Even if I managed to swim to one of them and find refuge, it would be short-lived since the water was still rising. So I elected to stay where I was, churning the water with my legs and treading the surface with my arms.

I estimated I had, maybe, a few more minutes. Fifteen at the most, before I would tire and begin to slip under the surface.

I would have welcomed the ability to project my soul out of my boy at that point, but this did not happen. Instead, I devoured myself. My soul, which had been hanging on the outside of my body, hoping for a miracle, instead of leaving, turned inward. It dove in through my skin and hair, past my flesh and through my bones and swam through the bone marrow and reached the center of my being where it kept going, as though it was able to take a left turn at eternity and continue on.

I followed. I felt the viscera of my body, the veins and blood and heat of my flesh. I moved with my soul as it tunneled and dug and journeyed. It moved at the speed of light and I struggled to keep up, but the struggle worked. I was able to trail my soul with a certain panache, as though I could hook a rope to it and follow along like a disabled auto towed by a truck.

That was about the extent of what I was able to do. My body, way way back there in the water, seemed to be okay. At least it was intact enough that it wasn't overwhelmed by the water all around it.

Meanwhile, I hung on for dear life. My only possibility of salvation, it seemed, was to hang on as best I could and not let go under any circumstances.

The journey, only the latest in a long series of them, continued through some awfully dark territory. There was no light of any kind and my eyes were unaccustomed to the darkness. They yearned for something to see and I believe I invented all sorts of odd objects and happenings in my surroundings at that time.

Lights were everywhere. Scenes from my childhood played out in phosphorescent dazzlements. I climbed trees and fell off bicycles and ate cotton candy. It was all there, spread out like a carnival of rides, all the exhilaration and adrenaline rush of life laid out before me.

But nothing after early childhood. Nothing from when I was eight or nine or ten. Everything was from my early days, from before I was seven years old. This seemed strange. Didn't I have a life after age seven?

I was sure I did, but you couldn't tell from my experience diving into my interior, following my soul's journey. I felt as though I had only a fraction of a life. All the years from seven to where I was now had disappeared, somehow, and I was adrift on a sea of undifferentiated years, as though I had no age, no way of knowing if I could be more than a child. This sobered me.

I set my mouth firmly, as grim as anything I could have imagined and I waited for some meaning from my later life to come to me.

Nothing.

There was running, a lot of running. I saw the landscape of my childhood rush past me like scenes from a movie. Was I always running then? By the evidence of my memories and images, it appeared so.

Falls. A lot of them. I scraped my knees, of course, what child doesn't? But I also broke my elbow once in a fall from a tree. I didn't care. I climbed the tree again the next day and talked to the birds and the squirrels. The bugs. They all had things to say to me.

I closed my eyes, to try to shake the mirages loose and bring new images on, but they wouldn't come. Even through my eyelids, I saw only what my faulty memories wanted me to see.

My surroundings were not completely black. There were hints of red in the murk, as though the blood and flesh held some sort of sunset, like the sky around me had lit up like a fireworks display and given me visions that would last forever.

That's the way it seemed.

The rope, for that is the way I seemed to conceive of our link, began to loosen. My soul began to slow down. I—whatever I was at that time—slowed down with it. The breakneck speed began to lessen and I felt some sense of relief, as though I was going to be able to rest now.

Eventually I came to an open area. A gash in the blackness appeared, like a thin lightning bolt. It did not fade away. Instead, it intensified, and I had to put my hand up in front of my eyes to protect them from the glare, which was white hot. It reminded me of a welder's flame, the way it insinuated itself on the surroundings, turning everything impossibly bright and white and blue.

This went on for some time. As my eyes grew accustomed to the glare, I let myself look more closely as the tear in the sky grew wider and wider and let in so much light that I was able to observe my surroundings with some comfort.

I was on a sandy beach. The sand was very clean and tan, like it had been filtered by something. Which it had, I suppose, filtered by the sea. Beyond the beach a stand of greenery. Palm trees, mostly, but others as well: wide ferns, some devil's club, lots of vines snaking here and there, winding around the trunks of the palm trees. The sea behind me was calm. Small waves broke on the sand with a pleasant and soft sound, as though someone was whispering to me.

Again, I had no words. I didn't understand what the surf was saying. This felt impossibly sad, but I did not dwell on it. Time for that later, I thought.

My body was still vibrating, like a bell that had been rung. Everything was trembling and shaking. I could not keep myself still. Nor did I want to. I wanted to move and grow and accelerate out of this situation.

I walked up toward the forest. The sand was warm and yielding. My feet slipped through the grains. I had to walk slowly, it was impossible to move rapidly through the sand.

A sun hung in the sky. I did not recognize it. It was the wrong size, somewhat larger than the sun I remember, and redder, as though someone had dipped it in red dye.

This was most curious to me. It brought to mind the picture of a retina I remember seeing when I was just a little girl. I put my thumb up and covered the sun. There was a trick I remembered about a blind spot everyone had. You found it by closing one eye and moving an object slowly, sliding against the background of the world until you found the place where it disappeared.

I tried that now, tried to make this foreign sun disappear. I spent quite a few minutes at it with no luck.

Eventually I gave up. My eyes retained multiple images of the sun, but it was not painful to look at the light from that sun. It was soothing in its way.

Meanwhile, as I watched, the sun dipped down in the sky, getting closer to the horizon. When it finally touched the edge of the planet, it seemed to sizzle on the water.

I thought I saw steam rise in billows and cloud over the sun.

Everything around me became obscured by the steam. My only sense of anything being wrong, however, was that I didn't know how to approach the fog. Should I remain where I was, or seek shelter? It was going to get cold, most likely, and I was not prepared for low temperatures.

I clutched my shirt around my neck, trying to keep in some of my heat. The air around me was not only wet, but became freezing cold very rapidly.

My feet were instantly cold. I moved backward, up the beach. The forest of ferns and palm trees beckoned, not in a visual sense, but as symbols in my mind. I knew they were there, even though I couldn't see them.

The sound of sizzling water filled the world. I bent my head down as I walked. It was an instinctual gesture. I didn't know where it came from, or what its purpose was. I felt as though I was under attack and needed to hunker down for my own protection.

In the forest, the air cleared up a little. Some of the fog or steam or whatever it was caught on the tops of the trees. Down at my level, where roots met earth, there was not as much fog clotting the air.

I looked for trails. There had to be some. I couldn't be the first one here, could I?

Not that I knew where *here* was. I had been in Nionc Tigo's skull, hadn't I? That's certainly what I had thought. But now—I wasn't so sure. Who has an island in their skull? For that matter, who has an ocean in their skull?

I wandered around the landscape, groping in the dark for the comfort of bark-coated trees. The ferns slapped at my legs.

And there were other plants as well. Bushes, some low-lying vines with berries on them. I wanted to eat them, they looked so good. But I thought it best not to until I had more knowledge of them.

A wind came up. It wasn't a fierce wind, but it was there.

The trees began singing with the wind. Or was it that the wind was using the trees to sing? It was hard to tell, and maybe, in the end, there was no difference between the two.

The singing sounded like a person. It startled me. I *knew* who that was. Or thought I did.

I stood still in the forest. In other circumstances, I might have been able to translate that sound. It would have meant something to me. Not then. It was just a voice.

A sadness, which had been hovering around the periphery of my consciousness, now penetrated straight through me to my heart and I felt heavy with melancholy. How could my life have changed so utterly in such a short time?

It was not the fact that I was adrift in a strange and unknown land. To some extent, it was what I had signed up for when I came to Slothin.

No, what troubled me far more, was that I no longer knew the words of the world. I could not translate any of the sounds that I used to translate with ease.

I found a fallen tree, one that was supported in the midst of the forest by the trees and logs under it, and I sat on it.

It was low enough to the ground that I could climb up on it easily. And it was high enough that I could swing my legs without my feet scuffing against the earth.

I wanted to cry, to relieve myself of the grief that had gripped me, but I found I could not. Something about the meaning of crying did not translate to tears anymore.

I pondered this anomaly. I had always been able to cry. It was never something I had to work at.

I kept trying. I wanted the tears to flow. They would cleanse me, take away some of the sadness. Wasn't that what tears were for?

Eventually the fog fell from the tops of the trees and flowed all around me. I had not expected that, but realized as it happened that I should have.

It was like the trees had shed their tears in my place.

The sizzling noise had long since ended.

Now the singing sounds subsided as well. The wind died down. I was still cold when I heard the sound of the an earth mover.

At first I didn't know what it was.

At first, I didn't even hear it. I *felt* it, the way one might feel the rumble of an earthquake far off. There would be no sound in that situation. All you would sense was some tremor in your bones. That's what it felt like.

I hopped off the log I had been perched on. I stood on the ground, trying to feel more of the rumble, to maybe discover what path I should run in to get away from whatever it was, since it felt like danger. Not an imminent threat to my life, but danger nonetheless. Enough to feel as though I should take some precautions for safety's sake.

I stood there, pondering my options. Go left, go right, go forward, go back.

I looked up, briefly. Couldn't go up. I didn't have wings.

I looked down. It was, maybe, possible to duck into the ground for cover, but that would take time and tools. I had neither. Or so I thought.

I began walking away from my perch. The feeling of the ground trembling grew more pronounced.

I felt undulations in the earth, like waves passing by. Land waves.

I knew they held some meaning, I yearned to discern that meaning, but as I have said, I no longer had that capacity.

Stars popped out in the sky. They trembled and vibrated against the blackness.

As the land waves continued to flow under me, and as the trees swayed with the undulations, my eyes, now accustomed to the twilight, suddenly saw a way through the woods.

If I went forward *here* and turned *there* and *there*, then I could get to the rise in the earth I saw a couple of hundred feet forward. It was defined by the region in the sky where I saw no stars.

Above that region, stars filled the sky. They had popped out of nowhere and were multiplying furiously.

The rise was not exactly a mountain, not by any means. But it was up there. I knew if I reached the top, I would be at the tallest point in the region.

Suddenly, that felt important to me.

I knew that islands sometimes grew up around volcanic regions. And I also knew that the vegetation in these areas argued for the primacy of island biodiversity in the world.

This thought filled me with trepidation. It was very possible that something lived on that rise that would not be hospitable to me. Might even want to kill and/or eat me.

The ground began to shake and vibrate like a bell.

I put my hands over my ears, suddenly realizing that I was no longer *feeling* the disturbance, I was *hearing* it.

My mind flipped over on itself. The sound was completely familiar to me. I had heard it many times. My husband made the noise in his sleep, when he had dreams of plowing through the earth.

He was a little boy, then, living his little boy dreams of operating earth movers. Which is what he did during the day.

Trees toppled in the distance. I hurried my pace. The top of the rise beckoned to me as a lover might call to me.

I wet my lips. They were so dry.

The sound of crashing trees followed me. I moved as quickly as I could.

There were no trees on the rise: only bare rock as far as I could tell. That filled me with good cheer, which I sorely needed a that point, as I had concocted some awful image of a giant earth mover slowly gaining on me.

I dared not look behind me. I thought if I caught a glimpse of the thing, it would frighten me so badly that I would be stuck in place and not able to move.

After a few minutes I broke free of the forest. The land at my feet rose quickly. I had to lean forward to keep from slipping down and before long I was climbing more than walking.

The forest, by this time, felt under siege, just as I had felt under siege.

The rock in the center of the island felt like the center of the universe.

For all I knew, it *was* the center of the universe.

I left the vegetation behind, except for some moss and lichen, which tickled my hands as I searched for handholds in the dark to help me up. There were fissures and breaks in the rock for my feet to climb up on.

I moved quickly, as though I had found some new energy and was using it to the best of my ability.

When I finally got to the top, I stood up. I was breathing heavily, but it was not a labored breath. I think of it, now, as more like a hearty partaking of the biosphere. I took in what was offered to me and released what I could offer in return.

Something about being up there, stark against the black sky and the impossibly fecund stars, gave me the illusion of a benevolent world. I knew better, but that didn't matter. Right then, I believed it.

When I dared to look down on the island, I saw what I had feared: many earth movers were there. They had their lights on to help them. They looked like industrious fireflies buzzing around.

I counted about twenty. I couldn't be sure, because they moved in circles and loops and changed their positions as I watched, but I'm sure it was no less than twenty and maybe a few more.

As the sweat on my skin dried, I felt the melancholy of my world being chewed up for no reason that I could discern. The earth movers ground into the rock and dirt surrounding me. Soon the water started coming in along the channels that the earth movers had created.

Troughs of water here and there. Phosphorescent water, probably from tiny creatures in the sea. The channels created some kind of pattern and the water, lit by the overhead stars, illuminated those patterns.

Was the island trying to tell me something? I saw patterns of channels that definitely created a certain look. It was as though letters had been carved into the island.

But I was unable to read any of them. All my language sense had disappeared and I didn't know where it had gone. I could barely understand my own inner voice.

I watched, helpless, as the earth movers worked to offer me some kind of information that might help me.

The script was flowing and loopy. There was exuberance in its look, the kind of writing that would look good all by itself. I studied the style, to try to discern some kind of meaning in it, or something familiar I could tie it to.

Nothing came to mind. I was a blank.

The earth movers worked for another hour or two. I lay down on the high rock and slept, sporadically, while their engines whined through the night.

They reminded me of mosquitoes cutting the air with their buzzing.

I woke several times, looked at what they were doing, then went back to sleep.

Eventually the sun emerged, phoenix-like, from the ocean. It rose slowly. I watched the curve of it scale the horizon, water dripping from its sides as it shook off the moisture the way a dog might shake off water from its fur.

It baked the sky immediately.

Color began returning. The stars dimmed, then finally winked out.

And what of my island? I rubbed the sleep from my eyes and stood and looked down at the island. The sun, still low to my back, illuminated the channels and the words. It gave them an orange-yellow tinge.

The earth movers were all gone. Where had they disappeared to? I scanned the beaches for them, but could not see them.

Instead, I saw their tracks cross the beaches, then abruptly end at the water line. They had crawled into the ocean? It appeared so.

I came down the slope, slowly. I had a day before me and I had a plan.

I would walk the channels the earth movers had created. That way I could internalize their message and then, perhaps, come to understand what it said.

As I descended from the heights of my perch, skree greeted the soles of my shoes and my feet slipped out from under me. I landed on my backside and skidded down the hill.

I scrambled for some purchase on the rocks, but the moss and grass was slick where the rock gave way to vegetation.

Branches and leaves slapped at my face and chest as I went by. I tried to grab some of them, but could not make my grasp work.

Ahead, I saw the rock split. A fissure was going to cross my path and I was not going to be able to leap across it. It was too wide and it was jagged and rough.

I put my hands down on the rock as it went by under me. My palms were stung and bleeding. I dug my heels in as best I could, but they wouldn't stay. It was as though the rock repelled me and wanted to push back at me.

I laid myself down, hoping my entire body would cause enough friction to keep me from continuing.

Eventually my leg caught on a root. It spun me around with a jerk. I felt something tear in my ankle. I was simultaneously relieved and frightened. I wasn't going to go over the lip of the fissure, but I might have a broken bone, which could mean I was not going to survive this odyssey.

I came to a stop with a jerk. My entire body hurt. My palms were bleeding and my back stung.

My head rang like a bell. I put my hand up to the back of my skull. There was blood there, although I couldn't tell if it was from my scalp or my hand. Maybe both. I wasn't sure.

I groaned and gingerly put my hands on the rocks beside me. The grit there hurt, but I didn't know how else to do what I needed to do. I pushed myself up to a sitting position.

The root that had grabbed me looked like the kind of vegetation that would as soon eat you as lie docile for your viewing pleasure. It had bright green bark, smooth in some places, but opening up in great gashes elsewhere.

Once again, as had happened so often in the past few days, I felt as though I was getting a message. The gashes seemed to be expressing some kind of pattern and meaning. But I was not able to understand it. Nothing was making itself understood to me.

I leaned forward. My bones groaned and my muscles ached. All of them, or so it seemed.

I was able to move my ankle out from under the root. As I did so I examined the root. It had risen out of the ground, then plunged back in a short distance later, maybe eight inches or so. The gap between root and ground was just large enough for my foot to fit inside.

I rubbed my ankle. It was bruised. I could see that already as I rolled down my sock.

No break in the skin, however, even though there was also scraping along the bruise. I gingerly put my hands over the ankle and the surrounding surfaces. There was pain, but not too much. I didn't feel a break.

A thrill of victory raced through me. I had escaped serious injury.

Behind me, the fissure in the rock gaped. I moved my hands to give me more purchase and rose up on my feet.

The ankle was definitely sore. No question. But it was not debilitating.

I thanked the root for its work, then began walking along the fissure. It looked like it went for quite some time curving around the mountain.

It expanded in some places, so that the gap was at least ten feet, and contracted in others to about three feet. Still too wide for me.

I would have to walk a good hundred feet or so before there was a possibility of stepping over the gap.

I did so, but kept my distance from the fissure. Didn't want to slip and fall into it now.

As I walked, the pain in my ankle got worse. I didn't know if that was normal with such an injury, or if it meant something bad. I elected to believe it meant nothing serious.

The crows returned.

I heard them before I saw them. They filled the air with their calls. They talked to each other. I talked back to them. I matched their sound, if not their meaning.

They poured out of the sky. Hundreds of them, flying in swirling cursive paths. If they trailed ink, they would have written something in the sky, I was sure.

It would have been something I probably could have translated back in the day.

Not now, though. It would have been gibberish. The whole world was gibberish to me now. No meaning at all. I only knew I wanted to get down from the mountain. Try to correct this lack in me.

The crows circled around me, like they were vultures. Or wanted to pretend to be vultures.

What's up with you all? I called to them.

They increased their volume, scraping the air with their shrill noises.

All of it was just noise to me. I felt the melancholy of my situation again. To not know the meanings of things brought only a helpless sense of futility. My spirit fled my body. Again.

I was distantly aware of my actions. It was as though I was watching an actor go through the rigors of developing a character and making that character move.

Now remember, you have an injury. Hobble if you need to. Make yourself into an injured person.

I tried. I responded to the pain. I watched myself respond to the pain.

But my motions meant nothing. That was the awful part. I could move in the world and I had a grammar of displacement. My arms waved and my legs worked and my lungs breathed. I had all the mechanics of meaning, just not the content of it.

Every step I took seemed to remove me even further from my true self.

The crows crowded my space. They circled around me in a thick cloud. If they were trying to comfort me, it wasn't working. Mostly they were spooking me. They had the demeanor of the hunter about them.

Or, more properly, the scavenger. They behaved like vultures.

This disturbed me, but it was just one more disturbance on top of many others. I wasn't going to let it bother me.

I got to a narrow gap in the fissure. No more than one of my steps wide.

I paused and prepared to step across it.

But the crows wouldn't let me. They flew at me and opened their beaks and cawed at me. I had never heard such a ruckus.

I was staring at a wall of bird flesh studded with beaks working in unison. They hovered and floated, individually, but taken together, they were the most intimidating wall I had ever encountered.

I stepped back. They continued to guard—for that is how it seemed—the fissure.

You don't want me to cross here? I asked. Is that it?

They made no move to lessen the volume of their noise. I felt them all around me, now. They had decided to surround me with—what? What could I call it? I felt like they were offering me some kind of protection, but it was a hostile protection.

Not an attitude of benign assistance, more a way of saying: Do this or else.

I looked up the way I had come. It would be possible to climb back up the hill, but it didn't seem like that would gain me anything.

I waved my hands in the air. That sent up a cacophonous noise from the crows. They increased their belligerence. They dove at me and spread their wings with what I took to be a menacing gesture, as if they could scoop me up and toss me into the sea.

Crows, I said. this is not helping either of us. Go back to your scavenging and I'll go back to my meanderings and we'll live in peace in the world. Or at least on this island.

I heard voices. I did. Lots of them. Each crow had a voice. Complete gibberish to me, but a voice nevertheless.

Also the trees. They spoke. The ground. The moss.

I was pretty sure the sea was giving voice. And the air. The sky, which, surprisingly to me, was distinct from the air. Huh. Who knew that?

The sun had a roaring voice. The island itself had a voice. They all spoke to me with vigor and intent.

Even today, years later, I wish I could know what all those voices were saying to me.

My own body had a voice. My bones spoke. My blood and sinews. My flesh and skin. The voices of the world coalesced to a kind of incessant static of sound and meaning.

I told the crows I had no patience for them. I kept flailing my arms and stepped across the fissure.

As I did so, the air dropped in temperature a good twenty degrees. It was already quite chilly, but now it was downright cold. I shivered, partly at the celsius count, but also at the shock of the transition, as though I had entered another world.

I could see my breath. Puffs of white dissipating as I breathed.

The crows, having failed in their attempt to keep me back, receded from me amidst more undecipherable noise. They liked to fill the air with noise, did the crows.

I glanced back, once, to see them fly up the hill to the top. Taking my place there? Or just flying at random. No meaning to their movements?

Impossible to tell.

I kept descending. Instead of going straight down, however, I adopted a more serpentine route. I walked in a zig-zag fashion, never going down too steep a slope. I believed this would keep me from skidding on the skree, which was everywhere underfoot.

It worked. It took me a long time to get down to the level where the earth movers had been, but I did so safely, never slipping once.

On the other hand, it took so long that the cold was beginning to affect me. My teeth chattered and my skin had goosebumps. My fingers felt numb. I hugged myself as I walked, trying to hold in some of my heat, but it was an attempt doomed to failure.

The cold snaked into my crevices.

It spoke to my flesh. My flesh spoke back. I think. I couldn't tell what they said to each other, but I felt the fury of their discussion. Each had opinions, strong ones, of how the world worked.

I couldn't tell what those opinions were from their conversation, but I could tell that each one was adamant in their positions.

I suppose cold was saying it needed to solidify things. It liked the simplicity of things *not moving*.

And I'm sure flesh was saying that it was fine for cold to have that attitude and to adopt it as a credo, but it had no right to spread its manifesto to material that was made to move and move constantly, like muscle and bone.

Then I'm sure, after stating their initial positions, they both restated them with gusto and vehemence. Then they might have tried to refute each other's positions. Maybe a little name calling ensued.

Anger, I'm sure, flared up. Each side thought it had the correct view and philosophy of the universe. How could each side not? They were made with certain tendencies and nature, in general, did not create entities out of place with their environment, since everything is part of the environment.

Meanwhile, as all this back and forth was going on, I tried to keep going. I had a feeling that as I got lower the temperature would go up. This did not, in fact happen.

Quite the opposite. As the slope's angle lessened and I got closer and closer to walking on a flat surface, I found that I was stepping on ice crystals. The ground beneath me was freezing.

My ears were numb. My hair had acquired frost in places. My fingernails hurt.

I looked at them. They were blue. As were my fingertips.

There was no wind, which was a blessing, I suppose. Unless a wind might have taken the cold away. I didn't know what might happen with a wind. I tried to think through the consequences. It was a simple thing to consider, wasn't it?

It should have been. But was not.

My thought processes had slowed way down and even my senses seemed sluggish, as if there was something slowing me down.

There was. The cold.

I pictured it like one of those ancient illustrations of a cloud with facial features blowing air across the world.

Fleetingly, I thought the crows had been right. I should have stayed away.

After a long time, I finally got down to the level where the earth movers had been. Their work plowing through the ground had left a network of canals filled with phosphorescent sea water, but that was now frozen solid.

I had no time to stop and admire the beauty. I felt if I did, I would freeze in place and never move again.

I stepped on the edge of the canal and gingerly moved forward. The surface was slick and flat. No gnarly bits to mar it. It was like I was standing on a mirror. I put out my hands, a painful operation in the cold, but necessary to keep my balance.

I pushed off the bank of the canal and skated along the first arm of the canal.

As I did so I tried to let my mind understand the meaning of what I was skating on. I imagined myself writing in ice. Glowing ice.

I tried to make my brain understand the strokes and the words.

I slid into a bank at the opposite end and ended up splayed on the ice, my legs and hands spread-eagled like a star.

Ha.

I was an asterisk. Not a real person at all, just a reference to something else.

This insult to my dignity did not deter me, although maybe it should have. I stood up, carefully, and pushed myself off the frozen bank again. My hands were even more cold than they had been before. I didn't think that was possible.

The canal was a good five feet wide in most places, a little more in others. It curved and turned, made corners and meandered. I followed the path, like a pen coursing over a sheet of paper.

I learned to avoid the banks. It took some doing, but I was able to use my shoes to change course. I also kept my speed to a minimum. If I went too fast, then I would lose control.

The crows were there, somewhere. I heard them far off. I guessed they were not interested in this cold.

I wasn't either. I saw it as a necessary task to come to some understanding.

I tried to shout out to the world. Tried to make my voice loud and ringing, but the air got stuck in my throat. The cold kept it from emerging.

So my voice stayed inside me.

This was most peculiar. I needed to express myself. Or thought I did.

It took me about an hour to traverse the script in the island. As I skated along the surface, I saw creatures trapped in the ice: sea stars and fish. Some barnacles. A few anemones.

I weeped for them. They had to die for the meaning of the script to be known?

The tears froze on my cheek. I brushed them away. They fell to the ice with a tinkling sound. I determined not to cry. No reason to lose moisture. The air was dry and I didn't know when I was going to be able to drink again.

But I couldn't stop.

More tears came. They emerged as little balls of ice and they fell to the frozen path. I moved away from them: they were too much like the skree on the mountain and I was afraid of what they would do to my feet and balance.

But there was no stopping them. The tears emerged from my eyes with alarming speed. They popped out like popcorn flowing from an overfilled pot. They cascaded down my face.

They punctuated the world with dings and pings. The sound of my tears falling was a song all by itself. I knew there was meaning in those sounds. I knew there was a pattern there and all language, all *meaning* comes from pattern.

But still, I could not grasp that meaning. It taunted me. I felt like all those time when my husband listened to the voices in the walls and I heard nothing.

By the time I finished traversing the path, I had left a long trail of frozen tears behind me. It heaped up in a channel down the center of the canals.

I stood at the other end. My travels had gone over every part of the island. I now stood near the base of the hill.

Above me, its summit seemed to reach for the sky. The sun was high, but not very warm. It couldn't cut through the cold all around me.

My brain was so sluggish that I thought I could take the sun and wrap it around me, like a warm blanket. I saw heat in everything.

The ground would warm me. The trees. The moss. The ferns.

My chest felt cold. I knew enough to know that was not a good sign. It meant my core temperature was dropping.

Nionc Tigo spoke to me at that point. She had the same soothing tone I remembered from before, but it was meaningless to me now. None of her words had any sense of language about them. They were just sounds pushed through the air to my ear. Or through my brain to my ear. Something.

I recalled a time when everything seemed clear to me: all languages, all patterns. The world was filled with meaning. Every sound, every image, every sensation was a large chunk of meaning and I knew it all. Never let any of it escape me.

I could tell you what the trees were saying. That was easy, I know. Everyone thinks they know what the trees are saying.

Next came the air. The breeze on my face was meaning. It told me there was love in the world.

Later the sensation of bugs crawling on my skin. They told me about family and perseverance. So many lessons from them.

Later the stings I got: mosquitoes and bees and wasps. My parents were horrified, but I internalized the message: be careful. The world can be dangerous.

Well, everyone knew that too, but I learned it from the stings.

The world was full of pattern, which meant the world was full of information. Meaning. Language.

The clouds told a story. The landscape, in its undulations, conveyed tales and histories and, well, everything. Everything was in the landscape.

Languages were living things. They grew and morphed and took in the world, then spit it out in bits and pieces called syllables and words.

I knew that early on. When I was just a child, all the world was there for me in the words and the meanings.

Which is why, now that I was stuck in this world without meaning, I was filled with grief and depression. I had nothing, *nothing* to hold onto.

Nionc Tigo kept speaking to me. I recognized her voice, but not the words or the meaning. It was as though static had invaded my head and would not retreat.

Once, way back at a time I could hardly imagine anymore, even static had its meaning. Even static offered pattern and life and recognition of the world. But now anymore. Static was just annoying. The static of Nionc Tigo's words were irritating and made me want to scream the way an itch that can't be scratched away can make you want to scream at the world.

My knees were weak. That, at least, was understandable to me. The machinations of a failing body was the new language for my head and heart.

I let myself slip down to the ground. The unruly mess of the island seemed to rise up to greet me. I gratefully accepted the cradle of its support.

In fact, with nothing else in particular at my disposal, I let the island envelop me and cradle me. Nothing would have surprised me more. I was not one to surrender to my surroundings.

But surrender seemed the only viable option on the island.

Nionc Tigo's voice grew louder and more insistent. I put my hands over my ears.

I stretched out in the mud and water. The cold seeped into me. It felt like it was freezing my flesh and trying to grip my bones.

For all I knew, it did exactly that. It wrapped its strange bony fingers around my bones and tightened its grip.

I do believe at that moment, with the swirling insults turning in my body, I would have welcomed death. That, at least, would have been a state of calm. Much better than the turmoil I was experiencing on the island.

Ever thought of swimming through the ground?

I did. I imagined myself taking a slow trip through the earth, breast stoke churning up the dirt and the worms and the soil. I'd throw off pattern and meaning as I went, fill the ground with words, maybe. Leave a story trailing behind me like a wake of tales.

But none of that happened.

Instead, I sneezed, sending a long stream of mucous out of me. I didn't even care. Didn't try to wipe it away or dignify myself by cleaning it from my cheek, where it lay.

I was in that position, undignified, weak, near death and frightened of everything when a short and stout woman appeared in my field of vision.

She wore what I took to be the traditional clothes of Slothin: sheep skin coat and boots, a tight cap with a wide brim, and rough and wrinkled pants. She stood over me with her feet planted wide and her hands on her hips.

I turned my head up to try to take in her face. I recognized her from the pictures on the dust jackets of her books. I tried to say something to her, to express my surprise at seeing her, but my own words were unintelligible to me. I heard sounds come out of my mouth, but did not recognize their meaning.

I felt even more bereft of hope at that point.

I didn't even know what hope was, but felt, somewhere deep in the interior of my heart, that it was something, some vague sense that hope was a necessary thing and without it there was no meaning.

So I tried to link in to that feeling.

In the meantime, Nionc Tigo kept talking. She clucked and tsked and emitted other sounds. I think I recognized them as words, which were things I should have known something about, but they were still meaningless.

She bent down and put her arms under me.

She couldn't lift. It was impossible.

Her arms slipped under my frame easily. She straightened her legs and I rose like a leaf blowing in the wind. I was floating in the air and suddenly realized I was much lighter than I remember. The previous days of not eating had taken their toll, it seemed. I was thin and weak.

I looked down at my arms. They seemed to exist somewhere else. They weren't my arms. Not really. And yet they were. They could be no one else's arms.

I tried to lift them, to put them around Nionc Tigo's neck, but I could not. There was no power in them at all.

Nionc Tigo obviously had no trouble carrying me, even though she was not a large woman. She moved her feet so that she faced away from the mountain and then she started walking.

Her arms were cradling me by my knees and my shoulder blades. My head was bent to one side, and banged against her shoulder. There was a soothing sense of calm and peace. Not to mention nurturing.

I welcomed the help from Nionc Tigo.

She talked the whole time. It all went into my brain, I think, but mostly I just accepted the help. Help I didn't realize I had needed until then.

We traversed the land of the island quickly and came to the sea. I expected her to put me down on the beach then, but she did not. Instead, she kept walking.

She splashed into the surf, kicking up waves and droplets everywhere. Some of them fell on me. They felt like raindrops. I was grateful for the sense memory. It made me think things were possible again. Or would be soon.

I spoke some more. I don't know where the words came from, or what they meant, but I made noises in my throat. Loud enough for Nionc Tigo to hear them.

She said things back to me.

I heard her, but did not understand. Still, all language was a mystery to me.

The water, though. It swirled below us. Nionc Tigo kept going into the sea. Its surface rose higher. She slowed her pace, but did not stop. She wanted to move us into the ocean. She was going to set up living arrangements in the water.

I had this sense of what I needed to tell her. Or ask her. I wasn't sure which. I needed to let her know that we were not made from water. She didn't understand water. She was from a landlocked nation. Water was a foreign nation to her.

All these things came to me. I wanted to tell her all of them. I needed to let her know that what she was doing now was putting us both in danger.

But the words would not form. I had the thoughts, but not the words.

As she walked, the sea floor must have moved higher beneath her sheepskin boots. We rose above the water, higher and higher. We went on this way for some time.

It was as though the ground under the water had its own rhythm and music. It was as though we were riding on its metrical meaning.

I found sleep again. Or, rather, it found me. It invaded my eyes, made them heavy. I don't know how long I slept, but when I woke, the island was gone. We were in the middle of the ocean, with no land visible in any direction. I craned my neck and looked in every direction I could find.

Nothing. Just water.

I looked up at Nionc Tigo's face. She was determined. Her jaw was set and her eyes were locked forward. What was she looking at?

By some miracle I could not fathom, we were still above the water. The ocean was only two feet deep in most places? I had not realized that. It was a revelation I relished, like finding out that flesh was really made of cheese. Now that would be something, wouldn't it?

The sky above me swirled and vibrated.

I had a sense that it was not really doing that. The effect was caused by my own delirium. My lack of water and food. My weakness in the face of the strange events.

I looked out again and saw the beginnings of something that might be called sanity. A wall. It looked exactly like the walls I had seen in Slothin. It was made of stone and towered above the water. It also looked like it went around the entire horizon, marking it like a gray crayon trail.

The wall accelerated toward us. It was as though the wall wanted to meet us.

Nionc Tigo's endurance was unflagging. She kept going. She also talked and talked and talked.

As I said, I didn't know what she was saying. I could hardly even determine what language she was speaking. My sense of meaning had fled completely.

As we neared the wall, I saw that it was going to be somewhat difficult to scale it. It presented a sheer face with little in the way of handholds or any kind of facility for climbing. I assumed we were going to climb it. And I assumed there was something on the other side of it.

Truly, the looming effect of the wall was overwhelming. It was as though I could not see the top of it once we got close to it. Nionc Tigo walked through the inches-deep sea and arrived at the wall, then stopped.

She was breathing very heavily.

Her arms, which had been strong and confident, now trembled a little. She let me down in the water. I put out my hands and braced myself against the sand, only a few inches under the surface of the water.

The sea. I was in the sea, but I was bigger than the sea. Deeper, at least.

I looked around me. The water was tepid here, not the cold I normally associated with the ocean. The sun was able to heat it all the way to the bottom of the water.

Tiny waves broke on the surface. They even had white caps, which surprised me. But then I wondered why anything should surprise me anymore. All the events of the past few days were a surprise, if not a revelation.

I stood up. Nionc Tigo put her arm around my shoulders and leaned into me. She said some words.

I nodded, as if I understood. And, in a way, I did. I couldn't tell you what the words were or what they meant, but I did understand that the gesture meant something. It was an expression of sympathy and friendship. She wanted to know how I was.

I'm fine, I told her, though I didn't feel fine. I was still hungry and frightened.

Are giants? I asked. Did we become giants, somehow?

She smiled at me, then waved and started walking along the wall. She twisted her upper body as she walked, so that her head turned and she looked at me. She waved me over to follow her, which I did.

We walked along the wall for a long time. I let my hand glide over the stones and the gaps between the stones, which were filled with concrete, or something similar. They kept the stones apart and held them together at the same time. Their gaps were a way of telling me that nothing was permanent, even though they were set in stone.

The filler material could disintegrate. And the stones, which were close and coherent, could separate as well.

My time in Nionc Tigo's arms had given me the rest I needed. I was able to walk along the wall and follow Nionc Tigo with ease.

My only thought was that I needed to keep up. That was all that mattered.

Like so many other events of that time, I am not now able to remember how long I walked. It felt like days or weeks. But that isn't really possible, so I must have construed the passage of time in a different manner than reality suggested.

In any case, my feet started getting uncomfortable from the water we kept splashing through. I felt blisters. The salt water was beginning to eat away at my shoes.

The threads went first. They disintegrated and fell away, bit by bit. The toe came undone first and the sole of my shoes flapped in the water, making a ridiculous sound, like I was talking to the birds and fishes of the sea. I was using water for my language, and sole flaps for my grammar.

Soon the rest of the threads holding my shoes together melted away and the sole separated from the rest of my shoe.

I took a few more steps with only the uppers, but that didn't last. They became an encumbrance rather than an aid to walking. I bent down and put my hands under the laces, preparing to undo them, but they had become so weak that my fingers broke right through them and the uppers floated away in the water.

Fish swam up to the pieces and nudged at them, like they were trying to discern if the pieces of my shoes were other fish.

They weren't. I told them so, but I don't think they understood.

Nionc Tigo, meanwhile, had gotten pretty far ahead of me. She was a tiny dot in the distance, crawling along the wall.

I was in bare feet now. I ran through the water to catch up to her. I made splashing noises and sent up waves and waves of water as I took long striding running steps.

The water splashed against the wall, leaving marks that I was sure meant something. If only I knew the language of water drops.

The bottoms of my pants came next. The salt ate away at the material. My pants were turning into rags. The ends of threads floated in the water like jelly fish. My skin was getting dried out from the salt, as well. I was worried that cracks were going to appear and I would take on infections.

I looked up. I was closer to Nionc Tigo. She did not turn around, though. She maintained her steady pace.

The wall went on and on. It curved, slightly, but not enough to matter, at least not to me, in the condition I was in.

I continued to splash through the water and slog through the sand. The bottom of the ocean had a changing quality. Sometimes it was soft and muddy, other times it was sandy.

I saw a couple of vessels at one point. They were far off, close to the horizon.

Or so I thought. They looked so tiny. But as I looked at them some more, they had details that didn't seem right. They were preternaturally detailed. I felt a frisson of strangeness rush through me. It was like I was looking at something I shouldn't be seeing.

I went away from the wall and through the water to get closer to the ships. They were passenger vessels. Large ones, but they were small.

My mind flipped over on itself. I had to readjust my perceptions. It had taken me only a few steps to get to the ship. I floated in the water and I was bigger than it.

Much bigger. I was a giant compared to this ship. I bent down to look at it.

Very tiny people scurried around on the deck. They didn't know what to make of this creature with the big eyes staring at them.

Me.

I was the the creature with big eyes.

I stepped away from the ship. I didn't want to wreck it or bring it to harm. I certainly did not want to hurt the people on it.

I called to Nionc Tigo. I said some words. They were just noises.

She turned around. An impatient look in her eye told me she had no time for me and my adventures, or misadventures, as the case may be. She had her hands on her hips.

I wanted to tell her about the tiny ships with the tiny people, but then I decided she must have already known about them.

I splashed my way back to the wall. Nionc Tigo waited for me.

She said words to the air. They appeared to be measured and melodic. Was she reciting one of her poems? I couldn't tell. Maybe she was just telling me she wanted me closer. Wanted to keep track of me.

I pushed on.

My feet contacted tiny sharp objects in the water. Coral? Shells? Fish bones? Rocks? One of these or all of these. I didn't stop to investigate.

When I got closer to Nionc Tigo, I saw why she had waited.

We had come to a gate.

It was made of wood, but had rocks embedded in the wood at the bottom, so that it kept the water from eating away at the door. She waited for me until I was right there beside her and the door.

She grabbed the handle and pulled it back.

I don't know, now, what I expected to see behind the door. More water, most likely. The ocean is vast, after all. No reason to think it wouldn't keep going on the other side of the wall.

That isn't what was there, however.

Behind the door in the middle of the wall in the middle of the ocean, I saw nothing more or less than the land of Slothin.

Its green fields extended way beyond the capacity of my eye to see. The sweet land of Slothin rose up from the altitude of the ocean and seemed to reach for the blue blue sky.

Nionc Tigo and I stepped up from the ocean onto dry land. We stood on the grass for some time. I felt the sun begin to dry my calves. The sound of sheep, distant, yet familiar, even to me, drifted in the air and landed on my ear.

The sheep sounds were pleasant not only because of their soothing quality, but because they were a reminder of Slothin.

I also understood what they were saying.

More grass. We like grass. We'll eat all the grass that's here. Just let us eat this grass.

Not particularly interesting conversationalists, but that didn't matter. I was able to understand them. My translation abilities were back.

I turned to Nionc Tigo. She smiled at me.

I knew what that smile meant. She was telling me she was glad we were here, together, and she hoped I would find what I needed.

Nionc Tigo, I said. I love your poems.

Thank you, she said in Slothin.

She gestured with her hand toward the grass. We stepped forward and walked to the sky.

There were walls within walls, exactly as I had expected. That was, after all, what Slothin was about: a network of walled enclosures.

Do you know where my husband is? I asked Nionc Tigo.

All in good time, she said. We need to get you some food.

Are we giants? I asked.

Everything you are, she said, is in your mind. Don't you know that?

I did, kind of, but not quite. I wasn't sure what was real and what was made up. Not anymore. Everything around me felt gritty and made of reality. But it also felt ephemeral and made of nothing.

I don't know how to understand anything that's happened to me, I said.

Well, said Nionc Tigo, you can think about that after you've eaten something. You have done bad things.

I have?

You have resurrected me from the dead. That's not good. Also, you have tried to take my poems. Equally bad. One is presumptuous. The other is theft.

I never mean either thing, I said.

I believe you, she said, but now I must take care of you. Our way.

I remembered that victims of crime were required to take care of the criminals. It seemed that, in Nionc Tigo's eyes, I was such a criminal and she such a victim. Then our relationship was clear. I needed nurturing.

We walked toward one of the walls that crisscrossed Slothin. Nionc Tigo wanted me to stay with her. She needed to watch over me and make sure I didn't do anything stupid or harmful to her or myself.

But I did not want to walk with her. I wanted to run free.

I broke from her company and ran to the stone wall.

I put my hands on the wall and pushed as hard as I could. At first the wall resisted, but under my relentless pushing, it gave way. My arms sunk into the wall all the way up to the middle of my forearms.

I was surprised by this, but not as much as I thought I would be. In a way, I expected it.

These aren't real walls, I said out loud, to the walls and the air as much as to Nionc Tigo.

The interior of the rocks felt cool and soothing. Not at all what I would have expected, which was rough and warm, like sandpaper in a sauna.

This was like pillows in the arctic.

Nionc Tigo walked up behind me and entered my peripheral vision.

So many ways to deceive ourselves, she said.

Like your poetry? I asked.

Yes, she said, exactly like that. Do you know those scribbles that the world is so interested in, they were not mine?

My arms sunk in the rock. I slipped down to the ground as they did so, pulling them with me. I plowed through the rock and mortar. Everything there was built up so nicely and we had the privilege of knowing that someone, somewhere had built the walls.

Are you saying, I asked, talking to the wall, but addressing Nionc Tigo, that you stole your work from someone else?

She laughed. Oh, nothing like that. What I meant was that the walls gave them to me. I was simply the receiver of their wisdom.

Walls have wisdom?

Well, said Nionc Tigo, my mother taught me that everything has wisdom, if you know how to look for it.

That's a wise mother, I said.

Nionc Tigo laughed, but it wasn't a harmonious sound. I didn't get the feeling that her laugh would ignite any kind of joy in anyone. I wondered why that would be, but then I remembered that Nionc Tigo was dead.

How can you be here, I asked, talking to me?

How can you be talking to the dead? she asked.

She had a point. I considered the question. My arms were getting cold. I pulled them out of the wall. As I did so, the wall spoke to me.

No one will care about you in a hundred years, it said.

I blinked.

Did you hear that? I asked Nionc Tigo.

Predicting the future? she asked.

Yes!

They do that, although their predictions are not particularly useful.

That's what I used to tell my husband, I said.

He listens to walls. He thinks they have wisdom.

Well, said Nionc Tigo, there's wisdom and then there's wisdom. Not all are created equal.

My arms felt like blocks of ice. I wrapped them around me. The cold from them penetrated my torso and seemed to grip my lungs and heart.

I think I left them in the wall too long, I said.

Nionc Tigo laughed again. A shorter laugh this time, but with the same bland joyless quality. It's easy to do. Such a strange sensation.

You're dead, aren't you? I asked.

Yes. Which brings up interesting questions for you, doesn't it?

I nodded. It means I'm dead too, doesn't it?

Oh, don't jump to conclusions. You're not an immigrant or a resident. Just a visitor. Come on.

She walked along the wall, treading on the grass. I followed. The walls of this doppelgänger of Slothin were just as extensive as in the real Slothin. They covered the land. We entered gates, walked through flocks of sheep, just as we had in the real Slothin, and tread on the greenest of grass one could possibly imagine.

The sky was blue as well. And the clouds were white. Perfectly ordinary and unremarkable things, but they seemed wondrous strange in this world. It was as though they had been newly minted from the forge of nature and presented to me for my own delight.

I didn't know where we were going, but I wasn't worried about it. Nionc Tigo would lead me where I needed to go.

Why couldn't I understand anything for a while back there? I asked Nionc Tigo.

She listened to my question but did not answer for a time. She pulled open a gate, we stepped through the threshold, then she closed the gate and we kept walking.

My question was the sort of thing that can hang between two people, unacknowledged, but impossible to ignore. It kept the air between us filled with portent, as though we both had unfinished business that needed attending to, but neither of us wanted to attend to it.

We came to the middle of this particular enclosure. Sheep flocked to us from every corner of the enclosure, probably twenty of them. They wanted something from us. I would have given them something to eat if I had anything.

I felt their bumps on my legs and behind. They were the gentlest of creatures, but insistent, as though they knew they were weak and needed the protection of something stronger.

Was I that something stronger? It didn't seem possible or right, but none of them spent any time around Nionc Tigo. I was the star attraction.

Nionc Tigo noticed that I noticed.

They aren't sure what to make of you, she said. They think you don't belong here.

I don't, I said.

Don't be so sure, she said. You came here for a reason.

I came to learn about you and to read your unpublished work.

And in the process, you lost your ability for language, said Nionc Tigo.

Yes, I said. It was very distressing. I was sure I had met some enormous calamity.

Only if you think of life as a calamity.

Was Nionc Tigo playing games with me?

I've never thought that, I said.

But it must have crossed your mind in the past few days, said Nionc Tigo.

A little bit, I said.

My feet suddenly felt cold. I shivered.

That's the ground, said Nionc Tigo.

What?

The ground. It's what's making you cold.

What? I said again and looked down. In the time I had spent standing and talking and letting the sheep bump me, I had sunk into the ground up to my ankles.

What? I said for the third time as I lifted my feet out of the ground, one at a time, and tried to plant them firmly on the grass.

Further proof, said Nionc Tigo, if you needed it, that you are in a foreign realm.

You don't sink, I said.

I'm not in a foreign realm, she said. I live here now.

And are you happy living here?

She waved her hand. Happiness doesn't enter into it. Come on. Let's keep going.

She stepped toward the nest gate. I followed. The sheep parted for us, giving us room.

If you keep walking, you won't sink, said Nionc Tigo.

Thanks for the tip.

If you stay too long, you'll sink all the way down and you won't know how to get back up.

How am I going to sleep?

You won't.

Ah. So, I said, I'll just have to keep walking?

We have a long journey, but you can handle it.

I wasn't at all sure of that. I wasn't at all sure that Nionc Tigo knew what she was talking about.

We traversed the island slowly, taking our time, so it seemed to me, even though we went at a goodly pace.

You never answered my question, I said.

Translators always have a lot of questions, said Nionc Tigo.

Really? I asked.

When I was still alive, I became famous. Not for my true work, my manuals, but for my other stuff. What I called my fun stuff. Things I tossed off in an evening, or spent a few idle hours fiddling with.

You're talking about your poetry, I said.

Yes. And some of the novels and stories. All that ephemera.

Ephemera.

Yes, she said.

That ephemera is what the rest of the world adores. It's what I came here to find.

Did you find it?

Yes.

In my nephew's house?

Yes.

Well, then, was it worth it?

I looked down at my feet. They were above the ground, thankfully, and they walked me across the land efficiently. They were cut and bruised, though, and they had the air of mystery about them, like they weren't really mine. I looked at my feet for a long time. I missed my boots, and wasn't at all sure when I had lost them. Nionc Tigo noticed my bewilderment.

Things disappear here, she said. It's nothing to concern yourself over.

I see, I said.

So, she said, was it worth it to come here?

I noticed that Nionc Tigo liked to avoid answering questions by asking her own. It was a tactic, I assumed. One that dead people used, maybe? I wasn't sure.

Those pages are back somewhere in the past of my life. Up there, maybe. I pointed to the sky, remembering that I fell out of the bottom of Slothin a long time ago to end up here.

You never read them?

No.

Well, you shouldn't bother. All the questions translators asked me were about little details of Slothin life and history. But, you see, I was no expert on that. I didn't know anything more than any other Slothin knew. I was just amusing myself with those pages.

I decided that perhaps the country's name should be Sloggin'. That's all that I was doing anymore. Dragging my feet from one place to another.

Well, I said, translators often know the words, but not the context. It's important to have that, otherwise the words don't mean anything.

Words never mean anything more than we put on them.

Yes, I said, I understand that. But translator's need to know what meaning the original writer wanted to put on a word. Otherwise you could use a dictionary to translate texts.

Or Google translate.

Yes, I said. Or Google translate. How do you know about that?

We get dispatches from the living world. We know things.

Which brings up another point, I said. Am I dead?

That's not for me to say.

But you are.

Yes, said Nionc Tigo, I am dead.

So why am I here if I'm not dead?

You're here because people in my culture look after those who have hurt us.

How have I hurt you?

So many ways, she said. You tried to determine my destiny. You shouldn't really do that. You tried to define my life. You shouldn't do that, either. You attempted to take my work from its rightful owner, the state of Slothin. Again, a big no no. You hoped to gain from my work. Shall I go on?

I had only the deepest respect for you and your pages, I said. I never wanted to place you in a compromising position. I would have done the best I possibly could on your pages.

She had this air of potency about her. Like she could take on anything in the world and it wouldn't faze her a bit. I was not like that, and I knew it. My skills were in words and their meaning. I envied the ability I ascribed to Nionc Tigo. Since it was not at all clear that she actually possessed these abilities, I knew that her way of being in the world was as much a fantasy of mine as a reality of the world.

It was like I was translating her reality for my own benefit. Is this the violation she had referred to? I wanted to stop and consider those possibilities, but I couldn't. If I did, I might sink into Slothin.

So I continued walking, following Nionc Tigo, who did not show any evidence of tiring or slowing down. Indeed, she seemed to pick up her pace as we went and I had to work hard to keep up.

We went through gates. We walked through stone-enclosed pastures.

She put her hands out to pet the sheep as we went. They seemed to love her. I didn't see any reason why they shouldn't. As we walked she appeared to take on a heavenly glow, as though she had picked up some light and draped it over her.

I looked at my own arms and legs as we walked. No glow there.

Hey, I called to her. Can you give me some of that light you've got?

She laughed. Translators, she said to the air, and shook her head.

Was I being rebuked? I couldn't tell. And how was this whole journey taking care of her violator? I didn't feel taken care of at all. I felt worked. Like a slave. Or a farm animal. Something.

The sun, which had been high in the sky, had arced down and looked like it was about to set. This startled me. We had been walking so long that the day had almost disappeared. I saw that I had lagged behind Nionc Tigo and hurried my pace again to get closer to her. I needed to be near her glow now that the evening was about to descend on us.

Your husband, said Nionc Tigo.

What about him?

He talks to walls.

Yes, I said. It's a hobby with him.

She laughed again. A hobby. Like my scribbles, yes?

I considered the question carefully, trying to fit my husbands's wall infatuation with Nionc Tigo's writing infatuation. I suppose, I said.

Do you know he's trying to access the walls right here?

I looked around. The stone walls were dim and gray in the fading light, as if they wanted to turn into ghost walls themselves.

How do you know?

He thinks he can find you in them.

Wait, I said. What do you mean?

You have left Slothin, you see. Now you're in the ghost Slothin. Your husband—how can I explain this? He believes in ghosts.

Yes.

He believes you may be a ghost. He's heartbroken. He should leave Slothin. But he can't. He needs to find you.

We stopped. Abruptly.

How long have I been missing? I asked.

The fire, you see. It swept over everything.

Yes, I said, Yes. I see. But how long?

It's hard to say, exactly. The realms have different metrics.

Yes, but *how long?*

Oh, she said, as though I had had wakened her from a dream. Forgive me. You are worried. I forget that you are not one of us. I believe in your time, it's been something like a year or so, give or take a month.

I swallowed. The only thing I tasted was the air. It had this aspect of bitterness to it. A sour feeling invaded my stomach and my throat. I felt like I was going to lose the contents of my stomach. I held up my hand and turned away.

So sorry, said Nionc Tigo. I assumed you had an idea of what was going on. Evidently I was mistaken.

I didn't have the energy to answer her or offer anything in replay. All I wanted to do now was get out of her realm and back to my own.

I leaned over and put my hands on my knees. I tried to suck in as much air as I could, but it was as though the oxygen had been drained out of the world.

She put her hand on my back. She said something I didn't quite understand.

The tracks on the island, I said.

Those were him. He got the earth mover in Slothin and tried to leave a message in the ground for you.

I felt the beat of existence course through me. It was as though my heart had taken on the characteristics of the world. Nothing I did had anything to do with this world. I was not of this world.

My face felt warm and I suspected it was redder than a rash. I straightened up. My head was light and felt like it was spinning on my neck. I tried to quell the feeling of nausea. It was trying to tell me something, wasn't it? But everything was trying to tell me something.

How do I get back? I asked Nionc Tigo, once I was able to muster the strength of speak.

I don't know, she said.

But you live here, I said.

She shrugged. You live in your city in your country. Do you know how to visit the ghost of your city?

What?

Just because I live somewhere, doesn't mean I know everything about it.

I breathed. I wanted to think she was helping me, but I felt no assistance from her. I felt more like she was toying with me.

Why am I even here? I asked.

You were in trouble. Buried under burning material. I was called in to help you.

Called in?

She indicated a shady spot against one of the walls. A gentle gesture, as though she was trying to find a way to cushion bad news and had only the resource of a cool place to sit.

If we stop, I'll sink into the ground.

It will be okay for a few minutes, she said. It looks like you could use the rest.

She was right about that. I was dog tired. I needed something to give myself back some energy.

We walked over to the base of a wall. The sun was behind the wall. As soon as I entered the wall's shadow, I felt immediate relief. A cooling sense of ease permeated my body.

Nionc Tigo stood over me for a few minutes. I looked up at her. She smiled down at me. I patted the ground beside me. My hand pushed through the surface of the ground. The blades of grass tickled the bones of my fingers. I leaned back on the wall and sunk into the rocks. They scraped against my shoulder blades. It was not an unpleasant sensation. It was as though I had someone scratching my back.

Nionc Tigo let herself descend to the ground.

You aren't going to sink down, are you? I asked.

No, she said. I have no mass. Or very little. I'm not yet sure which.

I'm going to sink.

If you get too far, I'll pull you back up.

You can grab hold of me? I asked.

He extended her hand. I grasped it in mine. It felt soft and yielding, but seemed to be made of something. Some material. Maybe not skin and flesh, but *some*thing.

She held my hand for a long time. I felt only a sense of strangeness. No human contact as I was accustomed to. There was a deep sense of other-worldliness, as though Nionc Tigo and I were visitors in each other's realm and there had to be a permanent barrier between us.

I'm very tired, I said.

You should sleep.

But the sinking—

Don't worry so much, said Nionc Tigo. You are under my care. Our tradition. You have wronged me and that means it is my responsibility to make you right.

Weirdest damned tradition I've ever heard of, I said.

It's worked for us for centuries.

Says you.

She looked puzzled. Yes, she said. I just stated that.

I smiled. I didn't know poets could be so literal.

Oh, that, she said. My being a poet was an accident. Always was. Always would be. I was never anything more than a competent make of instruction manuals.

I laughed. The funniest part of that was how she didn't understand how funny it was.

I did fall asleep.

I don't remember any dreams. Time passed very slowly. I wondered, or *thought* I wondered, if dreams were a part of this realm and I just didn't experience any, or if they were just not part of the ghostly realm that Nionc Tigo was a part of.

Time, of course, was fluid and strange. It passed in a kind of fog. I didn't know what to expect.

I woke with pressure on my armpits and a pulling sensation at my legs and feet. I blinked my eyes open. Nionc Tigo was pulling me out of the ground.

I thrashed my legs to try to help her. Not sure if I did. In any case, we ended up sprawled on the grass together. I tried to crawl back into the ground, but Nionc Tigo didn't let me.

Whoa, there, she said. You aren't going back. I just got you out.

The air was cool and dark. It was night. The next night after I fell asleep, or some other night? I didn't know and couldn't tell. A crescent moon hung in the sky. The stars were spread out over the sky like sparks from a welder's torch. I thought of my husband again, and my heart sank. Everything felt as though it was going to break.

I wasn't sure why I wanted to return to the depths of the dirt, but I did. Very strongly. It was as though I found peace and contentment there. Well, I *did* find peace and contentment there. I was asleep.

But I let Nionc Tigo pull me back.

I'm tired of this place, I said, without any energy behind the words. I was resigned to my fate, whatever that might be.

And I'm tired of you, said Nionc Tigo, but my tradition means I don't let that affect what I am supposed to do.

I'm tired of your tradition, I said. I don't want to hear about it anymore. It's the most ridiculous thing I ever heard. You don't *help* someone who wronged you. You wrong them right back. Double. *That's* how things are done where I come from.

Indeed, said Nionc Tigo. Then why didn't you stay there?

I liked your stupid poetry, I said.

Ah, she said. Art will get you in trouble quicker than anything.

So I've noticed, I said.

Have you finished your tantrum? she asked.

I looked at Nionc Tigo. She was not smiling, but neither was she frowning. She had a completely placid expression, as though she was waiting for me to apply an expression to her face. Waiting for my artistry to color her and give her some semblance of life, whatever that life might entail.

I wasn't aware I was having a tantrum.

Tantrum throwers sometimes don't. But everyone else around them knows it.

I stood up.

Let's get going, I said.

You husband has been asking for you.

So you told me. I'm going to meet him.

It doesn't work that way, said Nionc Tigo.

Then how does it work?

Come here.

She took my hand. I wanted you to sleep to give you strength. You don't want to try this if you are tired.

I'm still tired, I said.

But less than before. Yes?

I thought about it. I suppose you're right, I said.

Then *listen* to me, for once. I'm trying to help you. It's our way.

I wanted to curse her way again, but held my tongue. No sense in going over that ground again and again.

You need to go into the wall, said Nionc Tigo. Don't rush it. Go slowly, otherwise you'll scramble yourself.

Scramble? I said.

She looked up at the sky, as though hoping for some words from the stars.

Scramble, yes, scramble. You'll *separate*. Your soul will detach from your mass. You see?

I didn't, but decided she knew best. Or, at least, better than me.

Okay, I said. Go slowly.

Yes. Very important. It should take you a long time to get to the center of the wall. Hours.

I took a breath, wondering what substance I was taking into my lungs. Was it air, or some representation of air? Oxygen or a copy of oxygen? Ghostly molecules, maybe. I couldn't say for sure. And it suddenly seemed very important.

Nionc Tigo, I said.

Yes? she answered. She was alert to me, as though she truly did want to help me. Why did I doubt it?

Are you sending me to another realm? Because I don't think I can stand another transition.

Hard to say, she said. The wall is part of this world, and not a part of it. Something foreign, yet native born. It's a paradox.

I hate paradox, I said.

That's not true. You love the paradox of language.

Used to.

Not anymore? said Nionc Tigo.

No, I said.

Well, no matter. Once you do this, things will be clear again. Are you ready?

When is anyone ready for anything? I asked.

She didn't answer. Which was fine with me. Any answer would have been anticlimactic I was sure.

Now, she said, you will want to close your eyes. That's normal. But you must fight this.

Okay.

Keep your eyes open. You won't regret it.

Got it, I said.

Then she turned me around. I was facing the wall, so close to it that I could smell it. It reminded me of metal and something bitter. Not sure what, arugula, maybe. Not completely unpleasant, but not something I would want to spend a lot of time with.

Nionc Tigo applied pressure to my back. It was not so much a push as a nudge. Maybe the suggestion of movement.

I took the hint and stepped forward.

The plane of the wall passed through my face and eyes. My foot entered the mass of the wall.

Try to imagine being on fire and sandpapered at the same time. That's what it felt like. I wanted to close my eyes, but chose not to. I reminded myself that this was not real. This realm was massless. Anything I was feeling was my own body. Maybe my own perceptions. They had no real meaning outside of my mind.

The interior of the wall was a featureless gray, at first, then it resolved into separate bits of color and shape. It was like a phosphorescent kaleidoscope.

I kept walking. The wall gave the impression of mud and heavy water. There was no ease. I dragged my limbs through the murk and the resistance.

I felt the last of my body, my foot, leave the world outside of the wall and now I was inside it completely.

There was a cozy feeling, of sorts. It was as though I had something that cared about me wrapping me in protection. I understood that on a cellular level, I think. It bypassed my brain, or so it seemed, since my brain was screaming that this was unsafe, crazy, and other things of that nature.

I could not disagree with my brain. I did not *want* to disagree. I was willing to accept the strange weirdness of the sensations, but I did not want anything to keep me from doing what I wanted to be doing, which was to contact my husband.

I called his name.

A scratchy something scraped over my teeth and tongue. I gagged as the interior of the wall seemed to climb down my throat and threaten to explode my belly.

I knew this couldn't be true, but the feelings were there. It was as though I was swallowing rock and mortar.

Slothin walls are very thick. I knew that if I kept walking I would get to the other side, but that seemed like forever. Maybe I could walk backward?

Turn around?

I lifted my hands above my head. The process took a long time. I was moving through solidified rock. The bits of rock scraped against my skin and into my bones. The mortar felt like it wanted to break me apart. I tried to put all these sensations into some kind of coherent form, but they wouldn't let me.

To top it off, I was falling. Very slowly, but falling nevertheless. The wall material drifted up through my body. I had the uncanny sensation that my internal organs were being scraped down to nothing. My guts were shredded. My bones were being pulverized.

I opened my mouth a tiny amount, just enough to emit small sounds. I called my husband's name again. Several times. I tried to push the words out as hard and as firmly as possible, but the rocks, they kind of kept them close to me. I saw them fall from my lips and arc toward the ground beneath me.

I lifted my legs to get them out of the ground and adjusted my stance so I was back on top of the earth.

There were rocks here in the middle of the wall. Piles of them. I felt with my foot and stepped up on one of them. My body moved through the rock and mortar. I took another step and rose again.

It felt a little better to rise like that. It was as though I had some status in the world now. The mortar seemed a little thinner at this new altitude.

I opened my mouth again, a little wider this time and asked my husband where he was.

Silence.

Rock material seemed to crawl into my ear. I felt it scrape along my ear canal, through my eardrum, and slither into my brain. There's nothing like the sensation of sandpaper scraping through your cranial material to remind you that you are a mortal being.

As a cheese grater went to work shredding my brain, I also noticed that I was getting very warm. Sweat beaded on my skin and seemed to muddy the wall to some extent. I had wanted to be in here, but now that I was, I never wanted to be in here again.

I took a couple of more steps up. My head had to be near the top of the wall, didn't it? I wasn't sure. I had no guidelines for this, no way of understanding where I was.

Then I started falling.

I almost didn't notice at first. The sensations in the wall were so foreign that it was difficult to get my hearings in any case, and even more difficult to understand what those bearings meant. But after a few minutes I was definitely in possession of the sensation of having my balance offset by the littles amount. Maybe half an inch.

Then it got to be even more. I was still debating whether this was an emergency or not, when I lurched over a good inch or so, and was definitely going down. It was taking a while. The mortar and rocks were keeping me from going down quickly, but I was not able to right myself.

I probed with my big toe, trying to see what I had caught that would take me down. I found, amongst the rocks, bones.

At first I did not believe there were bones. I thought they had to be some kind of strangely shaped rocks. Or maybe lengths of mortar that had solidified into something that resembled bones.

But no. They were definitely bones. I could feel their smooth exterior, and as I pushed my toe in, the honeycombed frozen foam of their interior.

I knew what a bone looked like on the inside and this bone felt exactly what that would look like.

The next question that presented itself to my mind was what creature did the bones come from? Human? Animal?

All this while I was falling. Not sinking, as I had done before, but falling. In ultra slow motion. Like gravity had taken a vacation and left something much weaker in its place to housesit for it. The weaker version of gravity worked the same way, only with much less efficiency and zeal.

By this time I had gotten used to the wall's material invading my every free space and opened my mouth wide and called to Nionc Tigo.

What are these bones? I asked as loudly as I could.

I waited. No answer. Then I asked the question again, much louder this time. So loud that I felt the rocks and mortar and bones vibrate. That surprised me.

Still no answer, though.

I tried one more time, calling Nionc Tigo's name in long drawn out syllables, to try to make it clear that this was important. She should answer.

I waited. I held my breath. I felt sharp material scraping my every cell. I thought I must be bleeding. Blood must be pouring out of me and staining the wall red, dripping into the ground and coloring it crimson. My blood, my blood, it couldn't remain inside me under these circumstances. It must be flowing out into the world.

Such delirious thoughts.

I tried to turn myself around, but it was tough going. I couldn't get a grip on anything. The wall was simultaneously fluid and solid.

I was so tired. It was hard to fight the powers and forces keeping me in place. Despite the fact that I had been asleep not too long before this, I felt the urge to fall asleep again.

I fought it. Successfully. I remained awake.

About this time a voice became audible to me. It filtered out of the static of the wall, which had been roaring all around me the whole time. I had the feeling that the words had been swirling around for some time, but I had only just then become aware of them.

It was Nionc Tigo's voice. Her words had penetrated the wall and landed on my ears.

Think of the sheep, she said. What are they trying to say to you?

Well. I hardly knew what people were trying to say to me, let alone sheep. Was she serious?

I called to her again, as loudly as I did before.

Her answer came immediately because I had learned to find it in the swirl of undifferentiated sound around me.

The sheep, she said. All the answers are in the sheep.

Poets. Why don't they ever just say what they mean?

I wanted to shout at her again, but I had lost my voice by this time. It was hoarse and strange, like it was trying to use rock to make sound instead of air and it tried, valiantly, and even succeeded for a time, but had decided it was too ridiculous and was not going to go on with it.

I tried to force out words, but they wouldn't go.

I was almost prone by this time. My hands were before me, and my feet were pointed in the same direction. I was on all fours and had not even noticed that this had been happening to me.

My hands penetrated the ground at the base of the wall a few inches. I pulled them out of the ground and moved around.

I felt this overwhelming urge to eat some grass.

I wanted to graze the fields.

An alarm bell went off inside me. A chill froze my being and stilled my brain. I didn't move. Didn't *want* to move.

There were hints of my new form. No, not hints. Sledgehammer hits, more like it. It was as though my entire previous life had been swept away: all my thoughts, emotions, memories, yearnings, and hopes. The fears remained, unfortunately. I was afraid of death, mostly. Isn't that what all fear is about? The realization that death is the ultimate end game with no way out, not even if you cheat.

So death was still there. The meaning of it clear and undisturbed. The hope that death would go away was not to be realized.

Aside from that, there was nothing. I had gotten used to the interior of the wall. Its enveloping scratchiness gave me a kind of comfort. It complemented my wooly curls. They meshed rather nicely.

The only thing missing was grass. I wanted the grass. I bent my head down and nudged the ground with my nose, but the grass was gone. I felt some of it, snaking up my nostrils.

Or, rather, I felt the hint of old grass, long since crushed and killed. The juices of it were still there, in an aromatic way, as if it could not be expunged by the weight of the rock and the lack of sun.

So my stomach gurgled a little, in recognition of the power of grass. My insides wanted more of it. I sooted my nose along the ground.

There was a most curious level there, where the surface of the ground met the base of the wall. It was the border between worlds, or so it felt to me. I sniffed at it repeatedly.

It felt like so much of my life the past few weeks. I was between places. I was a being without a home, existing in the cracks between worlds.

But.

There was a difference now. I had a language. The language of grass.

It was dried up and dead in this space, but the remnants of it remained and I could take it in and work with it. The only thing it said to me was that I was going to be happy once I ate some real grass.

That was it.

But it was something. Some meaning here.

I heard a voice, too. Maybe more than one. But I couldn't understand what they were saying.

It didn't matter.

I walked along the wall. Or trotted. Or whatever sheep did. I encountered no other of my kind, which was a disappointment. I had hoped that I could form a new community with my new form. Maybe gather a flock around me. Move as one entity through the world. There was comfort in groups.

I imagined our woolly exteriors touching and comforting. There was language there: the language of consolation and tribe.

The wall was a corridor. I followed it.

I chose not to step out of the wall. I knew there was grass there, but I also knew there was nothing that I could eat. Not if wanted real grass, because I wasn't real. Or so I thought.

My brain activity was dull and sluggish. I knew that. It didn't bother me. I was a sheep. We were not noted for our cranial capacities. We had no way of navigating the shoals of intellectual shores.

So I walked and I walked. I came to a crossroads, where other walls intersected with my walls. I stood at the intersection for some time. I could go forward, left, or right. All paths were open to me. I could even, if I chose, go back the way I had come.

I could see only a short distance in front of me. It all looked the same. All directions had the same character and similar feel. I had no wind to guide me. No heat from the sun to tell me where the best grazing might be. No time to assess the nature of my options.

Such luxuries were for more complicated beasts than I was.

The language of choice did not enter into my vocabulary. I opened my mouth and baaed twice. The syllables rose up and out and flew to the surface of the wall.

That stopped me. I was able to send packets of sound and track their progress? This was amazing. I was amazed.

I sent out more sound.

I could almost watch the words, like bubbles from a child's toy, ascend through the rocks and mortar of the wall.

Such things were not in my experience, and they certainly were not in the sheep's experience. I sent out more and more sounds. I had no idea what I was saying, and it didn't matter, not really. There was joy, primitive animal joy, in simply releasing the air from my lungs as sound.

Once those sound packets crossed the barrier between wall and air, they were gone from me. I didn't hear them or see them. I had no idea what might have happened to them.

I did, however, exercise what little imagination I had and saw visions of them rising high into the sky. They clumped together, like frog eggs. I half recognized that this was simply my sheep's instinct for herding, which I transferred to the sound bubbles, but it didn't matter to me. Not then.

I gloried in the feeling that the bubbles were clumping for a reason. They had a purpose and they communicated with each other. They had meaning.

The walls just kept going. I walked.

I went down one wall and then another. I walked over the simulacrum of Slothin. I yearned for the outside, and yet I feared it.

Eventually, the voices returned. I heard two: a male and a female. Human, I thought.

Their words came funneling into the walls and snaked into my sheep ears. I let them flow through me, but I didn't know what they meant. I answered them. Or tried to.

Some of my words dropped out of my mouth and fell to the ground. They kept going, down into the dirt and mud that was caked there. I imagined them collecting way way down. Maybe at the center of the Earth after traveling for a long time. How long would it take?

I tried to do the calculation. If they travelled at 1 mile an hour, and the earth was about 8,000 miles in diameter, then they had to travel half that distance, which meant it would take about five months to get there.

Quite a journey. I had this vision of all the words of the world collecting there at the center of the planet. Maybe accumulating in big hot clumps, the heat of them building up to volcanoes of words spurting out of fissures in the ground. Had to. The interior couldn't hold them all indefinitely.

And what a gathering it would be. My sheep brain reveled in it and I didn't know why. Was the flocking instinct so strong in me?

Darkness penetrated the walls. This surprised me.

Maybe another way of putting it was that sunlight stopped seeping into the walls and they returned to their darkened state. I knew there were stars visible on the outside. Great clumps of them.

But who needed stars now? I was self-contained in the wall. I could have stopped. Maybe slept. But I didn't. I had some insatiable need to keep going.

I traversed miles of wall that night, going through them like a car on an interstate. I mentally flipped coins every time I came to an intersection and went where chance sent me.

I encountered lots of other bones. I recognized them as sheep bones. They had a kinship with me. I felt their heft and their pattern. I knew they were like mine.

I stepped over them. Sometimes stepped through them. It didn't mater what I did. They were the remnants of dead creatures like myself. They had been folded into the wall, most likely by accident.

Occasionally I stumbled across other bones. Different shapes. Different patterns and sizes. The first time I found these other bones I had to think about what they might have been. It didn't take me long to realize they were human bones.

Maybe some of the workers who built the walls got trapped in the walls?

I had a vision of workers working furiously on the walls, throwing up stones and adding mortar at breakneck speeds. They worked so quickly that when one of their own fell, no one noticed. The worker got thrown into the wall and engulfed there. The worker was just a part of the wall after that.

Once they noticed one of their own was missing, didn't they go back and see where he was? Surely the mortar would have been fresh? Surely it was worth their time to unearth the worker?

And yet, the evidence of the bones I encountered argued against that.

I found it difficult, at times, to leave the bones behind me. After I had run into a few of them, noting their poses, the arms stretched up, prone on their backs, the legs in a position that suggested they might have been kicking at something and frozen in mid swing, after this, I found the picture they presented too disturbing and I quickly moved on.

At one encounter, I noted a particularly distraught feeling from the old bones. It was as though the poor victim was still trying to claw his way out of the wall. He had his hands on boulders and he seemed to be pushing other boulders away with his feet. He seemed for all the world like someone who wanted to push the burdens of existence away but could not find the strength to do so. Or, rather, was exerting all of his strength to do so.

He gave me shivers. All up and down my sheep body. My wool felt like it curled even tighter than it had been curled.

I carefully stepped around the poor thing and kept walking through the wall I had found.

And then I came to a break in the wall.

I sensed it before I got to it. Up ahead, the wall had been breached. It had a jagged edge where something had broken through it. I wasn't ready to emerge from the wall yet. The outside world was too menacing.

I turned around to go back.

Then remembered the poor worker who had been frozen in the wall. I hesitated.

The wall was broken on one side and occupied by a dead person on the other. The bones of the dead person didn't have any power. Not really. They were just bones.

But my mind didn't wrap itself around that little detail. Instead, it wanted to tell everyone that there was no way I was going to go back to that spot. It felt like a graveyard and I wasn't interested in walking over a graveyard. Not anymore.

I turned in circles for a few seconds, then stopped.

My breathing was labored and difficult. Was it hard for me to breath in the wall? Why should it be? I kept the wall between me and the bones. The bones. They occupied a place I had to pass over.

A lot of time went by while I engaged my sheep's mind in trying to ascertain the best course of action for me.

The great outdoors beckoned, for sure. There were possibilities out there. Maybe I would return to my human self. That would be good. And then I could return to my own world. Even better.

And yet.

There was something very cozy about where I was. I liked the feeling of coarse rock. Breathing mortar had its charming aspects.

As I considered these things, and as I found myself telling my brain that I was nothing but a timid sheep, the feeling of helplessness grew. I was frozen in place.

That's when the voices returned.

I thought I recognized them. They had aspects that I could understand and map onto my knowledge base. One of them was Nionc Tigo's. The other was my husband's.

I *knew* this, and yet, I doubted it.

I doubted my sheeply abilities to comprehend anything. I doubted the news that funneled into my brain through my ears. After all, sheep ears are not my ears. At least not until just recently. They were ears that my body's makeup had taken on without any training in their use.

There really should be a way for new comers to the unearthly realms to get some guidance on daily living.

The events of those days are difficult to retrieve in order. What I am describing here must, necessarily, be a speculative reconstruction. I was not able to take notes, and even if I had been able, it would not have occurred to me. All I have now is my memory and the fact that I survived, so I know that whatever happened to me, it did not kill me.

Though there were times I was sure I would be.

As I stood between the broken edge of the wall and the ghastly apparition of the dead man frozen in the wall, a deeply resonant rumbling came up from the ground. It enveloped the wall and shook it.

The rocks and mortar vibrated and shook my sheepskin. My wool trembled. The rumbling was ominous and loud. As loud as anything I could imagine, and it was affecting the wall.

Above me, pieces of it were falling off. I heard them shake loose, and listened as they tumbled down the wall, scraping and blustering and popping all the way, to fall with a thud on the ground.

The rumbling, separate from the wall, rose up into the air again. It shook everything. It made my bones rattle and my teeth chatter.

I sought to dive into the ground, but it was slow going. I was not going to escape that way.

The voices got louder and the rumbling continued. More pieces of the wall broke off. I wanted to jump out of my skin. Wanted to rise and rise and rise. It was as though an earthquake was rattling me and the wall, and earthquakes don't want living things in the way. They'll rattle them to death with hardly a thought about it.

Just as the shaking of the earth got almost too much to bear, and just as I was about to lose all semblance of sanity, it stopped.

My ears rang. My body still trembled.

I pushed against the wall, not knowing where I was going. Not caring, really. I had the feeling the rumbling could start up again at any time and it would be very bad for me. I opened my mouth and let loose the loudest and most penetrating little sheep sound I could manage.

In the meantime, the bones of the wall maker I had sought to avoid, began rattling and dancing. At first I would not believe it. They were *bones*. Of a dead person. They couldn't dance.

And yet they did.

Instinctively, I pulled back from them. I snorted and huffed and walked backwards and let out alarming sounds I didn't know I could make.

I completely forgot about the break in the wall.

I ended up crossing that breach and tumbled out onto the grass.

It might not surprise you to know that I did not have the shape of a sheep.

No. I was my old self: a middle-aged woman with clothes and no wool. I was sprawled out on the grass. The blades seemed to want to tickle me and I seemed to want to get up, so I did.

I didn't stand on four hooves, but rather on my own two feet, the ones I had stood on all my life. I felt concrete dust was still covering me and I went to brush it out of my hair, but there was none there. Just my hair. My eyes still felt scratchy, but I was pretty sure that was more a memory than a current sensation.

I rubbed my eyes, pushing them back in their sockets with more force than was good for them. I saw phosphenes explode in my field of vision. Great splotches of color cascaded from some deep and dark place I couldn't fathom, and splashed down around me.

I tried to discern the meaning in them. They had pattern, that was clear, but there was randomness there as well. I had learned, over the years, to recognize those two competing characteristics as the hallmark of meaning. Languages had patterns to them. That's how you could recognize German, say, without knowing a word of German. Something about the pattern of sounds told you it was German.

On the other hand, if a sound was completely predictable, if it had no surprises, then it was devoid of meaning. It could convey no more information than a metronome.

The phosphenes were not completely metronomic, nor were they completely random. They occupied that middle ground that gave language its meaning.

So I fell into them. I wanted to know what they were telling me.

In some ways, it was like interpreting a dream. Nothing was given to me. Everything was symbol and I had to figure out the symbols.

I kept my hands over my eyes. It was like I was still in the wall.

Around me I felt grit on my ass and my legs. This must have been the dust that came off the break in the wall.

None of that mattered. The phosphenes. They had some meaning. I studied them. I invoked synesthesia. The colors became sounds. Language.

I listened with all my might.

And as I listened, I heard footsteps around me. They were soft and without menace. In fact, they seemed to offer some kind of solace, if footsteps can be said to do such a thing. I held my breath.

The phosphenes offered all kinds of sound. My mind took the sounds and filtered them through my language makers, the parts of my brain that knew what to do with all those noises that humans make.

At first I didn't know what to make of these sounds. They were clangorous and ugly. They threw up all kinds of contradictory meanings. In fact, I wasn't sure they had any meaning at all, and I wasn't happy about that. The whole point of human sounds was communication.

As I sat there with my hands over my eyes, I felt a kind of pressure on my shoulders. I shrugged it off, but it would not go.

A shiver went up my entire body. I knew that touch.

I let my hands drop from my face. The phosphenes stayed for a long time before they finally, gradually, faded. I looked up and blinked.

My husband's face looked down at me.

Beyond him a big yellow earth mover loomed high, dwarfing him.

You, I said. It was you. You broke the wall again.

Nionc Tigo said it was the only way to get you out.

He put his hand out and I took it. He lifted me up off the ground. I felt like I was ready to spring up to the sky. Maybe push the stars out of the way to make room for me and my husband. We would ride a comet to the ends of the universe.

He put his arms around my waist and I felt his weight against me.

You've been gone a long time, he said.

My husband had a beard. He never wore a beard. It looked like it was about a month old. Maybe more.

That, I said, and pointed at his facial hair, has got to go.

I can't disagree, he said.

You've been trying to get me back? I asked.

Ever since the fire, he said.

How did that go?

Look around, he said.

I pulled back from him, reluctantly, and let my gaze fall on the horizon. I saw charred buildings, half gone. We were on the edge of Slothin, looking in.

The town was devastated. No building I remember was still in its original condition. There were black bits of rock and wood everywhere. In some of the places, smoke still curled up into the air. Heat emanated from the wreckage. The sky was a dusty brown from the smoke and everything felt crisp, but not in a good way. It was as though the world had been toasted by a rogue storm of undetermined origin. Maybe from the ground beneath us.

Where's Nionc Tigo? I asked.

My husband blinked at me. She's dead, he said.

I know, I said. But I've been talking to her. We've been having a conversation. All kinds of things happened the last few days or weeks or how long its been.

I touched his beard. It felt real. He was real, wasn't he? I wasn't imagining all this. Or dreaming it. Was I?

I don't know where you went, he said, but there's no Nionc Tigo here. Look around.

I didn't look around. Instead I stared into his eyes. I wanted to make sure they were seeing eyes, not some fake eyes. Was there anything he knew that would explain what was happening here?

Why did you break the wall? I asked.

To get you out.

How did you know I was in the wall?

I talked to the walls, he said. All of them. I ran all over this country talking to the walls. I wanted to find you. After the fire came and wrecked everything, I thought you were gone. But you weren't. I heard you.

You heard me in the walls?

He grinned. Isn't that crazy?

I remembered all those years he listened to walls. I guess, I said, I can't make fun of your hobby anymore.

He put his arm around me. Let's go home, he said. He leaned close to my ears when he spoke. It was as though he wanted to bring me closer to him. I wanted to be close to him, too, but something nagged at my brain.

Nionc Tigo, I said.

Yes, he said. You mentioned her.

She was *here*.

He looked around. Where? he asked. He wasn't being unkind, or trying to make me feel bad. He really wanted to know what I was talking about. He needed to know for himself.

I don't know, I said. Not exactly. But Nionc Tigo and I had conversations. We had a connection.

I think, he said, that you might need to break yourself of this obsession with Nionc Tigo.

But that's just it, I said. I can't.

His mood changed drastically. He went from being affable and kind to irritated and somewhat belligerent.

I'm sick of her name and I'm sick of you talking about her. I've been dealing with the fallout from your ridiculous fixation on Nionc Tigo and this ridiculous country and I want it to stop.

I looked at him. I felt fear. I had never felt fear in the presence of my husband before. I stepped back from him.

I could see he wanted to step toward me. As though he wanted to intimidate me and solidify the fear.

What's going on here? I asked.

I breathed. The smell of him was familiar. He had the sweaty smell he often had when he came home from work. The mix of earth and body odor that I remember as not unpleasant. It was a way of him being in the world with me, that smell. It was his signature. His way of telling me he was of the earth, just like me. Just like all creatures.

He didn't crowd me. Instead he seemed to gather his wits and step back from my space.

I sought avenues of escape. I could step back and run. I could doge to one side or the other. The wall was still there on one side, broken. There was a big gap, strewn with remnants of the wall, that we were standing in. The bits and pieces of the wall could trip me up if I started running in the wrong direction.

I felt my hands tingle, like they wanted to get going with me. My feet had an itch in them. Everything in me felt light and vulnerable, as though I was about to be harmed.

All these things were so foreign to me. I tried to remain calm. That was foreign as well. I never had to try to look relaxed when I was around my husband. That was not something I needed to watch out for.

Come on, he said, finally. Let's get in the excavator.

Why? I asked.

You'll see.

I very seriously considered running. I told myself I needed to run. My husband was bigger than me, with longer strides, so presumably he could catch up to me if he wanted to. But he was also heavier than he should be, and he never ran much. It was entirely possible I could outrun him.

But then what? Where would I go? The entire country was grass and walls. Burned out grass and walls, at that.

He turned from me and began walking toward the excavator.

I breathed as I watched him walk away. From behind, it was easy to think of him as my husband again. Not someone who had strange ideas of what we were supposed to be doing in Slothin.

Reluctantly, I followed him to the excavator. He climbed up on the tread and into the cab. There was room for both of us. He put out his hand. A helping hand.

I walked close to the excavator, right next to the tracks. The thing rumbled and shook. The ground under my feet rumbled right along with it.

I couldn't read his face. I had no idea what he was thinking. Or what he wanted. Not truly. He was asking for my hand, but that wasn't enough.

Or was it?

I reached for him. His hand in mine felt real and right. I put one foot up on the track and he pulled me into the cab. I sat on the smooth leather seat.

My husband had been operating earth movers for many years and I had never sat with him in one. I suddenly seemed absurd that I had never done that. Weren't we partners?

He raised his voice above the rumble of the engine.

It isn't really the best tool for wrecking walls, he said.

I looked around. From this slightly elevated position, I could see lots of walls had been broken by the earth mover. I saw tracks leading to and rom the breaks.

You seem to be doing okay, I said, indicating the vast terrain with my hand.

He grinned. I guess you're right, he said.

Then he started up the machine and the rumbling broke through my skin and into my bones. It startled me pretty good.

I felt like I was going to shake apart, but I didn't. All that was behind me, I hoped. The uneasiness in the world, the feeling that I might drop out of existence at any moment. Nothing like it had ever happened to me before, and then it started happening on a regular basis.

To the point that I was ready to give up on everything.

My husband was in his element, and it felt good to be near him when he was like that. I smelled the sweat pouring off his body. Not a terrible odor at all. It was familiar and comforting, like the scent from a flower you knew and loved.

He said he thought he should be chomping a cigar as we went, but my husband was not a smoker, so that didn't happen. Instead, he tilted the hard hat on his head up a little, to give him a better view and proceeded to smash through the walls of Slothin.

Destruction felt like the proper course of action, for once. We needed to level what remained of the barricades.

My husband shouted above the sound of the engine.

I estimate it'll take me a good week or so to smash down these walls.

Why bother, I shouted back at him.

These people need these walls gone, he said. Once they're gone, they can join the rest of the world.

It seemed a strange thing to say.

You know, I shouted, there are dead people in these walls.

He acted like he didn't hear me, but I knew he did.

Are listening? I asked.

He nodded.

I heard you, he said. Dead people in the walls. We'll liberate them.

You won't liberate anything. You'll just disturb their bones.

He rolled over the grass, leaving tracks of disrupted ground behind him. He connected with a stone wall, and it crumbled in a crash. Bits and pieces of the rocks lay in piles all around us. The smell of diesel exhaust assaulted my nose.

I had been looking forward to the destruction, but now that I had witnessed one of them, I wasn't so sure.

I wrapped my hand around my husband's arm.

He hesitated, then stopped working the controls. He turned to look at me.

What is it? he shouted.

I indicated the ignition key. He reached forward and turned off the excavator.

It didn't go quiet right away. It still shook and rumbled and quaked for another five seconds or so. As if it was dying and didn't want to die so it put up one last futile fight. We waited for the death throes to stop.

Finally, the earth mover ceased shaking, a stilled fish that had been pulled out of a lake and flopped to the shore. We sat silently, letting the stillness invade our senses. My ears rang.

We can't just destroy this country, I said.

It's already destroyed, he said. We're just cleaning up. Don't you see? The walls have been holding them all back.

On purpose, I said. It has defined their tribe.

The fire killed everything, said my husband.

That's not our doing. Or our responsibility.

But we're here. We came here for a reason.

I just wanted to translate some of Nionc Tigo's works, I said.

My husband looked away. His gaze seemed to follow the horizon, which was studded with burnt our wrecks of buildings and even some trees, angular, like dark lightning bolts against the sky.

I've heard the voices in these walls, he said.

I thought you didn't, I said.

Since you went away. Everything changed then. It was as though they woke up.

And they wanted to talk to you? I asked.

Something like that.

I've been in them, I said. I've seen the inside of the walls. Nionc Tigo has seen the inside of the walls.

He didn't say anything. I saw the sweat on his forehead. This was something he felt strongly about, but I couldn't decide if I should support him or challenge him. Surely there was a way we could each have what we wanted. Wasn't that the key to life? Compromise?

I prodded him with an elbow.

What are you thinking? I asked.

When we first came to Slothin, he said, everything was strange to me. I didn't know how to react to the layout of the country. It was as though the land wanted me closed in. Didn't you feel it?

I felt strange, I said. Still do. But that wasn't the land. That was us. Me and you.

His hand twitched. I could see he wanted to start up the earth mover again. He wanted to wreck these walls.

The country needs to breathe, he said. I punch a hole in each of these walls, and the energy flows more freely.

I see that, I said, but the walls are centuries old. They've been there for a reason. If the people needed energy flow, they would have taken care of it, don't you think?

He shrugged.

I've always indulged your wall talking, I said.

He gave me a crooked smile. Indulged? he said. That's what you call it? I saw the twinkle in his eyes. He was trying to be lighthearted about this, but I also saw anxiety in his face. He wanted to do this and he thought if he didn't, then things would go very badly for everyone, including us.

Well, I said. Maybe not indulged. That might be a bad choice of words, but I've supported it, in my way.

In your way, he said with a voice that tried to echo my speech patterns, but only ended up sounding sad and pathetic. Yes, pathetic.

Look, I said. Why don't we put this project on hold for twenty-four hours? Let's find the prime minister and talk to her. She needs to know what we're doing.

I've looked, he said. I can't find anyone.

I took the keys from his hand. He didn't resist. I put them in my pocket.

These will be here if we need them again, I said. Right now, let's go find someone who *lives* here. Someone with a stake in what you're doing.

I climbed out of the cab and carefully made my way down the track and onto the ground. He sighed and followed. We stood next to the earth mover. Its bucket was banged up and covered with rock dust.

You've put this thing through its paces, I said.

He nodded. She's a good machine. I think if we ever want to do anything around the house, she would come in handy.

You mean like *wreck* the house?

He shrugged. You never know. Houses don't last forever. Just like people.

Or countries? I asked.

Or countries, he said, with a certain amount of satisfaction in his voice, like he had scored some points and wanted me to know it.

I rolled my eyes.

It's not enough you want to unleash destruction over this country, you have intentions of doing so where we live, too?

What's good for the goose, he said.

I dusted off my hands and turned toward the charred remains of the city that was once hospitable to us, and still would be, I conjectured, if it had the capability. We started walking, me first, my husband trailing behind. He still wanted to be in the excavator's cab.

I slowed down enough for him to catch up to me, then I quickened my pace and he followed.

It's hot, he said.

The sun *was* high and bright in the sky. I felt the heat waves coming off the ground and rising up to meet us. There was nothing in the air to prevent it. It was as though the fire was still present, or its ghost was, finding a way to inflict its heat on us.

As we walked I told him about my adventures. How I fell into the earth and what happened after that. I told him mostly what I have recounted here in this retelling of the tale.

Sounds like an *Alice in Wonderland* kind of thing, he said.

The worst part, I told him, were the times that I couldn't understand anything. Meaning was completely gone. I did not have the skill of translation anymore.

That must have been hard, he said.

I had been carrying my shadow for quite a while and it was getting to feel pretty heavy. I shifted it around some, trying to find a good place for it.

Nothing felt comfortable. If I pushed it up on my shoulders, then my neck felt crowded. If I pushed it down to the lower reached of my back, it made walking difficult. Anywhere else, and it felt like it was going to fall off.

Except it didn't fall off and wouldn't fall off. All it did was pull at my body, as though it wanted to wreck me.

My husband noticed. You need Nionc Tigo, he said. She would know what to do right now.

Nionc Tigo is an elusive spirit, I said. You never know when she'll arrive or when she'll decide to leave. I can't trust her.

You can't trust a dead person to remain dead? said my husband.

Something like that, I said.

I kept shifting my shadow around from place to place. It crawled down my arm to my wrist, where it wrapped itself like a rubber band. I let it stay there, even though it made my arm heavy and pulled me to one side. As uncomfortable as that was, it was at least something I could handle for a while.

We had to pull open gates as we went. The smell of burnt wood filled the air and only got stronger as we got closer to town.

I estimate we walked about two or three miles before the ground opened up in front of us. It started with a small fissure. We could have walked right over it, but we froze when it appeared, like a snake slithering. The ground came apart, leaving a jagged rip in the earth, reminiscent of a lightning bolt.

We stepped back. Our feet felt like they wanted to run, but we held hands and quelled the itch to flee. There was no where to flee to. The fissure widened and began to encircle us in a big loop.

What's going on? asked my husband.

The earth is mad at you, I said. It doesn't like how you've been plowing through it. Disrupting it. Making things difficult for it.

It's the *walls*, he said. I've been destroying the *walls* not the ground.

He kept stepping back. I grabbed his hand, but it was too late. He stepped right into the growing fissure. He stumbled. Tried to regain his footing, but it didn't work. He let go of my hand and reached up for——something. The sun? The sky? Me?

And then he was gone, fallen into the hole.

I dropped to my knees and looked down the fissure and called his name.

No answer. The fissure was dark, black as a cat.

I screamed for him.

Still no answer. I thought of my journey down. He had to maintain his optimism. He would come back. He would. But I didn't know if he knew that.

I remained there for some time, listening for a thud, or some other indication that he had met the bottom of the fissure. None came. It was as though he had disappeared into a zone from which nothing emerged. Or could emerge.

My skin was crawling with creepy feelings, as though centipedes, hundreds of them, were busily milling around on me. I wanted that feeling to go away.

I thought of jumping in after my husband. I didn't, and that confused me. I thought I loved him and would do anything for him.

But not this. I wouldn't do this. I had been down there before.

I rolled over on my back and felt the ground against my spine.

The sky descended.

That's the only way to describe it. The blue shell of the sky above me lowered itself. It compressed the air above me. I felt pressure and heat. The smell of burnt wood grew more pronounced. Sweat began popping out of my pores. It was as though I had taken a swim in wet air.

I let my arms flop to the sides. They lay against the grass like broken animals, unable to move.

I heard sheep bleating in the distance. It was not a good sound at all. They were in distress. I understood. My body screamed distress at me. Everything that had been happening to me was distressing.

I was so weary. Adrenalin was coursing through my system, I felt it in my blood, like fire tearing up my veins. My arteries were long fuses attached to bombs. I should have been up and mobile, animated.

But even all that energy could not get me going. I just wanted the sky to wrap me up and let me sleep.

Even though it was midday, things grew dark around me. The sky, it seemed, harbored shadow. As it descended, its shell made my world smaller and smaller. There were no outs, as far as I could tell.

Eventually, as I lay on the ground, my blood percolating in me with frenzied and animated abandon, the sky covered me completely, a great dark blue blanket. I immediately felt soothed and cared for. Some of the stars were a little prickly. They made my arms and face itchy.

I scratched at those spots and as I did so, the sky scratched at the back of my hand. It pressed down pretty hard and I had to move my hand away to keep it from getting all itchy.

The sky kept falling, falling. It covered me completely now and it was heavy.

Which, perhaps, I should have realized. But it came as a surprise.

It also kept getting heavier. The first contact, apparently, had been merely a prelude to the rest of the sky settling down on me.

I tried to think through the situation. Surely there were precedents for this. There must be a way to deal with the sky falling on someone.

The fabric of the sky was smooth and slick. I was able to slide away from it. My clothes snagged on the embedded stars, but it wasn't a true hindrance, merely an annoyance. I flipped myself over on my stomach and arranged my arms under my chest so that my face was above the ground, at least, so I could breathe.

I took in grass- and sheep-scented breaths. The weight of the sky was not merely a burden, it was as though I had stepped into a new world.

Yet again.

And the weight was increasing. I could not hold it back from me indefinitely. I called out for Nionc Tigo.

Help, I said, but not loudly. I could not speak loudly. The sky's mass was pushing down on me so hard that I couldn't work up the energy to get the words out in a bellow. It was more like a whisper.

Desperation seized me. I took in as deep a breath as I could, knowing I was on the verge of suffocating, and let out as loud a scream as was humanly possible for me at that moment.

Then from somewhere deep in a place I could no longer imagine, a voice rose sharply and loudly. It was Nionc Tigo.

You have fingernails, she said. Use them.

I began digging into the ground. I pulled out tufts of grass and sunk my fingers into the wet dirt. I pulled up hunks of earth. Small hunks. Barely handfuls, really, and tossed to the side.

This was to be my escape route? It didn't seem possible, but then, I seemed to be specializing in impossible situations lately.

I went on like this for a few minutes. Maybe less. Desperation distorted my sense of time.

Then Nionc Tigo's voice again, tinged with disgust.

No, no no. You're hopeless. You don't want to go into the ground. You aren't dead! I mean the sky. Rip open the sky.

Where are you? I asked.

Where I've always been, she said.

That's no help, I managed to say. The words were leaving me. The sky was too much pressure on me. I wasn't going to be able speak much longer. And soon after that I wasn't going to be able to breathe.

I let my body collapse on the ground. My cheek was in the grass. My lips touched dirt. Grit got into my teeth. I didn't try to spit it out. It didn't seem possible or worth the time.

The sky, pressing down on my back, pushed with such force that I thought it might break bones. I tried to take in Nionc Tigo's words. They were a path to survival, weren't they? I thought they might be.

For a moment, then, stuck between the sky and the earth, I felt like a butterfly on a pin.

You could say I had accepted my death.

I bid farewell to my husband the world. I said goodbye to myself. I thanked myself for being such a good companion to myself on my journey through life. I also cursed the fate that brought me to this end.

Dark shapes swam in front of me. They were the sort of thing that might show up in bad dreams.

I thought these were the shapes that populated the secret world, and I didn't even know what a secret world was. Not really.

Then I saw that the shapes were not shapes at all. Nothing was cavorting before my vision. I was not being granted a view to the other world.

No, what was happening was that death in the form of darkness was coming into my being.

It deployed itself in discrete clumps, like black clouds filling my space one fluffy clump at a time.

I felt a crushing sensation. I thought I heard bones snap. My bones. But I felt nothing.

Then, just as I was on the verge of leaving the conscious world, Nionc Tigo grabbed my hand and extended one finger and bent my arm back overhead and stuck my nail through the sky.

The resulting deflation was a wondrous thing.

Something spilled out of the rip in the sky. It was kind of like air, but also like water. Was it a substance born of both realms, perhaps? I can't say. It flowed out of the tear and into the ground very quickly.

Great gushes of the stuff went down, down, down. The earth, it appeared, had been waiting for this. Indeed, it seemed almost as though the earth had, perhaps, orchestrated the entire thing.

The sky, slowly being drained of its liquid, deflated like a spent balloon. The pressure was off me, and that felt good. I could breathe again.

But then a new situation, with new peril, emerged. The liquid built up quickly and soon began rising over the ground. A lake or sea was being built as I lay on the grass. The liquid was fluffy, like cotton candy, and wet, like water. The color was something between pink and green.

It looked vaguely disgusting, as though something rotten had expelled its essence.

I pushed myself off the ground. Nionc Tigo's voice rang through my head.

I wanted her gone just as much as I wanted the liquid gone. Neither of them was helping my demeanor and neither of them were going to be what I needed to survive this.

I rose up on my feet—with some effort—and stood as tall as I possibly could. I had pushed myself through the tear I had made in the sky, and I was looking at the empty space above the sky. No stars lived here. No planets. There was nothing.

I wondered what I was breathing, then realized I wasn't breathing anything. I didn't need to.

Nionc Tigo spoke in metered lines of verse. I did not understand the words or the language. I wanted to lift up the sky and put it back into place. What I got here was nothing but Nionc Tigo, and that was no substantial nourishment for anyone.

Something else nagged at my brain. The thought that my husband might be lost in the depths of the earth and was being inundated with the cotton candy liquid, even now.

Was it possible for him to survive this? It was hardly conceivable.

Nionc Tigo! I shouted.

But there was no sound. In this realm, no sound came out because, presumably, there was nothing to carry the sound. I heard it in my head, kind of, but it was a muffled, distant sound. It was as though the entire world of words and meaning had been ripped away from me.

I sighed.

No air came out of my lungs, but I made the motions anyway. I didn't want to escape the present. That was useless. We don't have anything except the present. Everything else is illusion at best.

But I was finally and totally bereft of motivation.

I knew I should try to help my husband, but I could not rally. I had no ability to muster the strength necessary. Was I going to follow him down the fissure?

I should. I should *want* to, at least. I needed to. Even if we were to die down there, it was better that we die together rather than alone.

I vaguely recalled a poem of Nionc Tigo's to that effect. It spoke of the power of loss when shared. Or was it that the loss was diminished when shared? It was difficult to remember. Her words were substantial.

I remember that. They rose and filled the void. Isn't that what poets are supposed to do? Take the emptiness and make it less empty?

About that time, a ship appeared in the distance. It was a sailing ship, fully rigged. I heard its sails flapping in the wind. At first I thought it was quite some distance away. Then I saw it was very close. So close that I could touch it.

I reached out. My arms seemed to sail across the cosmos. It swept over vast expanses of emptiness. I traversed the history of the universe in those few seconds and an immense brooding power seemed to hold me up.

I shook my head at the thoughts that were in me. My arms were not the instruments of the universe. They were just my arms.

And yet. My skin felt vast, vaster than worlds. My limbs were the work of divinity.

I moved confidently over space and time and arrived at the ship. My hands wrapped themselves around the ship and lifted it out of the liquid and brought it close to my eyes.

Probably nothing could have prepared me for what I saw next.

Nionc Tigo walked across the deck of the sailing ship. She seemed right at home. She waved at me, at my eye, which must have been like a giant's eye in her view. She jumped up and down on the deck. She danced and leaped and twirled around, like a child.

Other crew members were there on the ship. They went about their business, working the sails and the rope. Swabbing the deck. Making meals. There was a sailor in the crow's nest. The ship dripped gobs of cotton candy liquid from its bottom and sides.

None of the people on the ship seemed the least bit troubled by the fact that a giant had lifted them up and out of their sea.

In fact, the only person aboard that seemed to have any idea the ship was somewhere it shouldn't be, was Nionc Tigo.

I was absurdly enamored of this ship. It was like a giant toy just for me. I felt rather like a child and the feeling was most agreeable.

Where's my husband? I asked Nionc Tigo.

She was still dancing.

Stop that, I said. And listen to me. I'm asking you a question.

Nionc Tigo executed her dance moves with the precision and care that she executed all her lines of poetry. Nothing was left to chance. Every move of her feet could have been described with a mathematical formula.

I watched her for a few more seconds, then began to feel anger toward her.

I *said*, I said, what is it going to take to find my husband?

She laughed at me. It was as though she wanted to make me angry. I put the rest of my life on hold. Nothing else mattered except the thought that Nionc Tigo had the power to hold me, stuck here, maybe forever, looking for some way out of the trap I was in.

I held the ship in my hands, still.

I knew I was holding lives.

But I didn't care.

I turned the ship upside down.

Out tumbled a dozen of the crew. They fell into the glop from the sky. They flopped around on the surface. Some of them dipped under the surface. I heard tiny cries for help, and some gagging and gurgling.

I didn't care. Not really.

I would have been happy to let them simply drown. I don't, to this day, know why I elected to save them, but save them I did.

I put my hand in the water and under them and slowly raised my hand so that they ended up washed up on the shore of my palm. I held them, writhing and coughing, in my hand and carefully counted. There were eleven. Was that a complete crew? I had no idea.

Some of them stood up on my palm. They raised their fists at me. I laughed and jerked my hand very slightly so that they fell back down.

They were too funny. I laughed at them. Laughed and laughed. I laughed so hard that I was in danger of letting them fall back into the sea. That didn't happen.

Instead, I took hold my self and my emotions and put my hand next to the railing of their ship. They scampered off my hand back onto the deck.

Nionc Tigo herself was one of the crew.

How did I get to be so big? I asked her. And you so small?

You still ask questions that indicated you know nothing about metaphor, she said.

Her voice was so quiet I had to put my hands up to my ears to help me hear her words. She walked across the deck with purpose. I watched her.

I don't know what you mean about metaphor, I said.

Sure you do, she answered. You're a pie in the sky, aren't you?

Nionc Tigo had lost her mind. That was my first thought. She was going to end up in the Slothin equivalent of the loony bin.

Does your country have a place where crazy people go to get better? I asked. Or just to get out of everyone else's way?

Your humor is profound, said Nionc Tigo.

I don't think so, I said.

Let me show you something. She went to the stern of the ship and disappeared down into the hold. I watched the rest of the crew. They were still mad at me. I couldn't blame them. I had demonstrated that there was practically nothing they could do to prevent me from disrupting their lives. That's the sort of thing that would make anyone unhappy.

I reached out and tugged at the mainsail. It gave a little, and wrinkled under my pressure. The wind flapped at it and it did offer a certain charm to the world. I was not immune to it. I wanted to keep the ship, like a toy.

I wanted to launch it in my own private pond, one that my husband might have excavated out of the ground. I could imagine lazy afternoons watching the ship sail around the pond.

Eventually, waiting for Nionc Tigo, to return, I felt sleepy. I put the ship back down in the sea to prevent myself from dropping it. It bobbed smartly in the water, like it had a purpose. I pushed it out to sea. It turned slowly, pivoting on its keel, then caught wind and moved quickly.

Just as it was getting out of reach, Nionc Tigo came back up from below deck. She was accompanied by someone familiar.

I stepped closer, as the ship was gaining speed, but my stride was hampered by the viscosity of the fluid. I knew who that was.

I called my husband's name.

He called back. His voice was too quiet to hear.

Nionc Tigo had her hands on her hips and she was shaking her head at me. At me! Like I was the one who had brought this odd series of events to fruition.

Why are you cross at me? I asked. I didn't want to be here. I just wanted to translate some of your poems.

You still don't see it, she said. You're still blind to what's happening.

Her voice was barely audible. My words here, purporting to be her's, might not be. I had to interpolate what I thought she was saying.

Yes, I said. I'm blind. Tell me what's happening. What should I be seeing?

And then I could no longer interpolate. I listened, as attentively as I could, but I could not hear her words at all. My husband put his hands to his mouth and shouted something to me as well.

I heard nothing.

The ship, meantime, raced away at an ever increasing speed. A good strong wind had come from behind me and was pushing the ship with great force.

It was so strong, that it was pushing me along with it.

I suddenly had to fight to keep standing. I braced myself on the ocean floor and struggled to keep upright.

I hunkered down, bending my back so I could present a smaller surface to the wind, which had kicked up a few notches in speed in just the last few seconds. A few more seconds passed and I saw I was in a full blown storm. Clouds the color of night appeared above me. Rain began pelting down. The sea gave rise to huge waves. They rose up and slapped my face.

In the meantime, the wind grew even stronger. Objects appeared in the air. Dangerous objects. They included pieces of houses, roof shingles, siding, and the like. Also trees. Carts and bicycles. An excavator. That particular object flew around me in a circle for a few seconds before plunging into the water.

I put my hands up to cover and protect my head. Nothing around me could be called anything but chaotic.

If I kept myself above the surface, I was sure to be the victim of an impact with something big and heavy and lethal.

I saw swirling clouds of blackened wood. I saw boulders, some caked with mortar. The walls of Slothin, from all appearances, were being torn apart and sent over this ocean of sky. I took a deep breath, the deepest breath I had ever inhaled, and plunged myself under water.

Slothin was a land locked country. I knew that from the first bits of research I did before I ever even considered going to it. I also knew it from how we arrived at it.

Not only land locked. It was also reality locked.

That took me longer to figure out, but Slothin had no real connection to what most of us called reality. It had strange ideas of justice, even stranger ways of keeping their literary heroes alive, and even stranger ways of keeping them dead.

Not only that, but people like me were able to swim in the ground and fly in the air. We were also able to call down the waters, somehow. I still didn't know how that worked. The landlocked country became a flooded country.

All these thoughts swirled around in my head. I tried to flow into the swing of things. I tried to understand how all of this worked, but it was tough going, a long slog.

Nionc Tigo took me on this trip and she had no idea how to take me back to where I wanted to be, which, finally, at this time, was home. My own country. The place where things behaved as I wished them to behave.

In the meantime, I was swimming above landlocked Slothin.

I kept my eyes open, despite the sting that the water (or whatever it was) gave me. I wanted to be a fish. I wanted to fly.

After all, a bird was merely a fish with wings that swam in the air rather than the sea.

Or was it that a fish was a bird without wings, that flew in water rather than air?

I wasn't sure, but I pushed myself down toward the bottom of the sea.

I saw the entirety of Slothin laid out before me, all watery and murky. My eyes glowed. They sent out light beams into the water. I swept them from side to side. I kept going down, despite the niggling need I suddenly felt for some air.

I couldn't open my mouth and fill myself up with water. That would only kill me.

Wouldn't it?

I wasn't sure anymore. I tentatively inhaled some water.

It crawled into my nose and down the back of my throat.

My body extracted oxygen from the water and I breathed.

My need to exhale was assuaged.

I pushed harder with my legs and swept aside water with my extended arms.

The bottom of the sea looked much closer than I expected. Soon I was touching the bottom. It was composed of soggy grassy fields.

Slothin under water was just a flooded lawn.

I eased myself down on the grass and stood there beneath the sea. I took in great lungs full of water. It coursed through me like fire. Why was water burning?

Fish came to me. All kinds of fish. Their noses bumped into me. I saw fish with multi-colored stripes. Others with strange arcing fins that held images of Slothin on them, like pictures in a frame. Other fish that looked like sheep with tails.

I thought of Nionc Tigo's words. They seemed to be telling me that everything I thought I knew was gone. I was in a new world now.

Some of the fish had teeth. They pulled back their fish lips to reveal their chompers, sharp and delicately arrayed, as though an artist had rendered them. Maybe an artist had.

Some of the toothed fish made motions to bite me. They approached and bared their teeth. The sharp ends looked like they would pierce steel, never mind my skin.

But as I watched, bigger fish, with bigger teeth, arrived from the depths beyond and the first fish scattered. The bigger fish, about a dozen of them, arrayed themselves in a defensive position around me. They presented a formidable army and kept other creatures at bay very effectively.

I tried talking to them.

Hey, fish, I said, somehow pushing words into the water. What are you? Or should I say, *why* are you?

They laughed, these formidable fish. They let their laughter roll out into the water and fill the area with, well, not exactly glee, but some reasonable imitation of it. It was as though they wanted to present me with their chorus of sounds.

I listened carefully.

Sharks came from out of the depths. They looked menacing and large. They came racing up to me, but stopped short when they saw the chorus.

Other creatures came as well. Octopi, glistening and wavering, their colors moving from one to the other, disappearing and reappearing. They also backed off when they saw the shell of assassins enclosing me.

Soon many creatures of the sea arrived, all brought by the songs.

In a time of amazing and almost unbelievable events in my life, this event, this confluence of species at the site of these singing fish with their sharp teeth was perhaps the most wondrous.

It was as though the entire life of the ocean had stopped long enough to take in the concert.

I listened as the laughter turned to songs. Long, elaborate songs. At first they were strange to me. I did not know where they came from or what they sounded like. They were just a series of noises.

Clicks and twitters and warbles.

But as I listened, the meaning began to coalesce. I discerned something familiar in them. They were not so much songs as poems.

This realization dawned on me slowly. The rhymes were subtle and elusive. The meter, only a little less so. After a time the strange noises were clearly acting together to create a whole.

I searched my own memory and soon I had the source of the familiarity. These fish were reciting poems by Nionc Tigo.

I listened for some time. They were going through the entirety of Nionc Tigo's poetic oeuvre. I heard poems I had read before. I also heard some I had not read. Were they the ones that had been lost in the fire?

Perhaps.

No way to tell anymore.

The whole of her words were being recited by the fish shell around me and the rest of the sea was listening. It was as though the voice of Slothin, the *true* voice, was speaking.

I listened as well as I could. I tried to discern the ways in which Slothin's character came through her words. Slothin was no longer a land of grass and walls. It was a place underneath the water. It was a large flat surface covered in water.

My transformation into a water creature was also complete. I thought of the old saying that art can transform people. I tried to bring that saying back, but could not find it in my memory or in the surrounding waterscape.

Above me, the hulls of boats glided by in every direction. There was traffic up there. I wondered who was piloting the boats?

I saw sheep floating up there as well, but not for long, since the sheep's wool became scales, and the sheep themselves transformed into other creatures. Manatees, it looked like. At least, mostly.

Some of them were not manatees, but seals and dolphins. All of Slothin was being rinsed and shaken out and given new skins, with new ways of being in the world.

I dared not look down at my own skin. Did not want to know what I had become.

Nionc Tigo pushed her voice into my skull again.

You don't understand yet, she said.

I understand enough, I said. Where is my husband?

Oh, him, she said. He's safe.

What is he?

A shark, I think. Like you.

That startled me. I was a shark. I tried to see my body, but a shark's eyes don't move that way. I could see the fuzzy width of my jaw in my peripheral vision. And, as soon as Nionc Tigo mentioned a shark, I felt the strength of my appetite and movement.

I exerted my will, and water flowed past me. The merest ripple of my muscles made more water flow past me. The shell of fish around me, my chorus of Nionc Tigo, dispersed to the waters. I would have eaten any or all of them if I had been given half the chance.

I had an appetite for them. I moved quickly, silently. I flowed through the water. Everything flowed past me. I saw sheep (now manatees and dolphins and seals) and my mouth puckered with anticipation of the blood and flesh they held.

Careful, there, said Nionc Tigo.

Careful? I asked. Why careful? I'm the most feared creature of the deeps now.

That's why you need to be careful.

I found I was able to pick up speed very easily. I moved with an assurance I could not reconcile with my previous life. But that didn't matter. The body of the shark had its own instincts and ways of moving.

A few foolhardy fish, small ones, ventured near me. I chomped on them and chewed and swallowed. It felt good to introduce them to my system. I felt them inside me, being transformed by my stomach juices. I lurched toward the surface, then toward the bottom. Sideways, and, I think, maybe even upside down for a time.

The sensation of eating was intoxicating, like the feeling of being born.

I rolled out of that reverie and immediately began the hunt for more. I needed bigger fish.

I swam with purpose. My nose smelling out the merest hint of a blood molecule somewhere, anywhere in the vicinity.

I poured all of my energy into the effort. I swam and swam and swam, but my intent must have been telegraphed to the rest of the ocean. No creature would come near me. They all scattered away from me long before I encountered any of them.

I began to see that a shark's life was essentially lonely. No one likes a glutton, and even if they did, no one likes to be a victim.

Kelp swayed around, beckoning me to chew. I already had shark pride deeply embedded in me, and would not suffer to eat plants. I needed creatures. Big ones. I needed the heft of muscle and bone and skin, and I needed lots of it. I wanted to wrestle with the instincts of a creature bent on survival, but not having the ability to survive. Not survive me, at any rate. I was too much.

The sea, which earlier had felt exactly like my home, now felt like the most alien place I could imagine. Nothing here was for me. Nothing was made for my sustenance. It was made for its own survival.

I slowed my pace. There was still a lot of traffic above me. Boats going every which way. The people of Slothin appeared to have taken to water life with zeal and zest.

I angled my course upwards and broke through the surface of the water. My jaws leaped out of the water and grabbed air. I tried to bite down on the air, some infernal instinct taking over me, but, of course, there was nothing to bite down on, and I flopped back into the water, rolling to one side in an embarrassing display of futility.

I heard voices all around me. Shark! Shark! The universal distress word. Everyone knew to be frightened of sharks. Even a pathetic one like me.

The fish I had eaten earlier was long processed and gone. My stomach felt empty, and empty in a particularly awful way, like the juices there wanted to eat through the stomach walls and begin digesting me. My flesh and blood.

I needed something for those juices to work on.

A small wooden boat presented itself nearby. It contained a small crew: three young men. They sure looked tasty.

I moved toward them. They paddled away from me, or tried to, but they were much too slow. Their craft, far from being formidable, was a tiny wooden thing, barely strong enough to hold them, much less hold back my jaws.

I rose up, with what seemed like my last bit of strength, and began falling down.

Just as I was about to make contact with the boat, a *force*, which I did not see or hear, but which I definitely *felt* tossed me aside.

I fell, jaws over tail, and ended up tumbling into the water and going further down.

Nionc Tigo! I said to the water. Was that you?

No answer. I was broken, I could feel it. The bones of my spine were grating against one another. The pain was sharp and terrible. It pierced everything I thought was part of my life. Everything.

My memories were suddenly all shot through with immense and unbelievable pain.

My early attempts at translation were suddenly painful. All my growing up was accompanied by excruciating pain. It was as though an artist in discomfort had dipped her brush in pain and splattered my life with it.

I was a picture of suffering. A long, drawn out, epic of suffering.

My life with my husband, which had been pleasant and collaborative, was now difficult to contemplate for the torture of the events surrounding it.

All our meals together were agony.

All the trips we took: torment.

I had experienced pain before, of course. Most people do. It's nothing to get excited about, but this, this pain, was something else. It broke open my world. I felt like *I* had been broken open and my insides spread out across the sky without anesthesia. Indeed, it suddenly felt like anesthesia, or any pain relief, was not only remote, but impossible.

I continued to tumble down. I tried to move my shark fins, tried to swim again, as I had been, but it was no use. Nothing I did altered my course by the merest fraction of an inch.

I tried to see where I was going.

The sea floor and the surface of the sea revolved around me in a kaleidoscopic frenzy of color and motion. There was blurring, but not complete blurring. I saw some hints of clarity. My pain heightened my senses, it seemed, but beneath the all-pervasive pain, I was also filling up with dizziness.

Vertigo gripped me and wrapped my pain in disorientation.

I could not understand the world around me any longer. It was all too much, an assault of sensory information thrown at me with abandon.

At some point I completely lost consciousness. Blackness filled my world and continued to do so even after I thought that I had regained some sense of the world.

Time had passed, I was sure of it, but I had no idea how to tell how much time. It could have been a few seconds, it could have been a few decades.

I moved my body.

Or tried to.

I felt like a bag of meat that couldn't make itself do anything. I blinked my eyes open. No water covered them, only air, as far as I could tell.

A soft mattress pushed against my shoulders. Below that, I felt nothing.

I was not in complete darkness. It was a kind of gray soupy air surrounding me. As I kept my eyes open, they began to assimilate themselves to the light and I was able to discern some features of the room I was in.

First, it *was* a room, which surprised me. And a normal one, at that. There was a window covered by a curtain. The ceiling was a normal ceiling, off-white and made of, as far as I could tell, drywall material, just like most ceilings in most of the houses I had been in.

The walls were also off-white. Some pictures hung on them. A landscape of some rolling hills. Another picture of a flock of sheep.

On another wall, a large sailing vessel, with sails fully rigged.

There was a door. It was just slightly ajar.

I noticed that I was lying down, and covered with a blanket. I looked down at my feet and tried to wiggle them beneath the blanket. No motion came from that part of the blanket, which made my heart sink and my stomach knot.

I exerted all the will I could into making my feet move.

They would not.

I shed some tears, rapidly and copiously. They crawled down my face and dripped onto my pillow.

I had a pillow. My head was on a pillow.

I wanted my feet to move. I *needed* them to move, but they would not. Not an inch.

It took me a long time to realize that I *could* move my arms. I raised my hands close to my face and rubbed away the tears, one by one. I smeared them across my cheek, and a certain exhilaration, knowing I was able to move my arms, came over me.

I cried even more.

My tears made tracks on my cheek. I spread them around with my fingertips, creating meaning from the flow. It was as though I was translating them into something I could understand. They were like hieroglyphics on my face.

I laughed at the thought.

Here I was saying that I was relived. Here I was dipping into my past and explaining my memories to strangers, strangers who had some strange interest in me and my life.

Here I laid out the reasons for living. There were many and I took a long time to explicate them all, but in the end it came down to love. The only reason to live was to love.

After I had wrung all the emotion that I could out of my depths, I let my hands fall to the bed. Crisp sheets greeted them. I took an inventory of my condition.

It was hard to let go of the worst aspect of this, which was that I appeared to be paralyzed from the mid-back down.

As I tried to come to terms with this, a voice emerged from behind me.

Hey, the voice said.

A familiar voice.

My husband's voice.

Hey, I said back. His arms came around and touched my shoulders, then moved up to my face. He cupped my cheeks and then appeared in my field of view. Familiar face. Old face. Like mine.

I saw a clock on the wall beyond my husband's head. It read a time I couldn't decipher. I saw the hands, both of them, and the numbers in a circle, but the combination of them, how the hands overlaid on top of the numbers, none of it made sense to me. It was as though I was looking at a sculpture. A modern one that didn't give up its meaning easily.

The second hand swept past everything. Quick and inexorable.

I was worried about you, said my husband.

Why didn't you come for me?

I tried.

Hmmmm, I said, thinking that he didn't try hard enough. Then thinking that wasn't fair of me. I was in a crazy place, obviously, no place that anyone could ever have found me

I talked to Nionc Tigo, he said.

So did I.

No, I mean, right now. A few minutes ago. She's outside the door.

She broke my back, I said.

He looked startled. He blinked twice, as though that would clear up the confusion in his mind.

But it wouldn't. Nothing could clear up the confusions we had going.

Your back's not broken, he said.

Then why can't I move anything in the lower half of my body? Or feel anything?

That's not true.

It *is* true, I said. It is. You can't just say something isn't true if all the evidence contradicts that.

He grabbed me by the waist and lifted me up put of the bed in one swift motion.

I struggled against him. I pushed at his chest, but he wouldn't relent. He had me in his grasp and he knew it.

He had power over me. I was tired of that. I didn't want anyone or anything to have power over me anymore. I just wanted to be able to do things on my own without supernatural forces orchestrating things.

I kicked at him, and connected a few time with his shins. That must have hurt, but he didn't show it. Just kept moving me away from the bed and onto the floor.

My toes touched the floor first. I felt the smoothness of it on the balls of my feet.

See, he said. You moved your legs. You're fine.

He dropped me.

My heels touched the floor next. He let go of me.

I felt woozy, like I was going to tip over.

He gripped my shoulder. Not enough to hurt, but enough to keep me in place.

Now it was my turn to blink. I covered my eyeballs with blinks, dozens of them in a few minutes.

You look shocked, he said.

I couldn't *move*, I said. I swear it.

All an artifact of the process, he said.

Process?

That's all I can call it, he said. We were both going through something. I smashed walls, you smashed expectations. Or something. He shrugged.

I'm so thirsty, I said.

There's water by the bed.

I turned to look at the table next to my bed. So there was. I turned back to him to ask him to get me a glass, but when I looked at him again, he wasn't my husband.

Instead, I saw Nionc Tigo standing there. In the flesh. With her hand on my shoulder.

Expectations, she said. I always worked against them.

I was so startled that I stepped back from her and ran into the bed and fell onto it.

She advanced toward me. I saw a menacing woman. She was dead, after all, and yet she was here, in my life, talking and moving and causing me no end of distress.

She kept coming toward me. I scrambled away from her. The sheets tangled up around me, bunching into knots I could not undo. I was entangled in a strange place, as though I was dropped here from somewhere else that didn't want me.

Where's my husband? I asked.

Your husband, your husband, she said. He's just a wall breaker. Aren't you tired of him? Don't you want to live a life without him for once? Haven't you had more adventures in the past few days than you've had during your whole life with him?

She came forward. I swear, she looked as big as a giant and as menacing as a shark, which I no longer was.

The clock was still there on the wall. It kept going around and around, as though it had a purpose and wanted us all to know what that purpose was.

But Nionc Tigo, I said. Didn't I wrong you?

You did, she said. You tried to bring me back from the dead and I did not want to come back. I was content where I was.

So, I said, by your custom, you must take care of me.

She smiled. Her teeth were all crooked and yellow. Why hadn't I noticed that before? She had the air of a tyrant.

After all, she was made by a country that herded sheep. Could there be anything more tyrannical than people subjugating another species for so long and so thoroughly? The sheep were not their own entities. They existed to provide food and wool. Nionc Tigo was no better than a slave holder.

A slave holder who wrote poetry?

Why not?

There was nothing to say a facility with words and images meant someone was a good human being.

Well, she said. What you say is correct. Our people have the custom of caring for their oppressors, but have you ever wondered why that should be?

I only just learned of it not too long ago, so I couldn't have spent much time contemplating its wisdom.

Wisdom? she said. Is that what you call it?

Every culture has their ways of being. That's as good a definition of wisdom as anything I've eve heard.

When I was very young, said Nionc Tigo, I was given a lamb to care for. It is the way of my country. I gave everything to this lamb. All my time and all my attention. It did well for a long time, but then it began to have problems. It didn't eat and I couldn't make it eat. My parents were resigned to it dying. They told me lambs will do that sometimes. They refuse to eat and there's nothing anyone can do about it. I refused to believe that. I loved that lamb. I wanted all the best for it and I wanted it to continue living for as long as possible. After all, I was caring for it. If it died, then there was something wrong with me. I was not good enough to keep that creature alive and that thought was something I couldn't live with. I suppose I was a sensitive child. I grew up to be a poet, after all. But I didn't know that then. I sang to the lamb. I spent nights with it. My parents were worried about me, but not as worried as I was about that lamb. It grew weaker and weaker. I drew pictures of it. I told everyone I knew about this lamb, this beautiful creature, that had life, but that was being drained of life. Toward the end, the lamb became aggressive. It pushed me away. Whenever I came near to it, it would butt me with its head and try to make me leave her alone. None of the other sheep wanted anything to do with this lamb. They saw that it was on its last legs, on its last few breaths. If you can imagine it, it snarled at me and at the other lambs. It was a terrible thing to see because its eyes were so deep with sorrow. It didn't want to be an awful little thing, but it couldn't help it at all. My father wanted to slaughter it. He said it was best for everyone, including the lamb, who was suffering. I asked him why the lamb suffered. Why did it want to die? He had no answer. He said sometimes living things don't want to be living things. No one can explain it and no one can change it. It was my first encounter with the futility of life. It hardened me, I suppose, but also made me aware of the fragility of everything. The lamb struggled on for a few more days. She had no fight in her, that was clear. Resented life. You could see it in her whole way of being. She cried out for release, the release that comes from death and an-nihilation. My parents put her in a cage, they said for my own protection, since the wretched creature would lash out at anything. It tried to bite me several times and connected once or twice. Sheep have fairly dull teeth, but she was able to do some damage. I still have the scar on my arm from one of her bits. I remember at the time I didn't care that she bit me. It was a badge of honor to be her victim, however small. She died in the cage. I found her body one morning and knew immediately she wasn't sleeping. I opened the cage and lifted her out. I felt an incredible wave of love for the lamb. It weighed next to nothing. It was all wool with a little bone and flesh in the center of it, but it was easy to think there was nothing there. All air and emptiness. I cried the whole time I dug her grave. The tears fell into the hole in the ground and seemed to bless the space, even though I didn't understand that concept then. I suppose some of the meaning of the events came to me later. It's difficult to know what I was thinking then, now that I'm older and my memory has played tricks on me. My parents left me alone. They thought this was something I should do with the lamb. Afterwards, they made me a meal. I didn't want to eat but my father said, Don't be like the lamb, Nionc. I said I *should* be like the lamb, at least for a day. It's important to understand her. My father hesitated. My mother thought I should eat, too, but I think she might have understood the situation better. She told me and my father that it was okay if I didn't eat for one day, but only for one day. So I didn't eat a thing that entire day and for the whole night. I slept very well. Hunger gnawed at my stomach, but I didn't care. I was suffering for the lamb, you see. The lamb had wronged me by not accepting my care, by defying life and choosing death. But I was still honoring the life of the lamb. I was trying to understand why it did what it did. In that way, I was understanding the ways of my people. I was learning the lesson that we should always help those who have wronged us because they wrong for a reason, and punishment will not fix that reason.

Nionc Tigo spoke all these words in something approaching a mono-tone. I could see the pain of the lamb's death was still with her.

Did you every raise any more lambs? I asked.

I did, she said. Everyone in Slothin has sheep, but it was never the same for me. I always felt like that first experience made me unsuitable for rais-ing life. Instead, I turned to words.

She looked at me. Like you, she said. With your translation. You chose words over life, isn't that right?

I didn't think that was right at all. No, I said. I use words to bring life to the world. Words are a kind of life, I think.

You may be right, she said, but think about this: without life there are no words. But, there can certainly be life without words.

I saw her point, of course, but it did not matter so much anymore. The words she spoke meant less than nothing to me. I was tired of words. Hers, mine, anyones.

The room we were in did not feel like it was going to bring me any pleasure or closure. I wanted to get out.

I'm getting up now, I said.

She stepped toward me. I didn't tell you all of that so you could leave, she said.

But I don't want to stay. I want to find my husband.

Just as I said that, the wall behind me crashed in.

It crumbled and splintered.

The sound of the breakage was awe-inspiring, but also frightening. I cringed, and moved my head to the side, in case something would fly out and hit me. Nionc Tigo ducked down and covered her head.

The sound of the walls breaking continued. Dust was everywhere. I pushed the air out of my way. The *air*. It was heavy and oppressive. Nionc Tigo shouted something I couldn't understand.

The walls were done. I listened. Nionc Tigo jumped toward me and grabbed me around the shoulders and pulled me back from the broken wall.

The sound of an excavator filled the rest of the space.

I heard excited shouts down the hall in the other direction. Evidently, other people were shocked by the wall crumbling as well.

Walls, in general, were not supposed to *do* that.

Nionc Tigo pulled me out of the room. She had to drag me, because I did not want to go. I didn't care that the wall of the room was destroyed. I also didn't care that there was dust in the air. I knew exactly what was going on.

I pulled away from Nionc Tigo, but she had a strong grip one me.

No, I said. I want to stay.

Don't be ridiculous. You're in danger.

I tried to wrest my arm out of her grip. I tried to shrink back from her. She wouldn't let me. In fact, she reached her other arm around and grabbed me from the other end, so that she had a hold of both of my shoulders and was dragging me along the floor.

I resisted with all my strength, but Nionc Tigo was no weakling. She had me in her grip and was not about to let go.

I slipped down as quickly as I could, so that I fell to my knees and my shirt, which Nionc Tigo had a hold of, slipped off me. I was left looking at the floor, and she was left holding my shirt. We both froze.

The thundering sound of an excavator vibrated next to us. It was as though we were in the middle of a storm, a wild storm. The very dust in the air vibrated.

Nionc Tigo shouted something at the air. The excavator went silent.

I stood up. My back was still sore, a little, but not enough to keep me from standing.

I wavered in the air.

The dust seemed to be holding me up. It pushed at me. I felt the grit of it in my eyes and spit out some of it from my mouth.

I turned around.

My husband was climbing down from the excavator. He stepped out of the cab and descended the stairs one at a time, slowly, as though he was going to move the world with each step.

Maybe he did.

Nionc Tigo fell silent as well. There were still noises from behind her, noises in the hall. People running. A few peeked inside for a short time, then went on, disappearing from view.

I moved my feet, shifting my weight from one to the other.

My husband looked rugged and tall. Which was strange, since he was neither.

I stepped toward him and we embraced.

You my hero or something? I said into his chest.

Something like that, he said.

You sure took your time about it.

Not my fault, he said. The stars.

Were they arrayed against us?

Think so, he said. But they appear to be lined up right now.

You could have been a little more subtle about breaking down the wall, I said.

Slothin doesn't allow for subtly, he said.

I pulled away from. We looked into each other's eyes. I don't know what he saw, but I was sure I saw a sparkle and a glint. It was as though he understood something he had not understood before.

I always thought you would talk to the walls, I said. Not knock them over.

You were were trapped inside. I saw a way to get you out.

I turned back.

Nionc Tigo lifted her arm and waved at me. At us. She didn't speak. What happened to her words? I didn't know then, and I'm not sure I know now, either.

I pulled my will and my identity from out of the dust around me. It had been flitting away and I had had enough of that.

Nionc Tigo grew blurry and wavery in the light. I wasn't sure what to do about that. I reached out for her, but by the time I reached her, she had dissolved into the dust. Disappeared, actually.

It was as though she became dust herself. Her body faded and faded, the little bits of her becoming more and more tiny, until they shrunk to points, then winked out.

The dust around me was still settling out. The air was trying to reassert itself. It was as though the meaning of air was overtaking the meaning of dust.

Do you feel anything strange? asked my husband.

I had my arm around him, and he around me. I didn't remember when that happened.

I would welcome a moment that *didn't* feel strange, I said. Just one.

We turned to the excavator. I sat up on top of the mess around us like a candle on a cake.

We climbed up into the cab. My husband backed the excavator out of the hole in the wall. Then he turned it around and we traversed the whole of Slothin in that excavator. It took a long time.

We passed burned out fields and buildings, and lots of broken walls. Acres of them.

I don't think I ever need to talk to any of them ever again, he said.

I thought of Nionc Tigo as we trundled across the landscape.

Was her spirit here? I wasn't sure I wanted to know. It seemed that every time I thought of her, something strange happened. And I wasn't ready for anymore strange. I had had enough of strange for a long time.

Towards the end of the day, I saw a few sheep here and there, mostly on the horizon. They lifted their heads from grazing and stared at us.

We crossed the border of Slothin just as the sun went down.

In the instant we stepped across the boundary, a new day dawned.

The sun rose before us and we crawled toward it at a stately ten miles per hour, all the while feeling the cool air of dawn against our cheeks.

You just have read **The Translator's Tale** by Emen. Copyright © 2019 by Emen.

ISBN: 978-1-949644-57-9

This book by Emen. No fair for you to be copying this book, so don't do it, okay.

Picture of excavator: © Gerhard Gellinger | Pixabay

Emen no dedicate books so don't ask him for to dedicate book to you, okay.

Other books by Emen:
Assa's Eggs • The Ghost and the Machine
The Institute • Thieves • 20 Weird Love Stories

About the author:
Emen is much experienced with concept of translation because all Emen books translated from broken English to fixed English. Is process that give much interest to him. But Emen not lazy. No way. Emen work hard on making books that people want to read. Emen never used excavating machine. Then how he write about? Is called research. Simple stuff. How he know about translation? Is called research. Again, simple stuff, okay. Emen believes this first book that combine excavating machine with translation.